CW00539673

VENOMOUS

ADAM BLACK BOOK 3

KARL HILL

BLOODHOUND
— BOOKS —

Print ISBN 978-1-913942-13-7

ALSO BY KARL HILL

For the 'Old Soldier'
Who never gives up

1

Truth lies in the heart of combat
Hattori Hanzo

Adam Black had devoted an entire wall of his living room to the task ahead. Also, a good proportion of the floor. Files. Case notes. Medical reports. Psychologists' opinions. Photographs.

It was a task few would gladly have accepted. Why then, had he? He couldn't provide an instant answer. Maybe the challenge, the danger, the huge risks involved.

Or maybe something else. Something darker, bobbing always to the surface of his thoughts, like flotsam, incapable of sinking away. Maybe it was the prospect of dying, which in this case, was a likely outcome, and which, if Black were to bare his soul, was something he welcomed. Craved.

He sat on a chair, in the centre of the room, and gazed at the photographs he'd pinned to the wall. They filled almost every space, in neat rows and columns. Before and after. Photographs of ten young women. Pretty, fresh-faced, smiling, frowning, sad, drawing dramatic poses. Pictures of them growing up, as school kids, with parents, siblings, at birthday parties, Christmas time. Pictures of everyday life. Then more photographs of an altogether different sort. The same ten young women, in locations in various parts of Glasgow. Naked, mutilated, dead. Smiles and frowns vanished, expressions stricken.

In the centre was a photograph of a man. He was looking directly at the camera. It was taken on the day this man had pled guilty at the High Court in Glasgow for the abduction and murder of the same ten young women. Six months earlier.

Black stared at the face, which stared back. The eyes. They wormed deep into his soul.

And soon they would meet.

Black stared.

The Red Serpent stared back.

2

The room was at the end of a long corridor, at the back of a squat, stone-built, pre-war structure near the centre of Dumfries, a building drab and square and unremarkable, with tall metal-framed windows blanked out by closed blinds. The only indication of what it was used for was a small sign bolted onto the wall by the main front door – *Infrastructure and Development*. A "non-title", thought Black. As it had to be.

The front double door was entered by pressing a buzzer on the wall outside. A man, sitting at reception, unlocked it from a panel on his desk. He had greeted Black with a terse nod, unsmiling, entering his name in a book. Room 7. First floor. The interior was basic. Bare clinical corridors, devoid of any ornamentation. Tiled floors, white walls. Strip lights at regular intervals providing harsh illumination. There was no name on the door to the room Black was in. There were no names on any of the doors, in fact. Only numbers. More secrecy. Layer upon layer, until the truth became so hidden, it got forgotten. This was the world Black had been asked to enter.

He sat on one side of a large walnut veneered desk. It was clear, save a telephone, a tray of papers, a laptop, and two cups of coffee. Also, a single sheet of A4-sized paper. The walls were blank, except a clock. It was 8am. The room was large. At one end, a cracked dark leather couch, and some chairs round a cheap coffee table. In a corner, a drinks cabinet, glittering with bottles and glasses.

On the other side of the desk sat Colonel Stewart Mackenzie. A small, compact man. Neat features. Weathered skin. Grey hair shaved above the ears, a bristling salt and pepper moustache. Blue eyes, sparkling with inquisitive intelligence. Immaculately dressed – crisp white shirt, dark tie, dark suit. A military man, a lifetime serving Queen and Country, and he looked every inch of it. Black was less formally dressed. In fact, the opposite end of the spectrum. Jeans, open-collared shirt, somewhat-worn running shoes. He didn't give a damn about dress code. He openly rebelled against it. If it bothered the Colonel, the Colonel didn't show. Not that Black would have cared particularly if it had.

They each had a coffee. Black liked his strong, no milk, no sugar.

The Colonel spoke in a clipped, neutral voice. A hint of an accent. Perhaps Yorkshire. The Colonel had never volunteered his origins. Black had never asked.

"Thanks for coming, Adam. I wasn't sure you would."

"Your call was intriguing. Bordering on the theatrical. *A threat to national security*. Not something you hear every day. You caught my attention."

The Colonel gave a small sad smile. "That was the idea. And I wish it was theatrical. But this is a million miles from theatreland. This is more – how can I put it without being clichéd – the stuff of nightmares."

"You can't get much more of a cliché."

"But it describes the situation well enough. Read this."

4

The Colonel pushed the piece of A4 paper across the desk. Black picked it up and read the words typed on it.

Elspeth wakes screaming in the night. When she is lucid, her conversation can be stimulating, if a little distracted. But she is most revealing. She confides in me. She tells me all her secrets. And she has many.

I listen to Elspeth with the patience of a god. And when she reveals her last secret, when she has given me all she can, then we become eternal.

Like a circle. Like a serpent swallowing its tail.

She's Mummy's little girl.

Soon, she'll be mine.

Tick-tock. Tick-tock. Tempus fugit.

28th December, and counting.

Forever yours,
Red Serpent
x

Black placed the piece of paper back down on the desk top.

"The Red Serpent?"

"This is a copy. The original was sent to the Chief Constable's office. By special delivery. To avoid the Christmas logjam."

Black frowned. "Sorry for not catching on. What am I looking at, exactly?"

The Colonel lifted the cup of coffee to his mouth, took a sip, grimaced. "Hate instant shit."

"You should visit my office. I live on the stuff. You become hardened to it, after a while."

The Colonel placed the cup back on the desk. He cleared his throat. His tone was exact and clear.

"A twenty-two-year-old woman went missing four days ago. On the 26th December, to be precise. She was visiting Edinburgh to spend Christmas with some friends. Innocent enough. They'd gone to a club. She went to the bar to get drinks, and wasn't seen again. Her friends got worried and called the police that evening. The police responded instantly. They carried out an immediate search of the building and the surrounding area. But there was no trace. She'd vanished."

Black raised an eyebrow. "They called the police? And got an immediate police response? Wow. Things happen fast nowadays. A young girl getting drinks goes AWOL from a nightclub in Edinburgh at the height of party time. It won't be the first time it's happened. But yet, the police were called, and the police came running. Imagine that."

"Keep that thought," the Colonel said. "I dare say, under normal circumstances, matters would have plodded along, the police stirring after twenty-four hours or so, the wheels of law enforcement grinding into action."

"But the circumstances were not normal."

"Abnormal," the Colonel replied. "Monumentally abnormal."

"Which brings us back to my opening remark."

"Remind me."

"The Red Serpent."

"Ah yes. Him."

Black waited.

"It seems he's back."

Which was impossible.

3

The Colonel cleared his throat once again, as if about to commence a presentation. "I don't need to remind you of the details, but I shall. To give you context. Most of the civilised world followed the exploits of the psychopath referred to as the Red Serpent, christened by the media on account of his predilection for tattooing his victims in a particular and somewhat distinctive style."

"A serpent swallowing its tail." Black knew the case well. The Colonel wasn't exaggerating. The Red Serpent's antics had captured the interest – and fear – of an entire nation.

"Ten young women, over a period of five years. Two every year. A conveyor belt of death. He was methodical and consistent in his timetable. Two days after the initial kidnap, the police would receive a typewritten letter. In his later letters, he'd adopted his given name, referring to himself as The Red Serpent. I think he was rather fond of it. Exactly two months from the date of the letter, the victim would be dumped, in random places throughout Glasgow. Left at night, to be discovered the next morning. Maybe a park, a quiet street corner, a multistorey car park. Each victim mutilated and dead. A five-year killing spree. Until…"

"Until he was caught."

"Until he was caught," the Colonel repeated. "Six months ago. He pled, he was sentenced, case closed. The world rejoiced. One less serial killer."

"Which brings us back to the letter," Black said.

The Colonel picked up the A4 piece of paper, gazed at its contents. "The letter," he said softly. "The letter that shouldn't be."

Black took another sip of coffee. "We have what… a copycat thing going on here? Or, dare I say it, you got the wrong man."

The Colonel gave a brittle smile. "If it were so simple. The right man was caught. He admitted to things only the killer would know. Plus, the evidence was overwhelming. Victim's blood on his clothes, little keepsakes found in his house. And of course, he pled guilty."

"Compelling."

"Now the really compelling bit. The letter received two days ago is in the same style as the previous ones. Also, and crucially, it contains words featuring in every letter sent, details of which were kept from the public domain. He uses the Latin phrase – *tempus fugit*. Time flies. He finishes off, *forever yours*. Identical wording in ten letters. You see the conundrum we face."

"Right guy captured. No copycat. Looks like he had a pal. Not so much of a conundrum, more like one major fucking headache."

"Succinctly put," the Colonel said, "but it's only half the story."

"I wondered when we were getting to this. Her friends called the police, and they came immediately. Who then is Elspeth?"

"I thought you'd never ask."

8

4

The Colonel opened a drawer in his desk, took out a folder. In it were photographs, which he handed to Black. A young woman, smiling, in different settings. On a beach, with friends. In a library, sticking her tongue out, rolling her eyes. At a restaurant, toasting with a glass of wine. Loose blonde curls framed her face, delicate chin, pale clear skin. Blue eyes charged with intelligence and vitality. Appealing, thought Black.

"That's Elspeth," the Colonel said. "In her final year at St Andrews University, studying English and Politics. Twenty-two years old. On the cusp of a glorious career, no doubt. The promise of a full and happy life. Like a million other young women, I dare say. Only she's not. She's unique. Her full name is Elspeth Owen. As you've just read, she's *Mummy's little girl.*"

"And who's Mummy?"

The Colonel ran a fretful hand through his hair.

"Elspeth Owen is the daughter of the Prime Minister."

Black didn't speak, as he tried to compute. *A threat to national security* didn't seem to do the situation justice. More like one huge fucking shitstorm. The shitstorm of the century.

"How's the law?" asked the Colonel suddenly.

Black took several seconds to answer, mind adjusting to the switch in conversation.

"The law? As in my legal practice? Seeing as you've asked, ranging from torpid to profound boredom. Glad you're taking an interest."

The Colonel's face broke into a wintry grin. "How would you like a change of scenery?"

"I don't follow."

"Of course you do. Otherwise you wouldn't have come. You know I can offer you something no one else can."

"Which is?"

"First, let's ditch the coffee. A whisky perhaps?"

"It's 8.45 in the morning."

"We're both out of bed."

Black shrugged. "Why not."

"Let's sit."

The Colonel gestured him over to one of the chairs at the far side of the room, then went to the drinks cabinet, fixed two whiskies in little crystal glasses, gave one to Black. Black sat on a rather faded cloth armchair, the Colonel sat on the leather couch opposite.

"I asked you once if you'd like to work for us. The government. You never really gave me an answer."

"I was in the army for over twenty years. I think that counts towards working for the government. Then I retired."

"You retired? Really? That's an interesting expression. I don't think people like us ever retire."

Black hovered the whisky under his nose. Glenfiddich. Even in the morning, it had a perfect smell.

"You were a captain in the Special Air Service," continued the Colonel. "You won the Military Cross. You've fought all over the world, including countless excursions behind enemy lines, in both Afghanistan and Iraq. You were a guest in Saddam Hussein's dungeons, from which you escaped, and saving the lives of your men. I've read the dossier."

"I have a dossier? I'm flattered. All in the past."

"Bullshit. Let's confront certain realities. Your wife and daughter were murdered. As a consequence, you single-handedly wiped out of existence a Scottish crime lord and his drug empire. You destroyed an international paedophile ring, saving the lives of many children. Again, on your own. You've faced the most dangerous men in the world, and come through. You are a quite unique individual, Adam. Do you want to know why?"

Black cocked his head to one side. "There seems little point in answering, seeing as you know so much about me."

"Because you like it," said the Colonel, undeterred. "More than that. You *need* it. And you were trained to be the best. Which you are. Men like you feed on danger. Without it, what are you? Almost all your adult life, your job was to kill. Period. You don't turn that off. It's in your DNA. It's carved deep into your soul. I've been watching you for a long time, Adam. When this shit happened, I only thought of one man."

"One man to do what, exactly?"

"The impossible. Will you help us? Will you help Elspeth. Because right now, make no mistake, she needs someone like you."

Black took a long slow breath. The Colonel had given a fair assessment. But he didn't know the full truth. He didn't know the real reason Black embraced danger. It wasn't the danger itself which Black enjoyed. It was the killing. The killing of men. Evil men. And in the killing, he harboured a hope. The hope that in the process, he took a bullet and went straight to hell, where he believed he belonged, well and truly. The Colonel talked about his soul. Black didn't have one.

"I take it you have some sort of plan?" Black asked.

The Colonel gave a frosty smile. "Barely. And it's drastic. And it's life-changing. And you'll have to give up everything you know. How can I put it? There's no going back."

"Is that all?"

"Not quite. We're on the clock. We have until the 28th February, should he keep to his schedule, which we have to assume he will. *Tempus fugit.* What do you think, Adam?"

"I think I need a top-up."

"And you'll need something else."

"Yes?"

"A target."

5

Black got back to Glasgow that afternoon, was back in his flat for 3pm. He was hungry, but food wasn't an essential. The first thing he did was reach for the bottle of Glenfiddich he kept in a kitchen cupboard. It was something he found he was reaching for more and more. And he made sure, when he'd killed off a bottle, another was replaced with marvellous efficiency.

The drink helped. It softened the edges of the darkness. But the darkness still crept in, and as the years drifted by, its presence intensified. The operations, deep in enemy territory, Afghanistan and Iraq, had left latent scars. Sometimes, he would close his eyes, and they would come. The faces of those he'd killed, some just boys dressed in uniforms too big for them, holding weapons they didn't really understand, their eyes wide in childlike fear as Black put a bullet in their heads. Many of his friends had suffered from PTSD. Some indeed had paid the ultimate price. Suicide was common amongst veterans. Generally, it was an overdose. Or they drunk themselves into oblivion. One had jumped from a plane without a parachute. When Black left the army, he thought, at the time, he could handle it. And he did, for a spell. But it was never going to be easy, swapping a Heckler and Koch MP5 sub-machine gun for an office desk. A Glock semi-automatic for a Tesco trolley. And slowly, slowly voices began to whisper on the fringes of his mind. Whispers of the dead. Shapes hovered and floated. Images, flashbacks, scenes. Black had killed many people. Now they were coming back, blowing dark clouds in his head.

The drink helped. Death would be more complete. He sat in a worn armchair in his living room. He took a swig of the whisky, topped it up. A young woman had been kidnapped, and Black had a mission, bestowed upon him by Colonel Mackenzie. Probably because he knew Black was mad enough to undertake it.

Black wasn't mad. He was bone weary, and looking for an excuse to find the exit door. The Colonel had given it to him.

Black would take up the task, and do what he was required to do. And if he died in the process, then he guessed it would be better than jumping from a plane without a fucking parachute.

He finished his glass, and immediately topped it up, pushing out the darkness.

But it came anyway.

6

Death is watching you all the time, make no mistake. That's okay. Death watches everybody. It's when it smiles. That's when you have a problem. But soldiers of the Regiment know exactly what to do. They smile right fucking back.

Observation raised by Staff Sergeant to 22nd Regiment of the SAS.

The place was quiet. Pauline Jardine checked her appointment book. The first one was scheduled for noon. Nothing for the next three hours, unless she got a walk-in. Which she wouldn't expect. It was a bleak, freezing Wednesday morning in the middle of January. Snow wasn't far away. The air bit the skin, made the lungs tingle with every breath. People were either working, or staying indoors, if they had any sense. Popping early into a beauty salon in the south side of Glasgow was not something she anticipated happening. Not today.

She'd been in a short while, switching the heating on, the lights, tidying. Though not much tidying needed to be done. Pauline was obsessive about neatness. Everything in its proper place. Everything scrupulously clean. A little order in a chaotic world.

One thing was certain. Pauline Jardine's world at this moment was chaotic. Dangerously so.

She usually opened the salon at 10am. Pauline had worked in the industry long enough to know most ladies desiring a makeover were not early risers.

She had come in an hour early for a very specific reason. A meeting had been arranged. There was no way to avoid it. That had been part of the problem. She had avoided people who did not take kindly to being ignored. Her lip quivered. She took a deep inhalation of breath, fighting an urge to break down, sob into her hands.

A nightmare was coming. She glanced at her watch for the tenth time.

In five minutes, to be exact.

7

Pauline took up position behind the reception desk, and waited. There was nothing else for her to do. Her salon looked out onto the main road. Traffic was dwindling. Rush hour had ended. People waited at a bus stop across the road. People going to work perhaps, or into the city centre for any number of reasons. They could see her; she could see them. She'd kept the front window blinds open. Which was why she'd asked to meet here. Too public. Too exposed.

Surely they wouldn't try anything here.

Though if she were dragged into one of the back rooms... She couldn't finish the thought. She had to keep calm. They were businessmen. They would see reason. They would understand, consider, reach an agreement.

Who the fuck was she trying to kid?

As if from nowhere, two men stood outside at the door, peering in. One was smiling, and fluttered his fingers in a little wave. The other was not smiling. They entered. She stood up. A bell, fastened at the top of the door, tinkled.

"Hello, Pauline."

"Hello, Danny," she said, hardly able to keep the shake from her voice. "Thanks for coming."

"Thanks for asking us," replied the smiling man, his voice rich in sarcasm. The second man turned, and locked the door, flipping the sign over to "closed". Now both men stood, side by side, focusing on her, and all Pauline could do was stare back.

The one who spoke was dressed in jeans, a heavy parka, gloves. His features were regular, forgettable. Pale-blue eyes regarded her from a round, bland face, blond hair receding back from a smooth, slightly bulbous forehead. Maybe five-ten. A man who was in middle ground, between portly and just plain fat. Another couple of years, and he'd get there.

The other was altogether different – smaller, but broad, his neck wider than his head, close brooding eyes under a heavy brow, dark hair shaved almost to the bone. He wore a close-fitting sports top, showing off his physique to full effect, oblivious to the cold.

The first man was Danny Brogan. Money lender, pimp, extortionist, drug dealer, gangster. Highly intelligent. The other was Ian Johnstone. Full time thug. Brogan's enforcer. The man sent to maim and disfigure. The man who delivered Brogan's message, and then some.

"I have the strongest feeling you've been trying to avoid us," Brogan said. "I hope I'm wrong. Because that would be plain rude. Wouldn't that be rude, Ian?"

Ian Johnstone didn't respond. He kept his eyes fixed on Pauline.

Brogan continued. "How's your father keeping?"

Pauline swallowed back her fear, did her best to keep her voice level.

"Not so good. He barely recognises me."

"Sorry to hear that. Must be hard, seeing a man like that, your own dad, reduced to a shell. Like a husk. Nothing inside.

Hollow. All the lights switched off. If I end up like that, I hope to Christ they give me a pill."

Pauline nodded, but said nothing. She had nothing to say.

"But we're not really here to talk about him, are we, Pauline?"

"I suppose not."

"We're here to talk about money. And money makes the world go round. Doesn't it, Ian?"

Johnstone didn't move an inch.

"Money, money, money," continued Brogan. "Or lack of. You're late, Pauline. By two weeks. And you know it. Let's remind ourselves. You – or more specifically your father – came to us. We didn't come to him. And when people come to us, we explain in detail that we're not like normal lending institutions. If you can't repay the money and the interest within the allotted time, we don't send letters, or emails, or hire fancy lawyers, or any of that stuff. As you well know. We prefer to use other means. Which is why we're here."

Brogan tilted his head down, kept his eyes on her. The smile was gone. His voice was soft when he spoke, laced with menace. "Do you have the money, Pauline?"

Pauline had placed her handbag on the reception desk in front of her. She opened it, and pulled out a brown envelope, which she held out to him.

"It's all there. Twelve thousand pounds."

Brogan took it. He tucked it in an inside pocket.

"Aren't you going to count it?" she asked.

"You're short."

Pauline felt the heavy drum of her heart. "It's what was owed..." she stammered.

"Twelve thousand was the amount you owed before you were late. It's now £24,000. It's called *penalty interest*. So that's another twelve. And I want paid. Right now."

Pauline couldn't think of a response. She tried to speak, but her mouth was suddenly dry.

"Do you have £12,000?"

She shook her head. "Where can I find that type of money?" she mumbled.

"You managed to scrape this together," Brogan said, patting the pocket where he'd put the envelope.

"That was stock money. And six months' rent. I don't have any more."

"That's not strictly true. You need to open your eyes. Look around."

"I don't understand."

"You have all this. Your business. All the equipment. The products. Maybe we can put in some tanning beds."

"What are you saying?"

"Hear that," replied Brogan, nudging Johnstone. Johnstone looked immovable, like a chunk of granite. His gaze did not waver. Brogan continued in a silky voice. "I think she understands exactly what I'm saying. I think she's trying to be cute."

His lips curled into a crooked smile.

"What I'm saying, you stupid bitch, is that you work for me now. This is my business. I have acquired it. Which means you'll launder my money. And you'll work your little cunt off until the debt's clear. That could be a considerable while, what with compound interest, and penalties, and anything else I can think of. And you'll do exactly what I say, and jump when I say jump. You'll take the cash I give you, and put it through your books, and wash it nice and clean, and everyone's happy. Do you understand what I'm saying now? Or do you need more clarification?"

She couldn't help herself – her eyes began to well up with tears. "I don't want to go to prison."

Brogan cocked his head quizzically. "And that's your response? Seriously? Tell me, Pauline, what do you think's worse. Me, or prison."

She sobbed. "Please... I've paid what you asked..."

"She still doesn't get it." Brogan sighed and turned to Johnstone, standing beside him. "Looks like she needs more clarification. Such a shame. Such a pretty girl. Take her to the back room, and break her fucking face open."

Johnstone stirred, moved towards her. Suddenly the door rattled. Both men turned. A man stood at the entrance. Pauline recognised him instantly, but couldn't comprehend why, of all people, this particular man should be here.

The man was her lawyer.

The man was Adam Black.

8

He was a big man. Six-two, easy. Lean, unobtrusively muscular. Harsh cheekbones, flat cheeks, thick dark hair cropped short. He wore a close-fitting black tunic, pale-blue jeans. His office was directly above Pauline's shop. He'd sorted out her lease, and taken a token fee for the work. When she got behind in her rent, she'd asked him to try to negotiate with the landlord. He had asked if there were problems, and as if he were a priest, she'd unburdened herself. She had explained how her father had gone to money lenders, without her knowledge, to give her a start-up for her new business. She had explained her father had suffered a stroke. She had explained how she was struggling to find the cash. He'd listened patiently, saying nothing. And when she'd finished, he'd suggested her best option was to report the matter to the police.

At which she laughed, and realised there was no way out.

Yet here he was. At the front entrance. And suddenly he didn't look like a lawyer anymore. Suddenly, he was someone entirely different.

He gazed at her, through the glass door, past the two men,

stared straight at her. She tried to warn him away, with her eyes. *Danger*, she tried to convey. *Go away.*

But he looked at her, and did a strange thing. He smiled.

Brogan regarded him contemptuously, and gestured with his thumb. "Fuck off!" There was no doubting Black could hear. But he raised his shoulders, as if puzzled, and knocked hard on the glass.

"I don't believe this," Brogan muttered. He took three steps forward, so that his face was up close to the door, only the glass pane separating them. "Don't you understand. You need to FUCK RIGHT OFF."

Black nodded, grinning. "I understand. But I have the money."

Brogan turned his head to Johnstone. "What's he talking about?"

Johnstone twitched his broad shoulders, spoke for the first time, his voice a low growl. "Fucked if I know. But if he's got money..."

"True enough. If the man's got money..." Brogan swivelled round to Pauline, who had remained behind the reception desk, dumbfounded. "Is this prick your guardian angel?" He laughed. "Let's see what he's about." He turned back to Johnstone. "Open the door. Let the man in. It's cold out there."

Johnstone did as he was instructed. He unlocked the front door.

Black entered. They stepped back, allowing him room. He stood before them. Pauline regarded the three men. Black was big. Taller than Brogan and Johnstone. He had an easy stance, relaxed. Yet Pauline detected an undefinable presence. Something she had never noticed about the man before. Something suddenly menacing. She knew in that instant that he was home here, facing two thugs. Comfortable in such obvious danger. A strange comparison entered her mind – a fleeting thought. Two rabid dogs before a wolf. Dogs back down. The wolf fights to the end.

"This is a private meeting, between Miss Jardine and ourselves," Brogan said. "It's rude to interrupt. It could land you in trouble, friend."

Black regarded the two men. To Pauline, his eyes glittered. "I'm not looking to cause trouble," replied Black, essaying an easy smile. "I thought you might be discussing money. I thought I might help."

"What makes you think we were talking about money?"

"Pauline told me about her... situation. I understand you gentlemen are looking for the repayment of a debt."

Brogan flicked a glance back to Pauline. "You talked?"

Pauline stood, said nothing, two hands gripped tight on the edge of the reception desk.

Brogan resumed his attention back to Black. "She owed me £12,000. But I've had a change of heart. Because of the sheer fucking grief she's given me, the debt is now twenty-four. So that's another twelve grand. You have that type of money Mr..."

"Black. Adam Black. I have money."

"Then if you give me it right now, the debt's cleared. If you're fucking me about, then Ian here will break your arms, and the debt doubles. You understand?"

Black kept his gaze steadily on Brogan. Pauline watched the scene unfold, second by unbelievable second, heart in mouth.

"I understand perfectly. I've given you my name. I think, if we're about to complete a business transaction, you give me yours. As a courtesy."

"Of course. As a courtesy. It would be rude not to. My name is *none of your fucking business, prick*. Now, give me the money, or my friend here will get upset. He can get very mean and nasty. And you wouldn't like that, Mr Black."

"I'm sure I wouldn't. Here's your money." He took a one-pound coin from his trouser pocket, and tossed it at Brogan. It bounced off the front of his coat, and dropped onto the wooden flooring.

Brogan watched it for several seconds, then raised his head slowly. "What the fuck is this?"

"Payment. Exactly one pound. That's all you're going to get. You can take it or leave it. I don't really care. The debt's cleared. You'll leave Pauline alone, and you'll never come near her again." He turned to Johnstone. "And if you do, I'll rip your fucking heads off."

Brogan stared. His mouth drooped at the corners, his forehead wrinkled. Pauline thought of a sad clown. "You've got balls, Mr Black. You have no idea of the situation you're in, or who you're dealing with."

"I know exactly who I'm dealing with. Two small-time, scumbag fuckwits, who feel good about threatening women, and who, when it gets right down to it, are just a couple of gutless cowards. Am I right?"

Brogan licked his lips. Pauline could almost hear the cogs of his brain grinding. The large front window exposed them to pedestrians and traffic outside. One wrong move, one act of violence, and all it would take would be for someone to call the police. And she knew Brogan didn't want the police crawling all over his business. But his desire to strike out at Black was palpable. Pauline sensed it. It emanated like the smell of sweat. He had been insulted. He needed to respond. To save face. A silence fell. The two men stared at Black. Black stared right back. Pauline heard a noise – the boom-boom of her heart.

"This isn't over, Adam Black," hissed Brogan. "I swear to Jesus fucking Christ. You and that tart are dead. Dead fucking meat. You'll never know when, or where. Your life, my friend, is fucking over."

Brogan looked round to Pauline, and blew her a kiss. "Your

funeral." He nodded to Johnstone, who had remained as unreadable as a block of wood throughout the entire exchange. "Let's go."

Then Black reacted in a way Pauline could never have imagined. What he did made her gasp.

He stepped back, and blocked the door. He spoke in a quiet voice. "I didn't give you permission to leave."

Brogan and Johnstone stood, looked at the man before them. "What the fuck did you say?" said Brogan.

"You don't get to go. Not yet. This finishes now."

9

Pauline looked at Black from a suddenly different perspective. He was smiling. Behind the smile, she saw something which chilled her. She saw calculation and intent. And his eyes. His eyes gleamed. Like blue agate.

She shrank back in her chair. She was disorientated. She wondered if she should be more scared of the man she knew as Adam Black than the two gangsters trying to extort money.

Brogan took a step away, flicking a glance at Johnstone, from which Johnstone seemed to derive exact information.

"Big mistake, pal," Johnstone said, approaching Black.

Johnstone was easily six inches shorter than Black. But he was wide, built like a tank, thick neck and shoulders, long arms, head like a bullet, small, pinched features. A very dangerous man.

"Big mistake," echoed Black.

Johnstone lunged forward, swinging with one heavy fist. Black ducked, hacked with his hand at the side of the burly neck. Johnstone gave a grunt, stepped away. Black sprang forward, brought a momentous blow down on Johnstone's ear. Johnstone reeled back. Black followed up, striking Johnstone's face, using the heel of his hand, a crunching impact to the area between nose and upper lip. Johnstone staggered on his heels, into the receptionist's desk. Stuff scattered on the floor – leaflets; cards; a tray of the latest beauty products. Pauline jumped to her feet, screamed.

Black was on him, relentless. He swung a short, brutal uppercut, connecting under Johnstone's jaw. Pauline heard teeth break. Johnstone's head snapped back, his body flipping onto the desk. Black loomed over him, punched him in the throat, crushing his windpipe. Johnstone gave a wheezy choke. Black seized the front of his sports top, hauled him up, whirled him round. For a second, he stared into Johnstone's eyes. They were glazed, vacant. Black finished off, propelling him square into the front window, head first. Johnstone crashed through, glass cascading round him into a million pieces, to land in a heap on the pavement outside. A woman pointed, shouted. People stared, uncomprehending.

Black fixed his attention on Brogan.

Brogan had retreated back to the wall, and stopped. There was nowhere else to go.

Pauline watched. She became aware she was holding her breath.

"This ends now," Black said.

Brogan nodded. "Whatever you say," he mumbled.

Black looked round to Pauline. "I don't want you to see this. Go."

Pauline stood, transfixed.

"Go!" shouted Black.

As if woken from a trance, she snapped out of herself, ran to the front door, and out to safety, to join several other people, congregated on the pavement to watch the unbelievable events unfolding in her beauty shop.

Only yards from her, lying sprawled on the ground, was the

enforcer known as Ian Johnstone, suddenly no longer a threat, prostrate on a blanket of broken glass, unconscious, face unrecognisable, shaved head slick with blood.

What Pauline witnessed next, what everyone there at that particular moment witnessed, was like something from a movie.

A horror movie.

10

Black inspected the man before him. He was smaller, overweight. He was dressed for the winter, cocooned in a heavy parka, his movements restricted. Black looked into the man's eyes, the man called Danny Brogan, and saw something he'd seen a thousand times before. Fear. Undiluted. In its purest form.

"Who the fuck are you?" Brogan mumbled.

Black delayed answering for several long seconds. Let the silence heighten Brogan's distress. Black knew all about Danny Brogan. He'd been given intelligence by the best of sources. Brogan was small-time, trying to claw up the criminal food chain. Money laundering, drugs, extortion. Vicious and determined. Knifings and slashings, usually performed by his psychopathic friend Ian Johnstone, lying on the street outside. Perhaps dead, thought Black, though he hardly cared. It was Brogan's turn. A lesson was to be taught. Black felt he was qualified to give it.

He glanced round, at the crowd outside the salon. Maybe six or seven had gathered. And no wonder. It's not every day a body comes hurtling through a shop window in Shawlands. Let them see, he thought. Let them feast. The more, the better. Some had their phones pointed at him. The scene was set. He glimpsed Pauline's face, and felt a little sorry she should have to bear witness to the scene about to unfold. But his sorrow lasted all of two seconds. It was theatre time.

He turned his attention back to Brogan, who suddenly kicked out. Black caught his leg, gripping it under the knee, and pushed forward. Brogan yelped, lost his balance, and fell on the floor. Black was on him, jamming his knee down hard onto his collarbone, using his body weight to keep him pinned to the ground.

Brogan squirmed. Black leant forward, face close up.

"Who the fuck am I? Your worst nightmare, my friend."

He reached his hand behind him. Under his tunic, strapped to his belt, was an eight-inch red leather sheath. In it was a fixed Ka-Bar knife, favoured by the American Marines, carbon steel clip point blade, razor sharp. Black pulled it out, and held it in front of Brogan's face, four inches from his eyes. The blade gleamed under the salon lights.

Black heard someone scream from the crowd outside.

If you don't like it, then don't fucking look. Though that would defeat the exercise, he thought grimly.

"What the fuck are you gonna do with that!" gasped Brogan, words rattling out like machine gun fire.

"You picked on the wrong person this time," hissed Black, and began his work.

11

The High Court in Glasgow. Black was standing in the dock, a court officer on each side. He'd pled guilty to attempted murder.

The words of his friend and ally Colonel Mackenzie echoed in his head – *no going back*. The reality hit Black like a cold slap, here, in the lofty halls of Court Number 2. Too late now for second thoughts, for reconsideration. He'd slipped passed the Rubicon. It was worth it. So he told himself. A means to an end. *Buckle up*, he thought. *It's going to be one fucking rollercoaster ride*. Nevertheless, standing in the High Court, its power and solemnity weighing heavy in his mind, Black found it hard not to be overwhelmed. He waited for the Crown to address the judge.

The court was packed. Reporters, members of the public, and a large contingent of the Brogan family. There to gloat when Black was sent down. The dock was three steps up, then a waist-height varnished wooden box in which to stand. On a shelf was a jug of water and a glass. He was standing at the highest point in the court room, level with the judge. Below him, sitting round

32

a large circular table, were lawyers, clerks, court officials, hunched over computer screens, files stacked around them. They cast furtive glances in his direction. The place was hushed, waiting.

Counsel for the Crown Prosecution stood, cloaked in his dark court gown. Black was reminded of a crow, picking over the remains of the dead.

Counsel spoke, his voice rich and silky. Confident, thought Black. And why not – he'd made it easy for them.

"M' lord, Adam Black has pled guilty to two counts of attempted murder. On the morning of January fifteenth, in a beauty salon known as *Pauline's,* at 86 Kilmarnock Road, Shawlands, in the south of Glasgow, Adam Black attacked two men, Daniel Brogan and Ian Johnstone. These men were attending the salon to conclude a business arrangement with the proprietor of the business, Pauline Jardine. They were not seeking trouble. During the course of the meeting, Black entered the premises. He asked Mr Brogan and Mr Johnstone the nature of the business they were discussing. Quite rightly, they refused to divulge this information. Black, unprovoked, attacked first of all Mr Johnstone, striking him several times to the body, and then throwing him through the front window of the premises. As a result, Mr Johnstone suffered serious head injuries. He was taken to Queen Elizabeth Hospital, where he remains in a coma, assisted by a life support machine. The chances are, he will never recover.

"Black then focused his attention on Mr Brogan. After pinning Mr Brogan to the ground, he used a hunting knife he had concealed under his clothing to scar his cheeks, his forehead, his nose, and..."

The lawyer hesitated, turning a brief glance at Black, who stared impassively back.

"Yes, Mr Waters?" said the judge. "Please continue."

"Sorry, m' lord. Black used the knife to cut out Mr Brogan's tongue. Mr Brogan needed over three hundred stitches. He now suffers from chronic depression. He has been unable to leave his home since the incident, except for visits to his doctor and to the hospital.

"M' lord, the consequences of Black's actions have been devastating for his victims. They might never regain a normal quality of life. His actions were pre-meditated. He entered the premises that morning with the sole intention of killing these men. He brought with him a hunting knife, which he purposefully concealed. The only reason he was unable to fulfil his murderous intentions was through the bravery and quick response of the police, who arrived at the scene, and who were able to apprehend Black before he could inflict further damage. Though doubtless your Lordship would agree, enough damage had already been done. In the opinion of the Crown, he is a profoundly dangerous man, who lacks empathy or compassion. He is violent and reckless. Society needs protection from a man like Adam Black."

Waters, speaking for the Crown, sat down. He had finished his summary of Black's crime. Even summarised, Black conceded, it made for unwholesome listening.

The judge, after several ponderous minutes, finished taking notes. Then he turned to Black, scrutinising him with gimlet eyes beneath his white judicial wig. Then he spoke. "I believe you've chosen to waive legal representation?"

Black nodded. "Yes."

"That's unusual, given the circumstances."

Black shrugged in response.

"It's your decision. Do you have anything to say, in mitigation?"

"Not particularly. Except to say I'm sorry."

"That's something," said the judge.

"Sorry I never got to finishing Brogan off. Maybe next time."

People in the public gallery took a collective intake of outraged breath.

The judge kept a level stare on Black. He spoke in a measured voice. "I will not tolerate such comments in my court room, Black. You've had your say. Now it's my turn. Normally I would be seeking background reports, their purpose to assist me in coming to a decision about how I should proceed in sentencing those such as yourself. But in this particular case, I regard that as a waste of the court's time. As Mr Waters has said, it is clear to me that you are a dangerous, violent man, who has no regard for human life. You made it your business to try to kill these men. You concealed a knife to implement your dreadful intent. You carried out a ferocious attack. You mutilated an innocent man, inflicting horrendous injuries. And now you stand here, seemingly without remorse and without a single speck of contrition. The only mitigating factor is that you chose to plead guilty, thus saving the victims and their families the stress and hardship of a trial.

"Society has no room for this barbaric behaviour. You are a danger to the general public. You clearly believe the law does not apply to you, that you can do as you wish, causing harm and distress, without fear of reproach. Well, the law does apply. And it will be applied now. I have no hesitation in sentencing you to fourteen years' imprisonment. You will be taken immediately from this court, and begin your custodial sentence today."

The two court officials approached Black, ushering him from the dock, where a police officer waited. Black was handcuffed.

Someone shouted from the public gallery. "Rot in hell, Black!"

Black considered the remark, and agreed silently he probably would.

The words of the Colonel rang in his head – *no going back.*

Probably not. But Black had a mission. And the stakes had never been higher.

12

Rachel Hempworth worked for the Scottish *Evening Standard*, a broadsheet newspaper read up and down the breadth of Scotland. She'd been a journalist for over fifteen years, and this was, potentially, her biggest story yet. The Adam Black story. His crime was gruesome. The mutilation of a man's face, the use of a hunting knife, another man lying in a hospital bed in a coma. The facts were plain and brutal. And Black had ended up with a stiff sentence. But Rachel had a nose for a story.

And this had all the hallmarks of a great story. She knew Danny Brogan. Knew *of* Danny Brogan. Money lender, pimp, thug. The other one – Johnstone – enforcer and all-round hard man. These were choice items neither the public nor the court were aware of. And Black had pled guilty. No defence lawyer. And he'd made damn sure his assaults had been witnessed by a dozen people, recording everything on their mobile phones. The case raised a host of questions in her inquisitive mind. What the hell was a high street lawyer doing with men like Brogan and Johnstone? And how could a lawyer deal with such dangerous men in such a manner. Questions, questions.

She researched, pieced together fragments of his life to make a whole. She spoke to other lawyers who knew him, people at university who remembered him, tapped her sources in the military for information. And when she'd gathered up all the little vignettes of his life, and assembled a complete picture, the picture was compelling. Adam Black was more than a lawyer. Much more.

Straight after getting his law degree, he'd joined the army, like his older brother, who had been killed in Ireland. Black volunteered for the Parachute Regiment, then was accepted in the Special Air Service, where he was promoted to captain. The SAS. An elite combat troop. The most highly trained soldiers in the world. Adam Black was no slouch. Afghanistan, Bosnia, Africa, Iraq. Counterterrorism. He was a one-man killing machine. To top it all, he'd been awarded the Military Cross, the highest honour in the military. For uncommon bravery.

Then he left the army, to practise law in a small but prestigious law firm in the centre of Glasgow. Married, with a small child. A remarkable, full life, thought Rachel. From war hero to lawyer.

And then it got even more remarkable. Like something from a novel dreamed up by a thriller writer. More than remarkable. Unbelievable. But it was all true.

Black's wife and daughter murdered. Four years ago. In their house, by an unknown assailant. Killed at gunpoint, professional, clinical. Revenge killing? The police hadn't come up with any answers, other than the fact that Black must have seriously pissed someone off.

Then Black goes off the radar for a year. The law firm he worked for disappeared, amidst allegations of large-scale money laundering and gangland connections.

Black returns, setting up as a sole practitioner in Shawlands. Doing mundane stuff – conveyancing, leases, wills. From the remarkable to the banal.

And then he pushes one Glasgow gangster through a shop window, and disfigures another.

You'd have to be blind not to see a story here.

She now looked at the man in the dock. He was big, impressive. Handsome, in a hard-bitten way. Definitely not unattractive. Dark hair. Dark, deep eyes. She wondered what these eyes had witnessed. Savagery, violence, death.

She watched him as the High Court judge passed sentence. He remained impassive. Unmoved.

Did she detect a flicker of a smile?

Adam Black was no fool. He'd refused a lawyer. He'd pled guilty. What the hell was he doing?

To Rachel, none of it made sense. Did he want to go to prison? Rachel's nose twitched. She'd picked up the scent. When something didn't make sense, then her skill was unpeeling the veneer, to lay bare the darkness beneath.

She watched Black being led down, amid the jeers and heckles of the public gallery.

What are you up to, Adam Black? she wondered.

She would make it her business to find out.

13

The real name of the man referred to as The Red Serpent, was Oliver Pritchard. An unassuming name, in his own estimation. He had been bestowed the title of Red Serpent by the popular press, but he was glad of it. For once, they'd got it right. It reflected his true essence. Oliver Pritchard was a thing of the past, like an old suit he had once worn, and which he had discarded.

Or like a skin he had shed, as a snake might. Or indeed a serpent.

He had been incarcerated in his little box in Shotts prison for six months. He would die here. This knowledge did not trouble him. He lived on his memories. And his memories were capable of providing him solace and nourishment for the rest of his days.

He had his own cell, and he shared a section of the block with only seven other inmates. Four of them paedophiles, one of whom had killed two children. A mere shadow compared to his own activities. Pritchard's routine was simple and consistent. Early rise at 6.30. A short stroll to the showers, where a guard watched by the door. Breakfast in a small canteen where he ate with the other six. The food was tolerable, though he had to chew cautiously. Once he'd discovered a razor blade in his cereal. He never reported it. He kept it, tucked it in his sleeve. After breakfast, the routine continued – an escort back to his cell, where he was confined until midday. During this time, he would reflect, perhaps read a newspaper, which he was given every morning.

Midday, and he was allowed to exercise. He and his six fellow prisoners were led into a cordoned-off section of the recreational yard. A flat concrete square space, thirty feet each side, boundaried by brown brick walls fifteen feet high and topped with rolls of barbed wire. All the time, being watched by two guards. Forty minutes. Then back to the cell for half an hour. Lunch in the canteen. Then a trip to a room fashioned into a library of sorts, big enough for each of them to sit. There was a single television fixed high on a wall, the news channel showing constantly. Three hours. They were allowed to wander, out into the corridor, and into another common room, where there were couches, and tables, and even a coffee machine.

Then back to the cell for a short while, and then dinner. Then back to the cell, where they stayed, until 6.30 the following morning, when the process repeated itself, again and again.

But the blade – secreted in his sleeve. He had used it that night, on himself. Not in any effort to slit his wrists. Suicide was the very last thing on his mind. Before a mirror, he had cut deep into his right cheek. A symbol. The curling body of a snake. The mark he had left on each of his victims, on their faces. His mark. His brand.

Six months he had been locked up in Shotts prison, the most secure unit in Scotland, holding bank robbers, rapists, murderers, child molesters.

But none like him.

He was a god. Those around him were worms in the sun.

Six months. During this time, not one word had he uttered to anyone in the prison. He ate in silence. He sat in the common room in silence. Nothing could persuade him to talk. He had no inclination to speak.

Except for once every month, on a particular day, at a particular time. To a very special person.

And then, suddenly, his world changed.

14

The old woman sat by a burning hearth. Outside, the wind howled, the windows rattled. The wind was fierce even in the summer months, coming in from the ocean. But in the knuckle of winter, it possessed a demon quality. Cold enough to shrivel the bones, powerful enough to blow a grown man off his feet. She sat huddled under a layer of pullovers, a woollen shawl over her shoulders, her chair pulled up close to the flames. The wind wouldn't get her. Nor the cold. She'd lived with them for eighty years. The wind could rattle and howl as much as it wanted. The trees could bend and sway. The cold could frost her windows and freeze her rooms. But this didn't frighten her.

Her cottage sat solitary on the edge of a wood, through which a single path ran, like a slender black vein, to a village of grey-stone buildings. Stray off the path, and it was easy to get lost. In the dark, a careless person might wander away, and fall off the cliff's edge, and onto the rocks below.

She sat, and stared into the flames. She thought to detect shapes, images. Snakes leaping up from the coals.

A noise. From below. She shifted in her chair, unwilling to leave the heat. She pretended it was the noise of the house, groaning against the wind. But of course, she knew better. It intensified. She could not ignore it. She sighed, got up from her chair.

It was always the same time. When the woman kept downstairs roused from her drugged sleep, and realised she wasn't dreaming, that the nightmare was real.

The same thing every time.

Screaming.

15

Black, handcuffed, two policemen following, was escorted directly from a side entrance of the court building into a waiting police van. Another policeman was seated inside. Cameras flashed. The press were waiting. Front-page news, reckoned Black. The stage was set. Black got in, sat, still handcuffed. He was joined by a second policeman. The door closed. The van drove off.

The windows were darkened. The crowds they passed couldn't see him, but Black saw them. Cameramen lifted their lenses to take pictures through the windows – more in hope than accuracy. People shouted abuse. The van left them behind, taking the twenty-five-mile journey to the prison known as Shotts.

The two policemen started up idle chat, speaking as if Black didn't exist. To an extent, he didn't. Suddenly, he was no longer an individual. Now he was a number, at the behest of the state. Owned by the state. His rights were gone. From now on he would be told, not asked. He would be told when and where, 24/7. And if he chose to resist? Trouble.

He allowed himself a cold smile. Not so far away from army life.

He thought back to his previous existence – the life before he was married, before he was a lawyer. To when he was a captain in the SAS. He had been held prisoner before. Kept as a guest in Saddam Hussein's dungeons, carved from the dirt and stone, deep beneath his fabulous hundred-acre palace. At night, as Saddam sipped the finest wines in the world, beneath, his prisoners were subjected to the most brutal torture. Black had been one of them. Kept in the dark. Starving. Daily beatings. Mock executions. Water boarding. Constant noise. Forced to watch beheadings, hangings, mutilations. Every day. For three months.

Yet he had endured.

Shotts, in comparison, was a breeze in the park. Or so he imagined.

He had been handed down fourteen years.

Black had barely over a month.

Or the girl would die.

16

Colonel Stewart Mackenzie. Sixty-eight years old. Veteran of the Falklands War, the Gulf War, Bosnia. And throughout it all, running like a constant underground stream, always bubbling away, the Troubles in Northern Ireland. Now he was head of a small section of the government which had never been named. A name could cause attention. And attention was the last thing the Colonel wanted. From the public, from other parts of the government. From anyone. Except those in his room.

If shit needed clearing up, then he was the man to deal with it. Bad shit. Stuff no one else would touch, too scared to touch. Which was why he was given a free rein. He and his select band of men were given extreme flexibility. And virtually no accountability.

The job in hand was the worst yet. He watched a small television in the corner of his office, deep in the bowels of an anonymous government building in the town of Dumfries. The same office he and Black had sat in, discussing plans only four weeks before. He was accompanied by two men and a woman, all sitting on the somewhat dilapidated furniture, all eyes fixed on the unfolding news, listening, as the news presenter read out in a dead pan monotone the sentence Black had been given, the crime he had committed. Mackenzie watched as the camera caught a glimpse of Black, three inches taller than the two policemen beside him, being led from the court building and into the back of a van.

Mackenzie switched the television off. In his hands, he cradled a glass of whisky, an indulgence he was leaning to more and more. He gazed at its rich, gold hue. If now was not the time to have a drink, when the fuck was. He took a deep swig.

"So it begins," he said.

The man who sat next to him was large. A monster of a man, easily six-four. Dressed in full police uniform. Moist features in a round face, skin pale as the moon. Bald to the bone. Small ears flat against the side of his head. Eyes burrowed deep within folds of fat, his buttoned-up jacket straining to contain his bulk.

Chief Constable Frank Divers.

"It begins all right." He looked at the Colonel, small eyes accusing him from behind rimless glasses. Not the perfect advert to inspire young men to join the police, thought the Colonel. Fat, bald, short-sighted. A true leader of men.

"This is too far," he went on. "You and your department, or whatever the hell you call it – more like a circus show – have made a mockery of us. Even you can comprehend that, surely."

"Us?" said the Colonel.

"The Criminal Justice System." Divers pronounced each word slowly, a short space between them, to emphasise his point. "We don't need mavericks like you. Good old-fashioned police work, done properly, methodically," he stabbed one meaty finger at the Colonel, "and all carried out within the law."

"Drastic situation, drastic measures," broke in the other man seated. He was average height, wearing a blue pinstriped suit, blue silk tie, crisp white shirt. Maybe fifty-five, maybe older. Difficult to tell. Square, silver cufflinks gleamed. His aftershave dominated the room. His hair, silver like his cufflinks, was coiffured back from his forehead. Smooth, tanned face. But his eyes were old. His eyes had seen everything. And then some, thought the Colonel. His name was Ernest Stanford. Whitehall civil servant. A mandarin in the corridors of power. He'd survived six prime ministers, and would doubtless see off more. Like a mercenary, a hired gun, he was loyal only to those in power.

Not unlike his own position, reflected the Colonel.

"And let's face it," continued Stanford, "good old police work hasn't been an entire success."

Divers switched his gaze to Stanford. "We caught our man!"

"You did," said the Colonel. "After he'd tortured, mutilated and killed ten young women." He looked straight on at Divers. "And that's only the one's we know about."

"None of that matters," said Stanford. "It's the present we're dealing with. Sometimes rules have to be broken, when the situation merits it. This one definitely does. And this is from the very highest level – am I right, Katie?"

The three men turned their attention to the woman sitting next to them. She hadn't spoken. She was exceptionally good at listening. Listening, understanding situations, people. Katie Sykes. Dark hair, shoulder length, clear complexion, eyes azure blue. Slender, tall – maybe five-ten in her heels. Forty years old. She kept herself fit. Word was, she ran two miles every morning before breakfast, and hit the gym four times a week. You looked at her and thought – athlete. When she settled her gaze on you, thought the Colonel, how easy it was to be seduced. Fooled. But the eyes were blue steel. You didn't get to be the Prime Minister's Permanent Secretary, in effect the principal policy advisor and head civil servant, without being hard as nails.

"To quote the PM," she said, "do what it takes."

"Do what it takes," echoed the Colonel.

"Though there's no need for the PM to know the fine detail," said Katie. "Just the broad brush strokes. The less she knows, the less chance of... recriminations. Needless to say, her daughter's missing, so whatever you have to do, Colonel, you have her full support."

"Provided she doesn't know exactly how we go about doing it," replied the Colonel.

Katie twitched her shoulders. "It's the world we're in. It is what it is. A means to an end."

"And you're wrong," said the Colonel.

Katie raised an eyebrow. "How so?"

"Elspeth Owen is not missing. She's been taken. Let's not forget this."

"We have to keep this tight," said Stanford. "Your plan, Colonel, which some might describe as audacious, could still be politically damaging if it got out into the public domain. You understand?"

"This is a little beyond politics," retorted the Colonel.

"Nevertheless," said Katie. "It makes sense. The fewer people who know about it the better. Other than us, does anyone else know?"

Chief Constable Divers shifted in his chair. The buttons on his jacket gleamed like coins of silver. "I've informed the DI heading up the task force. She's good. She knows when to keep her mouth shut. I thought it prudent not to keep anything from her."

"What's her name?" asked the Colonel.

"Vanessa Shaw."

"Fair enough," said Katie. "Desperate times. We need to try anything. Talking of good old-fashioned police work, have there been any developments, Divers?"

Divers spoke, appraising everyone in the room. "I've got a team of over a hundred dedicated people working round the clock. The PM phones me every day." He was almost smug when he spoke. "We'll find her. I promise you. We just need time."

"Which is what we don't have," said the Colonel.

"For the record," blustered Divers, "I think your plan is foolhardy, reckless, and fucking irresponsible. And who the hell is this man, Adam Black?"

The Colonel sighed, took a sip of his whisky, and said, "Maybe our only hope."

17

S hotts prison. Situated on the outskirts of the town of Shotts, in that area of Scotland referred to as North Lanarkshire. Once a bustling mining town, but like everywhere else, when the mines closed, the town closed with it.

But the prison offered employment. The biggest source of employment in the area. Prison officers, IT professionals, cleaners, administrators, drivers, plumbers, joiners. Prisoners needed feeding, needed books, clothing. Without the prison, Shotts, and other places, would have shrivelled up and died.

It was maximum security. The entrance actually looked quite appealing. New high red-brick walls, clean and smooth. The double door entrance set in a turret structure. Modern, welcoming. Like the exterior of a sports complex. Inside was a little different. Concrete three-storey buildings, squatting in no apparent order in the Scottish wilderness, encircled by more walls and thirty-feet-high barbed wire fences. There was no doubting this was a serious prison. Holding over five hundred inmates. Six accommodation units, including a segregation unit, specially adapted to house those prisoners requiring protection from the general prison population.

New inmates were not taken to the main entrance. They were driven through electric metal gates, at the rear of the prison. Black was immediately installed in B Hall. His details were ticked off, he was given a plastic box, containing toothbrush, toothpaste, soap, shampoo, deodorant, other mundane stuff, and prison-issue jeans, polo top, underwear, socks. He was allowed to keep the clothes he was wearing.

He was taken into the main hall – a wide corridor, with metal stairs each side leading to the floors on the upper two levels. Doors upon doors, all open, men mingling on the corridors, or else in their cells.

Contrary to popular belief, prisoners were not required to share cells. He was led into a room on the ground floor, seven feet by ten feet, comprising bed, wash-hand basin, toilet, and a single cupboard with drawers for his clothing. One small window, with bars, offering a view of a courtyard, high walls, and beyond, a dreary flat landscape. It was clean, functional. Black had seen a whole lot worse.

He was escorted into his room by two prison officers. Big men, both about the same height as Black, batons secured to black belts, along with portable radio receivers. The three men entered. One of the guards closed the door behind them, locked it. The other one spoke. He had a head of coarse red hair, his skin pockmarked, the remnants of old acne. A twisted beak of a nose. He came up close to Black, his face only inches away. He had faint wispy eyebrows, flecked with tiny granules of dandruff. Pinned on the chest of his navy-blue pullover, a badge with his name – Fletcher.

"Adam Black," he said.

"That's me," replied Black.

"Don't fucking answer me back. Ever. Unless I say so. Understand?"

"Have I to answer you back?"

"Fucking smart arse. They said you were some sort of hard bastard. Well, Mr Black, no one's as hard as me. And right now, I am your worst fucking enemy. And will be for the next fourteen years of your miserable fucking life."

He leaned in closer. Black detected the whiff of onion. "You cut Danny Brogan's tongue out. You slashed his face. I've got seriously bad news for you, Black."

Black waited.

"Danny Brogan has lots of pals in here. Lots. And guess what?"

Black remained silent.

"I'm one of them."

He took a step back. He handed Black a form. "These are the rules. You break them by one fucking fraction of an inch..." He placed a hand on the baton strapped to his waist, "...then I break you."

The other guard unlocked the door, opened it. As they left, Fletcher turned.

"Watch your back, Black."

Black returned the statement with a cold smile.

18

Pritchard was led into B Hall. He was ordered to carry a plastic tray holding his personal effects. His other stuff – papers, books – he was told to leave in his cell. They would be transferred later. Not that there was much to transfer. There were no photographs or mementos of his earlier life. Nothing to indicate he'd even existed. He never got letters. Or cards. Nor visitors, except occasionally from the police. And that was only to resurrect old questions. Asking him about missing women. Missing children. Missing *anybody*. The Red Serpent was a mystery. It was the way he liked it. It was all about control. Power. He knew everything. They knew nothing.

He was accompanied by four guards. Throughout his six-month incarceration so far, he had never travelled further than the segregation unit. Now he was in a whole different world. He was taken up to the third level, to a cell identical to the one he'd left, except that now he was in a block with a hundred and twenty others just like it. And Pritchard was no fool. News travelled at blistering speed in a place like this. Like flames in a dry forest. He was the Red Serpent. He had little doubt every inmate in that place knew exactly the crimes he'd pled guilty too. The abduction, mutilation and murder of ten young women.

He felt a new experience – a flutter in his chest, a cold tingle in the base of his stomach. Prisoners watched him walk by. Someone said something, the word clear and unequivocal – *cunt*.

He was shown his cell. Bare. Four walls, a bed, sink, toilet.

"Welcome to Hotel B Section," said one of the guards.

Pritchard didn't speak. But for the first time in as long as he could remember, he felt unsure. Unsettled. Scared, even?

Which was ridiculous.

He knew what was happening. He knew why it was happening. It had all been predicted. And he was ready.

19

Chief Constable Divers and Katie Sykes left the Colonel's office together. They had pressing business to attend to. The same business – the safe recovery of the Prime Minister's daughter. Their timetables had been cleared. There was nothing else on the agenda. Divers would drive north, to Glasgow, to police headquarters in Pitt Street, where the task force was based. Katie would also head to Glasgow, but then a flight down to London, and then on to Downing Street, to brief the PM. To brief her about the abduction of her only daughter. Not that there was much to brief her about.

The Colonel and Stanford remained. The Colonel reached over to a plain wooden side table, upon which rested an open bottle of Bell's whisky, and he poured himself a large top-up. Stanford gestured with his glass. The Colonel replenished it.

"Your man Black," said Stanford. "He's got this covered?"

The Colonel gave a deep sigh. "Who knows."

"That's not quite the reassurance I was hoping to hear."

The Colonel lifted his gaze from the liquid gleaming in his glass. "But it's all you're going to get. The situation is unique.

And terrible. And time-sensitive. Adam Black will do what has to be done. He's already put everything on the line, just to give us a starting position. Now he has to see it through. I suppose my answer should be, if anyone can do it, he can."

"For your sake, and everybody else's for that matter, let's fucking hope so."

"And for the girl's sake. Let's not forget. There's a young woman out there, somewhere. God knows what she's going through. What about the PM?"

Stanford shook his head, just a fraction. "Not great. Her daughter's been abducted, but the country still needs to function. She's putting on a brave face, but she's cracking."

"Of course she is."

"And when the media gets a hold of this, then it all cranks up a notch."

"Maybe *if* instead of *when*. We can keep this under wraps, if we're careful. Black might get somewhere. If he does, and quickly, then the media need never find out. We could be lucky."

"Seriously?" replied Stanford, an eyebrow raised. "Please. The press *will* find out. They need to find out."

The Colonel stared at Stanford, uncomprehending.

"The twists and turns of Whitehall, my friend," continued Stanford. "When the news channels and newspapers hear about the Prime Minister's daughter having been... taken, then suddenly we have a nation in sympathy. And you know what that means, don't you? There's always a silver lining, once you rake away the shit."

Stanford fell silent. He didn't finish, didn't need to. He sipped his whisky.

The Colonel looked away, faintly disgusted.

A nation in sympathy meant one thing – more votes.

The Colonel didn't blame Stanford. He was merely a product

of the system. Nor did he give a shit about the political nuances of the situation. But he did care about getting the girl back alive.

The way it was looking, everything hinged on one man. One man prepared to walk a lonely and dangerous road.

Adam Black.

20

Elspeth Owen could not at first comprehend the situation she'd found herself in. It couldn't be real, but yet it was. It was simply not possible that she was sitting on a bed, manacled by a band of metal around her waist, connected to the wall by heavy link chain, just enough slack for her to use the toilet and wash her face and hands in a sink on the opposite wall. It was not possible that she was in a room of grey stone, with a bare stone floor, no windows, and a single door permanently locked.

None of this was possible. Yet here she was. Time drifted, becoming meaningless. There was no night, no day. A single light bulb suspended by a cord from the ceiling switched off, and then after a while, switched on. Operated from outside the room. She fell asleep, then woke, screaming instinctively when she realised the nightmare was real. That she really was a captive, in a prison. And that she might die.

She hadn't changed her clothes for as long as she could remember. She would stink. Jeans, a pale-blue crop top. The things she had worn at the club in Edinburgh, an eternity ago. Her shoes had been removed. She relived the final moments a thousand times – she'd gone to the bar to get drinks. She got chatting to a group of females on a hen night. She'd been drinking. The place was a swirl of lights and colour and faces. She'd felt suddenly light-headed. The ceiling rushed to the floor. She remembered hands on her back as she was navigated from the club, those around her insubstantial, like wraiths in the night. Into the back of a car. Then... nothing. Waking up, shackled to a wall in a room of stone. She had been drugged, her drink spiked, somehow.

The door in front of her was solid metal, painted bright white. There was a shutter at head height. Every so often – it could have been hours, or minutes, she had lost all sense of time – it screeched open, a tray slid out supporting a plate of food and a glass of water. Despite her terror, she still got hungry. When it came, she jumped from the bed and lifted the plate and glass. She would glimpse a pair of eyes. The tray would retract, the shutter would close.

At those times she would plead with the person behind the door. But it was like pleading to a rock. The door never opened. The eyes looked at her and through her, as if she didn't exist.

And then the voice. Deep and brassy. Mechanical. A machine of some sort distorted it into something bestial, unhuman. It came from nowhere, all around. It talked to her. It asked questions. Her name, her birthday, her friends. She gave faltering responses. She could feel it listening, absorbing her answers. What was her favourite colour? Her favourite rock band? Recently, it asked her personal stuff. Was she a virgin; how many men; how did she like it?

She ate, and cried, and screamed, and shouted. Pleaded. But no one came. Every waking minute was an ordeal in terror. A billion miles from the safety and comfort of London. Would she be found? Her mother was the most powerful woman in the country. She would spare no effort in looking for her. But as time wore on, the terror changed gradually to a dull, deep despondency.

She was here to stay, until whoever it was who had put her here, whoever it was who was speaking to her, decided it was time for her to die.

The lens of the camera was roughly the same dimension as the end of a cigar. Placed in a vent in the corner, it was undetectable. It would never be noticed.

Elspeth Owen's image was relayed to a coloured monitor. The picture was clear. Sound was picked up from a tiny microphone. Speakers were hidden in the walls and ceiling. The viewer had perfect access both on a visual and auditory basis. The image was also accessible via mobile phone. She could be watched, observed, anywhere, anytime. Buttons pressed, and there she was. A prisoner, captive. Kept. Terrified. And all aspects of her terror, from her screams to her moans, her pleads to her sobs, all of it was captured and gazed upon. Soon, she would understand everything.

Soon she would meet the Red Serpent.

21

The routine was simple. Breakfast, lunch, dinner. In between, shower, some time spent in the common room playing pool or snooker, or maybe the multi-gym. There were classes, for woodwork, metalwork, tech-drawing. Reading, writing, history, geography. A course on needlework and sewing. A library. Cells locked for 7pm. The same again the next day.

For Black, time was short. Something had to happen, and quickly.

The prisoner called Oliver Pritchard was on the third level. Black had been well briefed already, having spent hours reading his files, studying photographs, researching. He knew his face like his own. Pritchard hadn't changed particularly since his court appearance six months earlier. If anything, he looked healthier. Filled out. Clean-shaven, small, wiry, unremarkable. A sharp face, narrow forehead, blond hair grown past the ears, straggling over his collar, receding at the top. Who would ever imagine such a man was a walking, breathing serial killer?

Except the eyes. If they were windows to the soul, then Pritchard's soul was well and truly fucked. Dark, obsidian, like two black pebbles. Dead eyes. His victims would search them for a soupcon of mercy at the final moment, and find nothing.

Black had glimpsed him in a corridor. Also, in the refectory. Eating in the cells in B Hall was forbidden. No private dining for Pritchard. He was forced to join the congregation. Black, sitting at a table eating steak pie and chips with plastic cutlery, watched him askance. It was Black's second day of incarceration. Like Pritchard, he sat, solitary. The place was full, most of the tables taken, men huddled together, talking, muttering. Black sat at the back, at a table furthest away from the serving area. From this vantage, he had a view of the entire room. At the far end sat Pritchard. Black noted he was not the only person interested in Pritchard's presence. Others cast surreptitious glances towards him. Some not so surreptitious, openly stared.

Black understood the hierarchy in the prison system. Armed robbers were treated almost like movie stars. Rapists were almost rock bottom, a shade up from child killers and molesters. Pritchard had a whole new sub-level to himself. He had kidnapped, tortured and killed a long list of young women. If any convict were to be reviled, it was the Red Serpent. There was a long list of inmates keen and ready to dish out a little taste of pain and suffering, prison style. Which was where Black came in.

Black was suddenly aware of a man watching him, intently, seated at two tables pushed together, close to where Black sat. He was in a group of seven, all bunched up, eating lunch from plastic plates. Black kept his head down, concentrating on his food. He detected a presence. He looked up. The man was standing in front of him. Black smiled politely. He noticed the others were now watching.

Black resumed eating his lunch. The man didn't look like he was going anywhere fast.

Black continued eating, unfazed. The man took a step

forward, pulled out the chair opposite Black, and sat. He dragged it closer, using his weight, metal legs screeching on the wooden floor.

"Adam Black?"

Black considered the man before him. He was stocky, heavy brows, small, beetling eyes, his eyebrows one dark line. His hair was scraped back into a ponytail, a small blue tear tattooed on his right cheek under his eye. He placed both elbows on the table, clasping his hands below his chin.

"I asked you a fucking question."

Black shovelled a piece of steak pie into his mouth, staring at the man as he chewed, then took a swig from a plastic bottle of mineral water. "It wasn't a question. You said Adam Black. That's a statement. I didn't hear a question. Or like you, maybe I'm really stupid."

"You're a funny man. I know who you are."

"Excellent."

The man reached over and picked a chip from Black's plate, dipped it into the steak pie, and chewed on it, thoughtfully. "The scran here is fucking shit," he said.

Black watched him. "I've tasted worse."

"See these men at the table behind me?"

Black adjusted his position to look round. The six seated regarded Black with open stares, like hyenas measuring the weakness of their victim. "They're hard to miss."

The man picked up another chip, repeating the process, dipping it into gravy, and eating it, chewing on it slowly.

"They're all friends of Danny Brogan. You remember him?"

"Difficult to forget."

"He remembers you. He thinks about you a lot. I would go so far to say he's fixated with you. He's glad you're here, with us. You want to know why, Adam Black?"

65

Black shrugged. "You're certainly a man who likes to ask questions."

The man smiled, revealing gaps in his teeth. "Because he knows you're going to get so fucked up. And that's a promise."

"A promise?"

"Too fucking right."

Black leaned closer. "Then let me make a promise in return."

The man gave a wide grin.

"If you take one more chip from my plate," said Black, his voice barely above a whisper, "then I'll break your fucking arm."

The man stared at Black for several seconds. Black stared back. Daring him.

The man sniffed, wiping his nose with the back of his hand. Black tensed. These people were used to swift violence. Black was just the type to dispense it. And something in the man's demeanour told Black that he knew, instinctively, Black was not bullshitting. That he was a man of his word. The man sniffed again, stood, and left to join his friends.

Black smiled at them, raising his plastic bottle of water. "Bon appetite."

22

Pritchard made one phone call the first day of every month. He used the public phones available to prisoners, in an annex off one of the main halls. He telephoned at the same time on the same day. Once a month. Needless to say, the authorities were intrigued. Pritchard had no known family. His mother and father were both dead. He had no friends. He was a loner.

He had worked as a librarian at Glasgow University's main library, providing, so he claimed, the means by which he chose his victims. Each of the young women were undergraduates. They visited the library daily. He picked them, observed them, studied them. Then killed them. He was a solitary individual. He hovered on the periphery of society, an outsider. He was invisible. Which rendered him all the more lethal.

The phone call had aroused interest initially but it diminished as the months wore on. They had their man. He was serving life, and would never see the light of day. There were other murders, and thus other murderers to catch. Glasgow was, and always had been, a busy place in that regard. As was only natural, the police and the public lost their appetite for the Red Serpent.

But Elspeth Owen had been taken. Suddenly there was renewed interest in Pritchard again, and in particular his monthly phone call.

The Colonel, with the agreement of the Prison Governor and the Crown Office, got a warrant to wiretap each phone in the annex. There were twelve telephone cubicles. If he stuck to his timetable, Pritchard's next phone call was on the third day of Black's interment, the first day of the month. The telephone lines in the prison building were hardwired the evening before. Specialists worked through the night, and it was expensive. But expense was not a concern. Not in this particular case.

And exactly on cue, Pritchard made his call. The only time he ever chose to speak.

The Colonel listened. He was sitting behind his desk, in his office in Dumfries. He had on headphones, connected to a hard drive. Pritchard spoke. The voice was low, hushed. The Colonel detected something else. Excitement. Barely contained. It leaked from every word, every syllable.

"You see the past, the present," Pritchard said. "And you see the future. I am in the company of insects. Slime in the sun. Their presence disgusts me. Soon I will... transcend."

No response. Only breathing from the recipient.

"I can feel the power rising in me," Pritchard said.

Again, only the sound of breathing.

Pritchard's voice rose. "We are three. A trinity. When we each move, then we move as one. Can you feel it too?"

No response.

"You are the hand. I am your instrument of death. And him. What is he? Is he a god?"

No response. The Colonel strained to hear something, a background noise, a telltale sign of location. But nothing. Except breathing.

"What is he?" repeated Pritchard, his voice shrill. "What is my brother in all this?"

Then the other person responded. A voice deep, booming. Unnatural. The Colonel jumped at its ferocity.

"He is the death bringer," came the voice.

The line went dead.

The Colonel stared into space. *What the hell just happened.*

Words echoed in his mind.

Death Bringer.

There were three.

23

Black had never been more conscious of the time, or lack of. Every minute slipping by was a minute wasted. The Red Serpent had been most exact in his timetable of murder. Two months between the date on his letter to the police, and the discovery of the victim. The victims spaced out over five years. His prolific spree was matched only by his efficiency. Production-line killing.

If indeed the perpetrator was the same person.

It was lights out. The sky was cloudless and freezing. Through the thick window, and the bars which enclosed it, a full moon glimmered, pale and perfect, casting a bluish sheen on the world. A strange, witchy quality, thought Black, as he gazed outside. Was Elspeth Owen looking up at the sky now, he wondered? Or perhaps she was trapped somewhere cold and dark, terrified and alone.

Or perhaps she was already dead.

Black had no answers. But he had to find some. Quickly. Clock was ticking.

Tick-tock.

~

The telephone conversation between Pritchard and his cohort had been recorded and listened to by Chief Constable Divers, Ernest Stanford, and the PM's private secretary, Katie Sykes. As Black lay on his prison bed, contemplating the plight of Elspeth Owen, the Colonel was waiting in a room at 10 Downing Street. A meeting had been hastily arranged. The conversation Pritchard had was revelatory. The PM wanted an update – first hand. The Colonel had taken a flight down from Glasgow Airport, then a taxi from Heathrow.

And here he was.

The Colonel had visited several times before. Different governments, different leaders. He thought back – he'd been asked in as a member of the War Council, both for Iraq and Afghanistan. His advice had been sought. Strategy; management; deployment. This time, he reflected, the situation was intimate. Personal. The Prime Minister's daughter was probably in the clutches of a psychopath. Maybe a serial killer. The issue was not an abstract debate. It was real. It was etched in the Prime Minister's face, her movements, it shone from her eyes. Fear. Real, tangible fear. Her daughter might die. Could be already dead. It was up close and personal. And she was entrusting the Colonel, and a few select others, to get things sorted.

The Colonel took a deep breath, and prayed for the millionth time he was up to the task.

He had been asked to wait in a sitting room, designed for invitees. The Colonel had always been impressed with Number 10. Its understated elegance. Its subtle display of power. Nothing showy, nothing gaudy. The ceilings were high, textured with complicated, exquisite designs. The coving was gold and silver filigree. The wallpaper was finest quality, midnight blue, smooth as silk. The furniture was old – antique old. The couches and chairs were possibly Edwardian, he reckoned, though he was no expert. The carpet was thick, luxurious. Pale cream. A real coal fire burned in a massive oaken hearth.

A young man ushered someone in. The Colonel recognised him instantly. The enormous bulk of Chief Constable Divers. The Colonel nodded. Divers nodded back, face shining with sweat in the glow of the soft chandelier lights.

The young man spoke. "Would you both please like to follow me?"

The Colonel got up, and they were led through a corridor, up some wide stairs to the upper landing, to a black, glossy door. The Prime Minister's private study. The young man knocked gently, opened it. He looked in. He turned back to the two men.

"The Prime Minister will see you now."

The Chief Constable blustered forward, the Colonel following.

The room had the same vaulted ceiling, but more intimate than the one he'd been waiting in. A smaller hearth crackled on one wall. A large gleaming mahogany desk stood by a wide bay window, and on it scattered in no apparent order, papers, files, notes, books. Behind it sat Prime Minister Owen. She stood when they entered.

There was no display of cordiality. Time was too short.

"Gentlemen," was all she said. She gestured them over to comfortable chairs by the fire. Across the table from her, sitting, were the Permanent Secretary, Katie Sykes, and the lean figure of Ernest Stanford, dressed in a silky dark suit fashioned by tailors from Savile Row. He gave the Colonel and Divers a fractional nod. The five took seats by the fire. The Colonel covertly scrutinised the Prime Minister. She was small, angular. All elbows and knees. Deathly pale. He knew her real age – sixty-one – but her eyes were old beyond her years. Ancient, exhausted. Blue pinpoints peering from hollows in her face. She was more stooped than he remembered. The burden of the country on her shoulders. The burden of her missing daughter crippling her heart, shredding her nerves. He was four feet from a mother whose daughter was being held prisoner by a psychopath. He could not begin to comprehend the hell she was going through.

Her voice was quiet, the tone terse. She looked around her before she spoke, encompassing each person there in her gaze, bringing them in.

"I've heard a recording of his conversation," she said. "What does it mean?"

They each looked at the Colonel, as if he were the font of all knowledge.

Before he could respond, Chief Constable Divers broke in. "We've already had our forensic audiologists analyse the voice, the background noise, ma'am."

"And?"

"The voice is not real. It's been modified by a voice modulator."

Christ, thought the Colonel. *Thanks for the stunning observation.*

"The accent is virtually undetectable," continued Divers. "From the little that was said, we know he is educated, and probably English is his first language. There were no other sounds beyond the voice itself. Therefore, the assumption is that he spoke in an enclosed space. Possibly a room with extremely good soundproofing. Maybe a basement, or perhaps a lock-up, or a..."

Divers looked down, not finishing.

"...or a?" asked the PM.

Divers darted a glance at the Colonel.

"The young women murdered in Glasgow were kept in a

dungeon," finished the Colonel. "Pritchard never revealed the location, but that's how he described it in his statements. His *special place*. If the person speaking was in such an environment, then I imagine it would be insulated from external sound."

"Which really tells us nothing at all," snapped the PM, staring at Divers. "Was the call traced?"

Divers shook his head. "The mobile number was a 'pay as you go'. A burner."

"But the content?" asked Ernest Stanford. In the glow of the fire his hair gleamed like spun silver.

"Whoever Pritchard was talking to, his tone, his words, were respectful, reverential," replied the Colonel. "He obviously treated him in great esteem. I would almost say, he spoke in awe. Pritchard believes he is special. Above normal men. I think he sees this other person as almost godlike."

"He mentioned a brother?" said Katie Sykes. She looked officious, dressed in a dark-blue suit, cream blouse, dark necktie the same colour as her hair. Solemn. Exact.

The Colonel pursed his lips, measuring his response. "Not in a literal sense, I think. We know Pritchard had no family. His mother and father are both dead. No siblings. He wasn't married. So, *brother* in the conventional way doesn't add up. But..." The Colonel looked at the PM, his face lined in scepticism.

"Speak up," she said. "Say what's on your mind." Her voice faltered, her face softening. "Please."

"Maybe it has religious, or mystical connotations," said the Colonel. "It would also reinforce the idea that there are three parties acting. That perhaps there have been three all along."

Katie Sykes frowned. "I don't understand."

"Me neither." The Colonel sighed. "Not really. But he could be alluding to a mirror image of the Father, Son, and Holy Spirit. The Holy Trinity. And he specifically used the word *trinity*."

"Mirror image?" It was the Chief Constable who spoke.

A short silence followed before the Colonel answered, punctuated by the crackle of flames.

"The Unholy Trinity," he said quietly. He felt the eyes of Prime Minister Owen burning into him.

"Satan, the Antichrist, and the False Prophet. Deception, hatred. And evil."

24

Adam Black had been a prisoner of HMP Shotts for just over three weeks. Nothing of consequence had taken place. Which was not as Black would have wished for. Yet there was tension. He felt it, breathed it. If anything happened, it would be swift, unexpected. Explosive. Black braced himself. He lived, second to second, minute to minute, nerves stretched.

Pritchard tended not to stray far from his cell. He ate silently, on his own, at a corner of the canteen. He went straight to his room afterwards. Black would make it his business to saunter past. Sometimes the door was closed, sometimes open. Pritchard didn't seem to care. If he was nervous in his new surroundings, he didn't show it. He read a lot. He had books in his room. And he was given a collection of newspapers every morning. A man who liked to keep up with current affairs, mused Black. Which they knew already. And which had formed the backbone of the plan.

Black telephoned the Colonel every day. The number used was the Colonel's own private mobile. Daily updates. But there was nothing to report. Clock was ticking. If something didn't happen soon, the girl would die. Then something did happen, both swift and brutal.

Pritchard changed his routine. After lunch, he decided to visit the library. Black followed nonchalantly behind. The library was situated on the west wing of B Hall. It was one large vaulted room, sectioned into squares by four-foot-high shelves of books. In each square were tables and chairs, allowing prisoners to read, study. A prison guard sat behind a reception-style desk at one end of the room, watching. The walls were crammed with posters of famous people, with associated quotes. Winston Churchill: *It's not enough that we do our best, sometimes we have to do what is required.* John Lennon: *War is over... if you want it.* Other pictures, other quotations. To inspire. Black gave a sardonic smile. Not an easy sell to the crowd in this place.

Pritchard hovered about a small section entitled History, then moved to General Fiction. He chose a book, sat at a table, and began to read.

Black pretended to browse books in a section opposite, watching Pritchard askance. Pritchard was hunched over, studying the open pages, oblivious to his surroundings. Black wasn't. He read the signs as soon as they began to take shape. The officer behind the desk got a call. He spoke in short monosyllables – *Yes. No. Right.* He suddenly stood, casting a swift glance at Pritchard, then left his station, and out of the room. Black waited, nerves tingling. This might be his chance.

A harsh looking man entered. He was small, and powerfully built. Black recognised him from the exercise yard, and the gym. He lifted weights. Heavy weights. He wore a plain white T-shirt, moulded over muscled shoulders and upper arms. His neck was thick, corded, one side tapestried with a tattoo of a woman's face. Hair shaved to the bone, revealing a scattering of old scars. By no means a man to be taken lightly. Not the type to frequent a library. He ignored Black completely. He honed in on Pritchard, sitting with his back to him. Black glimpsed something in the man's hand. A shiv. Primitive, but effective. A toothbrush with a razor blade stuck on the end. His intentions were clear.

The man approached Pritchard, now looming over him. Black didn't hesitate. He strode forward. He held a heavy hardback book. He battered it across the man's face. The man reeled back against the wall, the blow disorienting him. Pritchard jerked up, swivelling round at the commotion, eyes wide in shock. Black followed through, bringing the book up and connecting under the man's chin. The man grunted, but seemed to absorb the blow. He lashed out, slicing the shiv in the direction of Black's face. Black leaned in, blocked with a forearm, struck the man on the throat with a hard jab, crushing the windpipe. The man staggered, gasping for breath, both hands clutching his neck. Black punched him in the groin. The man doubled over. Black clasped the back of the man's head, brought his face down hard into his upraised knee. He felt teeth break. The man gave a rattling groan, swayed on his feet. Black swept his arm across, using the edge of the book, bringing a thunderous blow to the man's temple, knocking him across the top of the shelves, and into the next compartment.

Black turned to Pritchard. "We need to go."

Pritchard jerked to his feet, wavering, shocked, ashen-faced, dark eyes darting from Black, to the book in his hand.

"I'm not out to get you." Black gestured to the man on the floor. "But he was. We have to leave. Before the guard comes back. Or more of his pals."

Pritchard took several seconds, as if digesting the sudden, extreme situation he was in. Then he nodded. The Red Serpent was into self-preservation as much as the next man, thought Black.

They left the library, together, walking quickly. On his way out, Black glanced at the man with the tattoo on his neck, sprawled on the ground, twitching, a small oasis of blood pooled round his head. Looked like half his teeth were missing. Looked like he was dead.

Too bad.

25

The prison was in lockdown. A prisoner was dead. In the library. By a bloodied hardback book. Cluedo didn't have a look in, thought Black grimly. The governor, a small martinet of a man called Walter Shipley, was in an apoplectic rage according to the rumour mill. Questions were asked. Heads would roll. The man killed was Charles Swinton. Serving five years for selling class-A drugs. Nicknamed *Tank,* on account of his physique. He was popular in the prison. And presumably had friends in high places. The video CCTV fixed in one corner of the room was faulty. Nothing was recorded. The guard was disciplined for leaving his station. Forensics were examining the scene. Black had wiped the book clean before he'd left. Zero fingerprints. Or so he hoped.

The prisoners were confined to their cells, except for mealtimes. The morning after the incident, the heavy bolt on Black's door unlocked, the door slid open, to reveal the large figure of Fletcher, accompanied by another guard. Fletcher remained at the doorway for several seconds, appraising Black with narrowed calculating eyes. They entered, and rummaged through Black's belongings, silent, focused. They checked his cupboard, the shelves. They upended his bed, checking through the sheets, the pillows. Black stood to one side, watchful, waiting for what was to come next.

They finished. Fletcher turned his attention to Black. He stepped forward, his face an inch from Black's. They were about the same height. Black was in far superior condition. A lifetime as a trained combat soldier gave Black the edge over most men. But Fletcher had the weight of the Criminal Justice System on his side. A big advantage.

"I fucking know it was you," hissed Fletcher. "I'm not stupid. But you're not being reported. No way. That would be way too fucking easy. We've got other plans for you. Big plans. I could give you a taste right now. You want that, Black?"

Black tensed, but said nothing. If he ended up putting two prison officers in hospital, then the plan was blown, and the girl was as good as dead.

Fletcher nodded, smirking. He unclipped the baton at his side, brought it up, placed it under Black's chin, tilting it one way, angling Black's face to the side.

"Cat got your tongue," he said. "I could break your head in two, if I wanted. Right now. Spill your fucking brains all over the floor. Then make you clean it up. No one would say a word. No one would give a damn. Now that's real power, Black. Real fucking power. And you have none. Nada. I can do what I fucking want." He leaned forward, whispering in his ear. "And I will. Make no mistake. You're what is described as a fucking dead man walking."

Black waited, breath held. Anything could happen. If Fletcher lashed out, Black, instinctively, would lash back.

Fletcher curled his lip into a crooked smile, showing yellow teeth. He waited, daring Black. Black did nothing.

Fletcher stepped back, shaking his head. "Knew it," he said. "Big man, big fucking coward."

He glanced at his colleague. "Let's go."

They both left Black's cell. On his way out, Fletcher banged the door with his baton. The impact echoed through the corridors. Fletcher turned back. He gestured, using his two fingers, pointing into his own eyes, then towards Black, to signify *I'm watching you*.

Black released a pent-up breath, trying to keep the tremble from his hands.

If Fletcher had tried something, then matters would have escalated beyond Black's control. One dead prison officer, and there was no going back.

But Black had sight of a far bigger picture. He had a mission.

To save the girl.

And time was running out.

Tick-tock.

26

Elspeth Owen dreaded the dark in her new world. It was solid, tangible, like a living thing. She would open her eyes, and think she was blind.

When the voice spoke, she jumped. Sometimes it would speak in the darkness, sometimes when the light was on. There was no pattern.

It asked questions. She would respond. Initially, she pleaded to be let free, promising to keep quiet, not tell a soul. But such pleas were fruitless, she came to realise. The voice would never let her leave. As time drifted by, her responses were a mixture of defiance and despondency.

"Do you believe in God?" it asked.

"Do you?"

Silence.

"You can't," she said. "Or else you wouldn't do what you do."

"Do you believe in God?"

"No. Yes. What the fuck do you care?"

Silence, for several seconds.

"I care what you think," spoke the voice. "I care a lot."

"Then let me go."

"I think God loves you."

"I'm glad."

"But he doesn't love you as much as me. My love is... all. His is fickle."

She bit her lip, trying to fight back tears.

"You will be changing soon," said the voice.

"I don't understand."

"Changing."

"I heard you the first time!"

"Then you will be ready."

"Ready for what. What do you want?"

"Like a snake, shuffling off its skin. And then it's renewed. Resurrected."

"I don't understand!"

"You will."

She waited for it to explain, but there was only a deep silence. She sobbed, quietly. She heard a noise – a scrape of metal. Suddenly her eyes were heavy, her surroundings whirled. She realised dully that she'd been drugged. Her food had been laced. She lay back on the bed, the ceiling circling, then growing distant, as she slipped into oblivion, vaguely aware of a dark shape approaching.

Then nothing.

27

The crime unit established to find Elspeth Owen was based at police headquarters in Pitt Street, Glasgow. On the same floor as the Chief Constable Frank Divers' office. That way, he had direct and instant access to developments.

He'd placed Detective Inspector Vanessa Shaw in charge. She was clever and ambitious. A law graduate who'd got fast track promotion. She had worked on the Red Serpent case from the very beginning, five years earlier, so knew the background.

She was in his office, sitting opposite, as he was briefing her on the meeting with the PM. She looked good, he thought. Fit. Divers was divorced, and wanted to fuck everything that moved. The woman sitting before him was appealing. Medium height, trim and agile. Dark hair, shoulder length, hazel brown eyes bright with enthusiasm. Clear, fresh complexion. The type who didn't need to wear make-up to look good, in his opinion. She was a black belt in aikido. She was a regular at the police gym. She cycled to work. Unmarried, though she talked about a boyfriend. Lucky bastard, thought Divers. Here was a keeper.

He scrutinised her from across his desk. Imagined her naked. Spread before him. Submissive. His heart raced. He experienced a powerful erection. Sometimes, Divers had what he described as *moments*. When the red mist would descend. He had needs. And he had very specific requirements to satisfy his needs. His moments. Requirements no one could ever know about.

"The PM has been made aware of Pritchard's telephone conversation," he said. "She's as confused as we are."

"Then we should go public with this. Somebody might have seen something. The greater the exposure…"

"The greater we could fuck up," finished Divers. "A plea to the public? Then what happens. This psycho panics, kills her, disappears. Until the next time. Plus, think of the response we'll get. The PM's daughter's been kidnapped by a serial killer. A killer copycatting another one currently in prison. We'll get swamped by calls from every oddball under the sun. And suddenly resources are stretched to the point of being worse than useless. Counterproductive, Inspector Shaw. Plus, it wouldn't look good."

Shaw cocked her head, puzzled. "How so, sir?"

Divers had to grit his teeth, swallow back his frustration. He was fed up explaining the obvious. "What do you think? People, the press, the whole world, will think the one thing we don't want them to think. That we caught the wrong man."

"Maybe we did."

"That's really not helpful. We caught the right man, no problem."

"Fair enough, sir. And what about Adam Black? Anything further there?"

Divers looked down at his desk top, which was bare, except for a pen and a blank A4 pad. The Adam Black thing was a mess. The involvement of this man worried Divers. A fly in the ointment. It could prove disastrous, for everyone. But he was still part of the plan to find the girl, and as such, Divers had kept his

Inspector informed about him from the very beginning, when the whole crazy scheme was hatched by Colonel Mackenzie.

"Nothing. And I suspect nothing will ever come of it, except deep embarrassment for all concerned."

Vanessa Shaw cleared her throat. "I think something's happened, but it might be nothing."

"What?"

"It was pure chance I got to hear about it. Normally these things are dealt with internally. There was an incident at Shotts prison yesterday morning. A man died. When I heard it was Shotts, I became curious."

"And?"

"It looks like a man was murdered. Bludgeoned to death."

Divers was immediately interested.

"Surely it wasn't Adam Black?"

"No. Maybe it's coincidence, sir. But only weeks after Black's introduction to Shotts prison, a man is dead."

"Coincidence," muttered Divers. "Prison life. When you sup with the devil."

Vanessa coughed, fidgeted in her seat.

"What are you not telling me?" said Divers.

"I've met Adam Black before. I think he's dangerous. Maybe even insane."

28

Divers sat back, the chair creaking under his gross weight. He was intrigued. He let her comment linger for several seconds, then he spoke. "Explain, please."

He stared at her, waiting. With his position – the highest-ranking police officer in Scotland – his stare could be a powerful weapon, which he often used. Divers had no trouble with intimidation, if it got him what he wanted. He enjoyed watching her squirm. Power. It was all about power.

She took a deep breath. "Black has a law office in the south side, Shawlands. Had. You probably know that, sir. Three years ago, a woman was raped in Queen's Park, a half mile from Black's office. It was bad. One of the worst cases I'd seen. We'd set up a specialist task unit, and I was doing door to door. Routine enquiries. I met Adam Black. It turned out he knew the victim. Turned out she was a client of his. That he'd been her lawyer when she purchased her flat. He remembered her. I can't forget his reaction."

"Which was?"

"He's a physically powerful-looking man. Striking, almost.

But when I told him, his reaction was... not quite what I expected."

"Yes?" *Get to the fucking point.*

"He remained still. I mean perfectly still. Now normally, when I talk to people, people in the area, they respond. They react. They dialogue, get involved. Show *empathy*. With Adam Black, it was different."

She looked at Divers, but her look was faraway. She was searching her memory, he thought, casting her mind back, choosing the right words to describe what she remembered.

"He never said a word. He showed nothing. As if he were... empty. What made it peculiar was that he knew the victim, by his own admission. Had it been a complete stranger, then perhaps his lack of emotion would have been a bit more... well, understandable. But his was strange. I don't think I'll forget it."

"He's a hard man. Background in Special Services. They're not built like normal human beings."

"But there's more."

"Yes?"

"The man who we were looking for was Polish. In fact, he'd tried to rape another woman in the same area. When we established it was him, he had already absconded back to his home town. Krakow. We sought extradition. We were too late."

"Too late?"

DI Shaw paused, then spoke. "He was found. By the Polish police. At a rented flat. Badly beaten. His face scarred beyond recognition. Blinded in one eye by the point of a knife. Legs and arms broken. He died in hospital shortly after. Brain haemorrhage."

"What are you saying?"

"What I'm saying, sir, is that there are similarities. The man Black attacked in the beauty salon – Danny Brogan? His face was scarred, mutilated. Christ, Black cut the man's tongue out with a hunting knife. I think they're connected."

"And what are your conclusions?"

"That if Adam Black carried out these attacks, then the level of ferocity tells me one thing."

Divers waited.

"That he enjoys it," said Vanessa. "He enjoys killing. That's why I think he's insane."

Divers couldn't disagree with anything his DI had said. But whilst she knew some of the facts, she wasn't privy to them all. He'd told her Black was inside Shotts prison, to get close to the Red Serpent. That was all. The mutilation which she had referred to? The excision of Brogan's tongue? Divers knew the truth. It wasn't insanity on the part of Black. Far from it.

It was madness of sorts.

But planned.

To Divers' mind, Adam Black was a loose cannon, a maverick. The very last person to be counted on. But the Colonel had final say, and that came directly from Whitehall. There was little Divers could do, except wait. Wait until the whole thing backfired in the Colonel's face, and then Divers would choose his moment – to gloat, to cast recriminations and point his finger. The finger of blame. A talent Divers was especially good at.

29

Life resumed as normal three days after the killing, if normal was the appropriate word to use for prison life. Black decided it was time.

Twelve thirty pm. Lunch in the canteen. The place was crowded as usual. Men queuing with trays, waiting to be served. Men sitting at tables, eating, talking. Two guards at the entrance, another guard waiting by the queue. CCTV cameras everywhere.

Pritchard, as usual, sat alone. He seemed unconcerned at the stares levelled in his direction. He was a cause cèlébre in prison society. For all the wrong reasons. Black collected his food, balancing it on his tray, and made directly over to the table where Pritchard sat.

Pritchard watched him approach, eyes never wavering. Black hadn't realised just how pale he was, under the white glare of the ceiling strip lights. Pale white skin, smooth like a shark, eyes like two black holes, set deep.

Black stood facing him. "Mind if I join you?"

Pritchard's stare was unflinching. He didn't reply.

Black shrugged. "I'll take that as a yes."

He sat opposite, lifting the plastic plate of steaming food onto the metal table, a bottle of mineral water, plastic knife and fork. He placed the tray on the ground.

"If you ever wondered what shit tastes like," said Black, "then I recommend the shepherd's pie."

He nodded at Pritchard's plate. "Though you're more of a vegetable man, I see. Good for the digestion."

Pritchard's plate was a combination of green beans and broccoli.

"Close call in the library, don't you think?" continued Black, through mouthfuls of food.

Pritchard's gaze never wavered. Unsettling, under normal circumstances. But the circumstances were far from normal. And Black didn't have the luxury of feeling unsettled.

"You're a bit of a sensation around these parts. Look about. You'll find everyone's interested in you. You're famous. Or is it notorious? I'm not certain there's much of a distinction in a place like this. The attack was poorly planned. Maybe just a lone strike. Next time, it might be better orchestrated. Maybe three or four guys. And I might not be around. What will you do then?"

Black continued eating. Pritchard continued staring.

"Maybe you don't care. Perhaps you want to be scarred. Though I see you're already partial to a bit of self-mutilation."

Black used his plastic fork to point at Pritchard's face; more specifically the DIY design of a snake Pritchard had engraved with the razor blade on his cheek, under his right eye.

"I like that," said Black. "I really do. It tells me you're not afraid of showing those around you who you really are. But I'm only guessing the guy in the library wanted to scar you. Maybe he wanted to shove that shiv into your guts, and twist it round a bit. Do some real damage."

Another mouthful of food. Black was almost conversational.

"The price of fame, my friend. And as I've said, I can't be the angel on your shoulder all the time. Or is it devil? Anyway, it seems to me, you need to watch your back. And I'll do my best to help. I only hope it's good enough. You'd better eat those greens, before they get cold. Though if they taste anything like they look, I can understand the lack of enthusiasm."

Pritchard, who had both his hands on the table, palms facing down, rested them on his lap. The movement was slow, careful.

He tilted his head forward by the slightest of angles, and for the first time in six months, he spoke to another human being face to face.

One word. A whisper, almost.

"Why?"

30

The PM was about to crack. Or so it appeared. Ernest Stanford and Katie Sykes were in touch almost hourly. The PM had cancelled meetings, debates, conferences for the next eight days. Feigning illness. The leader of the opposition was capitalising, naturally, as were the press. Questions were being asked. Answers were required. Demanded.

Katie Sykes, who was at the PM's side permanently, like a shadow, was also struggling with the pressure, thought Stanford. Her function was to deflect the constant barrage of questions. She couldn't lie. That would bounce right back, if the truth were ever revealed. Thus, she had to appease with generalities – *the Prime Minister is dealing with urgent business; the Prime Minister will respond shortly; the Prime Minister regrets not being able to speak today, but promises she will address the issues raised... blah blah.*

Stanford had asked to meet her. He waited in the Green Room at Number 10. A room of regular dimensions, the carpet pale olive, the walls decorated in tapestried wallpaper the colour of fresh lemon. Sunlight streamed through stained-glass windows, creating soft hues of green, yellow and red. Beyond was a small enclosed garden, a neat lawn shimmering with mid-morning frost, as if someone had sprinkled tiny white jewels. Under different circumstances, the scene would have been almost uplifting. But Stanford was in no mood for quaint English gardens. A tray had been set on a low table, upon which was placed petite porcelain cups and saucers and a silver teapot and a little stand of cakes and scones.

The door opened. Katie Sykes entered. Impeccably dressed as ever. Elegant. A simple black dress, a slender silver belt at her waist, her dark hair glossy in the sunshine, artfully tousled.

She nodded at Stanford, sat opposite. A man entered behind her, waited until she'd seated herself, then poured the tea into the cups, and left.

"Milk?" she asked.

"Thank you."

She poured milk from a miniature silver jug into both cups. "She's in her study," said Katie, launching straight in. "No sleep last night. Divers has been in constant touch. She waits for the phone to ring. And when it does, she fights to stop crying. But she cries anyway."

Stanford sipped his tea. Darjeeling. He said nothing.

"She's at her wits end."

"Understandable," he said.

"I don't know what we do from here."

"We wait. Let people who know what they're doing, do it."

"The police? They took years to find the Red Serpent. And we don't even know if they got the right man. Too desperate to get a conviction. And this other man? Are we really pinning our hopes on him?"

"The fearless warrior, Adam Black." Stanford's voice dripped with sarcasm. "God knows. A hair-brained scheme. Concocted by the Colonel. The PM puts a lot of faith in an old soldier. Whether that faith is misplaced, we shall see soon enough."

"What then? What if her daughter…" Katie swallowed, clearly unable to articulate the consequences. The worst-case scenario.

Stanford reacted with a gleaming smile, revealing pearly white teeth, set in a perfect row. A man who took extraordinary care of himself. Lean, as a result of a strict diet, who resisted salt and sugar, who preferred Strathmore mineral water to alcohol – though he could be tempted by a malt, and fine red wine. Delicate features, high, aquiline cheekbones. A keen cyclist. Tanned, a result of four holidays a year to a small beach-side bungalow he owned in the Caribbean, though he had been born and raised in Scotland, before graduating in International Law and Politics at Cambridge, first-class honours, and then further graduating to the lofty corridors of Whitehall, where he'd risen through the rank and file of civil servants at rocket speed.

People knew little about him, which was the way he liked to keep it. He spoke rarely of his family. It was no one's business but his own. Unmarried, though he still had his mother. He knew people suspected he was gay, and he did nothing to quell the rumours, the speculation. He thrived on the mystery.

Ernest Stanford was a private man. Jealously so. Some described him as something else. Secretive.

"What then?" he echoed. "Let's not be squeamish about this, Katie. You're not the squeamish type. If her daughter ends up dead in a ditch, then that's that. You think the PM can go on? I hardly imagine so. She'll resign. And then her job's up for grabs. And then the whole thing's one fucking mess. Unless we… *pre-empt*."

She glared at Stanford. "What way is that to talk? What do you mean – pre-empt?"

Stanford relaxed back on the green velvet couch, gazing at her with pale-blue eyes. Eyes sharp and intense, capable of making the most seasoned politician baulk.

"The party is doing as badly as it's ever done. Our Prime Minister, despite her best intentions, is universally hated. Popularity is down the shitter. Or have you been sleeping? They'll lose the next election, beaten in tsunami proportions. Some say they might never recover. But..."

He leaned forward, took a sip of Darjeeling from the white porcelain cup. "But..." he continued. "If there was a leak."

"The PM was most specific. As was the Colonel. And everybody else. If this gets out, then we don't know how the kidnapper will react. We have to assume the worst. He'll kill Elspeth, lay low, disappear. The whole thing has to be... clandestine. For as long as possible."

"For as long as possible," said Stanford. "Sometimes you have to see the bigger picture when you're planning your masterpiece."

"I don't understand."

"If you press your nose up to the canvas, you never will. If the newspapers get wind of the abduction, what then?"

"Disaster."

"Wrong. Salvation. Suddenly we have a metamorphosis – a reviled politician to a stricken mother. She'll still resign, of course. But everything changes. Imagine that."

"I'm trying to. I don't know if I like a single word of what you're suggesting."

"Then you really have to try to expand your horizons, darling. And then, if the girl dies – tell me what we have then?"

"Tragedy."

He leant back again on the couch, his smile widening.

"Resurrection."

31

Let him wait, thought Black. But not too long. Time was not on Black's side.

"Later," was all Black said, when asked *why* by the man known as the Red Serpent. Black left the table, feeling his stare on his back. Sitting across the table from a serial killer creeped him out. But Black had a job to do. To complete it, he would rip the world apart if it meant saving a young girl's life.

Black sauntered back to his cell, collected things, and made his way to the multi-gym. The place had extra security. More prison guards watched the corridors, the various annexes. The surveillance system was overhauled, beefed up.

The gym was impressive. Physical well-being was promoted actively by the prison institution. A large room, with rows of treadmills, rowing machines, cross trainers, weight machines, free weights. Black had always made it a point to keep in shape. A memento of his life in the military. Video cameras fixed in each corner. Plus, a guard had been placed at a seat by a table. Watching. If he needed a toilet break, he would be replaced by another.

Black had never been a fan of weight training, though he

understood its importance. Nevertheless, he found it boring. He trained a half hour every day on the machines, by way of habit, rather than enjoyment. He also ran 5k on the treadmill, still keeping his time under twenty minutes.

He got changed into gym gear in the locker room. Like everywhere else, a camera in the corner pointed down at him. He made his way into the gym, heading for one of the treadmills. The place was only a quarter full. Most hovered round the free weights, in little bodybuilder cliques, testing each other, comparing biceps.

One of them noticed Black, made a comment to his group of friends, and nonchalantly crossed the room in Black's direction. Black was in the process of setting up the treadmill. He nodded at the man – the same man who'd spoken to him in the canteen. The man with the tear tattoo on his face. He nodded back.

He leaned against the machine, as if Black was his best friend.

"Danny Brogan says hi."

Black smiled at him. "I don't think Danny can say hi to anyone, seeing as he no longer has ownership of his tongue."

"That's very true, Adam. He's got you to thank for that."

"I aim to please."

"You sure do. And you've got a new best pal, too."

"Really? Who's that?"

The man gave his gap-toothed grin. "The Red fucking Serpent. That was some move. You killed Tank. With a fucking book. Never heard that done before. Not the wisest move, friend. Now everyone wants a piece of you. See the big guy over there?"

He turned, nodded towards the group of six men congregating around a bench between two metal stands, supporting a barbell with heavy weights fitted on either side.

One of them was staring intently at Black. Six-six, easy. Massively muscled. Coarse black hair. His head seemed out of proportion with his bull neck and wide shoulders. His features were pinched, squeezed under a jutting brow. His mouth was a gash; his nose flat. Black noted his right ear was a misshapen lump of gristle. He smiled at Black, and gestured with his hand, running it horizontally across his throat. A gesture used worldwide, the intention clear. Black had seen it many times in his career. Often in his direction.

"That's Freddy. He's known as Hammer. You know why he's called Hammer?"

"Similar level of intelligence?" ventured Black.

The man gave a hollow laugh. "He killed a guy." He leant closer. "Hammered a fucking six-inch roof nail through his eye. Hammered it right fucking through."

"Wow," said Black.

"And that's why this is not good for you. Because guess what?"

"What?"

"Tank was Hammer's best pal. And he's Danny Brogan's cousin. So you are in the middle of one fucking shitstorm, my friend."

Black pursed his lips, considering his response. The man and his pals were a distraction, which could prove costly.

"You've got colourful names. *Hammer, Tank*. But you've never told me yours, which is just plain rude."

The man straightened.

"Swifty."

Black stepped off the treadmill. He was easily eight inches taller than Swifty, and twice as broad. He towered over him. Swifty took a step back.

"Two things," said Black. "One is a statement of fact. The other is a request."

Swifty swallowed, his demeanour changing suddenly from

self-assurance to self-doubt. He flicked a glance to his friends at the other side of the gym. A million miles away.

"The first thing," said Black. "Understand that I am not your friend, you fucking piece of dog shit. The second thing – introduce me to Hammer. I'd like to meet him."

"When?"

"Now."

32

Rachel Hempworth was interested. And she had contacts. The two combined meant that if there was a story out there, she would dig and dig. Relentless. Which was why she was regarded as the *Evening Standard*'s best reporter. And one thing she loved beyond all else was the whiff of conspiracy. She was on the little guy's side, regarding herself as the proverbial knight in shining armour. Fighting injustice against big corporations, institutions, the government. The Establishment.

She got to hear about the death in Shotts prison because she knew one of the guards, and when Adam Black had been shipped out there after his trial, she kept tabs. Her nose was twitching. She just *knew* something was going to happen. Call it instinct. And she was right. Something did happen.

She got a call. A man dead. Assaulted. Perpetrator unknown. Ongoing investigations.

But Rachel didn't care about the simple facts. They told her nothing. She was interested in the rumours, the gossip, the stuff lurking between the facts, where often the underlying truth could be found. Sometimes a hint, a flavour. Of something bigger.

The incident had taken place in the prison library. The CCTV camera hadn't been working, which was strange. More than strange. The room was unmanned. Again, strange. Rumour had it, the mass murderer Oliver Pritchard – aka The Red Serpent – was the target. He'd been transferred from the segregation unit only a short time before, and straight into the general population of B Hall, which was itself unusual and inexplicable. The man was an instant target. Not even the guards could blame another inmate dispensing their own brand of prison justice. *Christ*, the guard had reasoned on the phone, *the bastard killed ten women!*

The consensus was, Tank had tried to get him, in the library. No way could Pritchard have killed a man like Tank. Tank was a heavyweight hard man, enforcer for the Glasgow gangs. So, the conclusion reached was that someone was looking out for Pritchard. Obviously, someone able to take care of themselves.

And one man who could possibly fit the bill, was the new guy called Adam Black.

Adam Black. The guard and his colleagues had come up with that idea. Rachel agreed. She listened to her gut feeling, and usually her gut was right. Black had stepped in. He'd saved the Red Serpent.

But why?

Something massive was happening. And she wanted to be part of it.

To achieve that, she had to do one thing.

Something which filled her with a heady mixture of emotion.

Excitement.

And dread.

33

The Colonel had received a text message from Detective Inspector Vanessa Shaw. There had been a development.

He had booked into a cheap hotel room at a Premier Inn only a half mile from Pitt Street Police Station, and was available 24/7. His own office in Dumfries was now redundant. Glasgow was where the task force was based, and as such, the Colonel ensured he was close by, having been granted full access to the ongoing investigation in the search for Elspeth Owen. He made it his business to keep in touch, not only with Chief Constable Divers, but the task force generally, and in particular DI Vanessa Shaw. He found her bright, interested, enthusiastic. In his opinion, one day, she might make Chief Constable. She was, in his opinion, the very opposite of the current Chief Constable, who he found obstructive, negative and into arse-covering big style.

The Colonel was no city dweller. Far from it. He lived in a white-walled cottage by a stream, in a village called Gate House of Fleet, in border country between Scotland and England. A cluster of shops, houses, a hotel, and little else. But the land was green and lush, the forests ancient and dense, and on a summer's day under a blue sky, the Colonel could forget, for a little while, the atrocities he had witnessed, the many friends he had lost in the grand theatre of war. But there were things he could never forget – his wife who had succumbed to breast cancer; the sunny smiling face of his daughter. A lasting snapshot in time, before she'd been killed in a car crash. She was twenty-one. The smile, he would never forget, nor want to. He thought about it every day, and would give everything he had to see it again, for just a second.

Perhaps Vanessa Shaw reminded him of his daughter, what she could have been, as he watched her, busy, in the incident room.

The room was large, cluttered with desks and laptops, behind which sat policemen and women, working, poring through paperwork, speaking on telephones, gazing at computer screens. One wall was a whiteboard, upon which were scrawled names, arrows, addresses. Lots of question marks. The attempted creation of a timeline, prior to the abduction. Also photographs. Friends, relatives, past victims. A picture of the Prime Minister, an older one with her husband, before cancer had taken him. In the middle of it all, was the most recent photograph of Elspeth Owen at a party, smiling archly at the camera, holding a stem glass of red wine, dressed in a winter parka by an open pit fire. Taken only a month before she'd been abducted.

Beside the photograph was a blown-up version of the letter sent to the Chief Constable's office, purportedly by the Red Serpent. It had been analysed by the best forensic experts in the land, who had come up with zero, other than it bore strong similarities in style and content as the ones received before, during the killing spree. There was nothing they could add. No fingerprints, other than those belonging to the people who had handled it when received. The paper was cheap and common and found in a million shops. The ink was from a common brand of cartridge found in printers up and down the country. The postmark was Brighton. Every letter sent was from a different part of the country. What did that say? Nothing, other than the perpetrator was mobile.

But the Colonel had received a text message from Vanessa Shaw. There had been a development.

They'd received another letter. With a little extra.

34

Elspeth Owen found consciousness, but it was a gradual thing. A fuzzy greyness, as if the world was consumed in fog, rendering the world around her to outlines and silhouettes. The fog dissipated, wafting away, like tendrils of smoke in a wind, until her vision cleared. At first, she couldn't understand where she was. Then it all flooded back, like a torrent. She sat up suddenly, her chest filling with fear.

Same place. Her stone prison. Still manacled to a wall by a length of chain. But things were different.

Before her was a full-length mirror, standing in a far corner. It was framed in wood, on a little trestle.

She stood up, swaying. She concentrated, staring at her image. She saw herself, threefold, whirling, reducing to two, then a single image. Her reflection, looking back.

It was her. But not her.

She wore a red dress. Medium length. It fitted her perfectly. Hugged her body, accentuating her contours. Cashmere. Red high heels, matching her dress. Her hair had been cut, tidied up, a shade shorter, styled.

Lipstick, lip-gloss, blusher, highlighter, eyeliner, eyeshadow, mascara. All applied with care. Meticulous.

Around her neck, a silver chain. Attached to it, sitting three inches below her collarbone, a little red jewelled heart, the size of a thumbnail. On her left middle finger, a dress ring – amethyst set on a simple yellow gold band.

She shook her head – the image in the mirror was an illusion, she thought.

Then the voice came. It startled her.

"Look at yourself."

"What have you done?" she croaked.

A silence. Then –

"Presented you."

"I don't understand. Please let me go." She could feel the familiar wave of tears coming on.

"Soon," said the voice. "Soon you'll be ready."

"Ready for fucking what?" The words rose as she spoke, verging on the hysterical.

"Ready," the voice repeated, "to transcend."

35

"If that's what you want," said the prisoner called Swifty. Suddenly, his composure had returned, his doubts vanished.

He sauntered over to the group of men, Black following. Others watched him walk by. They stopped what they were doing. Something was happening. Their prison antennae for imminent violence tingled. The talking ceased. A hush descended. The air was electric.

There were seven men altogether, noted Black, including Swifty. The biggest one by far was the individual referred to as Hammer. They each stared as Black approached. The smile on Hammer's face never left, as if set in concrete. They had formed a small circle round the bench. There were four cameras. So far, nothing would indicate to the guards watching in the surveillance room that there were any problems. Black had to keep it that way.

Swifty didn't speak. He merely gestured with his head, towards Black. The circle parted, allowing Black in, and closed behind him. Nothing was said. Hammer stood at the top of the bench, where the barbell rested on metal stands.

"Afternoon, gentlemen," Black said.

If they attacked in unison, he was a dead man. He kept his focus on their leader. Nothing would happen without his say-so. But all it took was a glance, a cue, the miniscule nod.

Hammer stood a clear four inches taller than Black.

"Swifty tells me you're not a happy man," said Black.

Hammer's face straightened, in mock indignation. "I'm fine. I'm the happiest fucker you're ever gonna meet."

A trickle of laughter.

"I'm happy," continued Hammer, "because I know I'm gonna kill you, Black. You and that fucking weasel, Pritchard. But you're first. You want to know how? I'll shove a blade up your arse, loosen things a bit, then pull your fucking lungs out. But done real slow. What do make of that, Black?"

"I think you have a vivid imagination."

"Glad you think so. You are coffin bound, my friend. Headstone's ready, with your fucking name on it." His broad jaw broke into a grin. "You're not gonna know when or where." He leaned his head forward, veins in his neck thick and blue. "But it's gonna happen."

"I think you're mistaken, Hammer."

Hammer arched his back, raising himself up, hands on hips, a towering presence. "What the fuck are you talking about?"

"I plan on being cremated. You can forget about the headstone."

Hammer's grin wavered; his face creased in a mixture of puzzlement and anger. It was all Black needed. A flicker of hesitation. There were cameras on each corner of the room. But for any onlooker, he was sheltered by the crowd of men around him.

Black struck.

The last weight on the end of each side of the barbell was a small two-kilo. The weights weren't locked in by collars. It only took Black a second to slide it into the palm of his hand. Before Hammer understood what was happening, Black swung the weight up, connecting under the big man's chin. The movement was swift and dramatic. Black's audaciousness took everyone by surprise. Hammer's head snapped back, the strength of the blow lifting him off his feet. He landed on the concrete floor, the back of his head hitting the hard ground with a slap. Black followed up, stamping twice on his testicles with the heel of his training shoe. Hammer gave a reflexive spasm, lay still. Blood began to well out from his head, forming a glistening red pool.

Black swept his gaze round the men, eyes glittering, hand still grasping the weight, daring them.

"Who's next?" he growled. "Who wants a piece of this?"

No one moved. He'd neutralised their leader. The wind had been well and truly sucked out their sails. They would need time to regroup, rethink. Plan. By which time Black would be finished and gone.

He gave Hammer a cursory glance. Possibly a skull fracture and dislocated jaw. Definitely stitches.

"Better get him to the doctor. This man's had a nasty fall."

He glared at them, taking care to meet each pair of eyes, locking for a second, moving to the next. Their demeanour had reversed, from careless swagger, to amazement, fear.

Black knew one thing. Not one of them would talk to the guards. Squealing was a mortal sin in this place. Silence was displayed almost like a badge of honour. Black knew all this, read it in their shocked expressions. They would call for help, sure. But they wouldn't talk. Not even the mighty Hammer would wish that. Instead, they would wait, allowing rage to bloom, and then cut him down at some later time.

Black didn't care. He'd made a statement, and bought himself a little space.

"Not one of you fuckers talk to me again," he said in a low voice. "Or I'll kill you all."

He tossed the weight onto Hammer's face, hitting his cheekbone, then sliding on to the blood.

Black gave a thin-lipped smile, and returned to the treadmill.

He still had his 5k to run.

36

The letter followed the same pattern as before. The Red Serpent had taken the time to send two letters to the police prior to the eventual killing. As before, the words were printed on cheap A4 paper. Good spelling, punctuation, grammar. Full marks. The letter had been sent direct to the Chief Constable's office. The postmark was Harrogate. It was picked up immediately by staff, slipped into a sealed polythene envelope, and taken to Vanessa Shaw, who had opened it with the care of a surgeon, wearing blue latex gloves. It was photographed, as was the envelope, then returned to forensics.

"We tend to get our mail late," explained Vanessa. "We have our own internal sorting office, based in another building, in another part of Glasgow. It arrived thirty minutes ago. It was picked up instantly. And here we are."

The Colonel sat in a small darkened room, with nothing much in it, except chairs, tables, a single window with the blinds closed, and on one bare white wall, an image blown-up from a projector. The latest letter from the Red Serpent. Expanded, every letter large and clear. The jottings of a serial killer, mused the Colonel. He read it, reread it.

Art imitates life.

Odd that few believe this to be true. It's there. All you have to do is look.

Transcending. It's a process, you understand. Open your eyes.

Tremble in excitement. And anticipation. And fear.

Don't believe me? Open your eyes. She looks magnificent. But that magnificence is nothing, a speck.

You're liars. You hide from truth. When she becomes, then you cannot hide. Look. Open your eyes.

Behold all of you, for what she will be, for when she emerges. To become eternal.

I will pick the place, the time. Open your eyes. Look, and everything is revealed.

Liars. Tick-tock. Tick-tock. Tempus fugit.

X

The Colonel stared at it for several long seconds. "It doesn't make sense."

Vanessa nodded in agreement. "Indeed. It's different from the others."

The Colonel understood her observation. The previous letters were inherently logical, despite their bizarre content. Their intention was to relay a message. This letter, however, did not seem to make any internal sense. It lacked structure. Random. There was no obvious connection between each line. Inane ramblings.

"What do you think?" he asked. "Someone else?"

"I don't know. Could be. It doesn't seem to be consistent. But that's not all."

The Colonel waited. Vanessa left the room, returned, and switched on the lights. She'd put on gloves, and was holding a sealed polythene bag.

"This is about to go to forensics. I wanted you to see it first. It came with the letter."

She laid it carefully on one of the tables. The Colonel got up from his seat, leaned over to look at it.

It was a black and white photograph. Of a headstone. Behind it, a stone wall and trees. The inscription had been crudely blanked out by white marker. In its place, handwritten in blue ink and in block capitals were the words –

DIED FOR THEIR SINS

5541214161I

"What the hell does this mean?" said the Colonel.

"God knows. We'll get it analysed. For fingerprints, fibres, anything."

"You'll find nothing, of course."

"Probably not. Might it be a code of some sort?"

"Our friend the Red Serpent isn't into codes and secret messages. That's never been his thing. He wrote his letters to taunt. To impress. The posturing of a psychopath. This is different. Have you shown this to the Chief Constable?"

"We can't reach him."

"Christ. He needs to see this."

"What's his game, I wonder," said Vanessa, more to herself than the Colonel.

The Colonel chose to reply. "That's exactly it. Suddenly it's become a game. Which doesn't make any sense. Something's changed."

The door opened. A young man, no older than twenty-six, wearing a dark-grey suit, grey tie, his face pale with tiredness, stood in the doorway. Detective Constable Gavin Chiltern. Economics graduate, joining the force straight from graduation and part of the fast track promotion scheme. He licked his lips, as if summoning up the courage to speak. Vanessa snapped her head round.

"Yes?"

"Ma'am, we have one major problem."

"What is it?"

When he told them, the Colonel flopped back in his chair. The girl would never be found now, he thought dismally. She was as good as dead.

37

Pritchard sat on the bed in his cell. He wasn't frightened. Everything so far was as he had expected.

As he had been told.

And now all he had to do was wait. There was little for him to do, other than play his part.

He was allowed books. Books he took from the library. Also, newspapers. He had requested, in writing, that he be allowed two every day. Those in authority agreed. He kept cut-outs of stories and photographs which interested him. Of course, he didn't use scissors, but rather he tore round the edges of each particular section with great deliberation. He was an exact man. He had worked in Glasgow University's library for over ten years. Administration was his strength. He was methodical, organised, tidy. And very careful.

He had been careful with each of the dead young women. He dismembered with a surgeon's skill. The mark he left on each of their bodies was precise and detailed. He'd always had an eye for detail. The mark of the serpent in the act of consuming its tail. Cut deep into the face with the point of a needle. The skin dyed red. A tattoo. A brand. His brand.

He kept each piece removed from the newspapers in a thick A4 writing pad, improvising as a scrapbook, each stuck to the pages with Sellotape. The pad was checked occasionally by guards who leafed through it, showing only casual interest.

Lately, a singular piece of news had interested him. Fascinated him – the man who had caused a minor sensation because of the ferocity and macabre nature of the violence he had inflicted.

Cruel and unusual were clichéd words. But here, they fitted perfectly.

And now he had spoken to him.

The man called Adam Black.

It was Black's move. Pritchard would wait. His patience was his strength.

The trap was almost set.

And the trap was perfect.

38

Chief Constable Frank Divers was the acting head of Police Scotland. As such, he carried considerable responsibility. Lately, the responsibility had escalated geometrically. The Prime Minister's daughter had been kidnapped. On his watch. In his capital city. It looked bad. But as he entered through the arched doorway of his house, the girl was not on his mind.

Divers lived in a village fifteen miles from Glasgow, called Kilmacolm. A rather upmarket pocket of Scotland, where houses were mansions, where seclusion was a given, where the rich liked to settle, away from the grime and dirt of the city. Where Divers liked to live a very private existence. And for a man like Divers, privacy was high in his priorities.

Divers was a wealthy man. The police pay was substantial, but he had private means. His parents were both dead, and his inheritance had been large, with no siblings to share. He had divorced his wife – or she had divorced him – creating a dent in his resources, but a dent only. She'd asked for x, he'd given her that plus more. A sweetener. To buy her silence. She'd grabbed the money, and immediately bought an apartment in the South of France. He hadn't seen her or heard from her for three years, and had no desire to again. He rather hoped she was dead, and if not, that she would drop dead soon. Then he would know his secret was secure. In the meantime, he had to content himself with the money being enough to shut her mouth. He had threatened. If she tried anything, if she resurfaced, using what she knew as leverage for more money, then he would break her. Snap her spine, twist her head off, and pound her fucking bones to powder. Those were the words he had used, in private, whispering in her ear, when they left the lawyers office.

And he knew she believed him. Every word. After what she'd witnessed. To her mind, he was capable of anything.

Divers thoughts were not on Elspeth Owen as he entered his plush, five bedroomed mock-Tudor house, sitting on an acre of manicured lawns, nestled in the shade of Duchal Woods, within earshot of the River Gryfe. A curious onlooker might have described the place as magical. Somewhere plucked from another time, another world.

Divers unbuttoned his jacket, loosened his tie, took off his peaked cap, tossed it on the stairs. He made his way through a wide, high hallway, to the kitchen. He switched on the lights – the place lit up. Open-plan, broadening out to a large living room, one wall all glass with bi-folding doors, beyond which, the back garden enclosed by stone walls, and beyond that, the shadow gloom of the woods.

Divers first port of call was the fridge. He got a cold bottle of Bud and some pizza, which he didn't bother to heat up. He was starving. He was fat, had diabetes, had been told to watch his diet, but he really didn't give a shit. He had urges. One was to eat whatever the hell he wanted.

And the other was just as compelling. When he felt the red mist descend.

Which was now, after talking to the slut, DI Vanessa Shaw. How he wanted to crush her, break her down. The thought consumed him, made his heart beat fast, his hands tremble, made his cock hard as iron.

His mobile rang. He checked the number. He answered. He knew exactly who it was. The call he had been waiting on.

"Get here now," he said, cutting straight in, ignoring pleasantries. "I'll have things ready."

He hung up. The conversation was entirely one-sided.

He had to get prepared. He left the kitchen, through the living room, into another hall. He unlocked a door, switched a light on, and went down several stairs, coming to another door. This one was gun-metal grey, new, and opened by a coded keypad on the wall. He pressed the five digits. The lock clicked open. Lights came on, automatically. He went through, the door clicking closed behind him, and down more stairs.

To his basement.

39

Nothing was said. No one talked. An accident in prison life was not uncommon. A fall, a slip. Broken bones resulting from a loose shoelace. A tumble down the stairs. The warden, the guards, they were not naïve. The prisoners closed ranks. To get someone to talk was like turning water to wine. It would need a miracle. And HM Prison Shotts had seen very few of those.

Hammer did not have a fractured skull. He suffered concussion. His jawbone was cracked and he lost some teeth. Plus, twenty stitches to the back of his head. Plus, double vision which turned out to be a detached retina in his right eye. He was taken to the Southern General, where he was handcuffed to a bed. Word was, he would be back in two weeks. Word was, he was in a mad-dog rage, and the man called Adam Black was a dead man.

Black had to move quickly. The threat of Hammer didn't trouble him. No one would dare make a play against him. Not while Hammer had marked him out. Which meant he had time to deal with Pritchard without glancing over his shoulder every two minutes.

The day following the incident in the gym, Black found Pritchard in the library. Sitting in the same seat when Tank had tried to razor-shred his face. Clearly not the superstitious type, reflected Black.

He picked up any book, and sat opposite. A guard was positioned at his station yards away, watching closely. There would be no repeat performances of the last debacle.

Pritchard looked up. If Black's presence had any impact, it wasn't reflected on his face. His expression remained impassive. Impossible to read. He stared at Black with his dark eyes, and Black was unable to fathom the motivations behind them.

"Mind if I join you?" Black asked.

Pritchard didn't respond.

"What are you reading?"

Pritchard had placed his book flat on the table, front cover face down. Delicately, he turned it over, and swivelled it round so that Black could read the cover –

Captain Blood by Rafael Sabatini. Hardback. The cover, somewhat battered, depicted a sailor, gazing out to sea from the prow of a ship.

"Really?" said Black. "I'm surprised it's still in print. It must have been written a hundred years ago."

Pritchard's lips twitched. A semblance of a smile. He slid the book back in front of him. Black noticed how soft and slender his fingers were. The hands of a pianist, he thought. Or perhaps an artist. Also, his fingernails. Long. Sharp. Like talons, almost. When he was eventually caught, forensics had scraped underneath them and found particles of skin. Skin from his last victim. The police report at the time recorded his reasoning – *because when I tear their flesh, they experience a flavour of the pain to be. Call it an aperitif.* Black had read every report, every interview. There was little he didn't know about the Red Serpent.

Suddenly Pritchard spoke. "You know your books." His voice

was low, quiet. "It was published in 1922. Hollywood turned it into a movie."

"I recall that," said Black. "The Golden Age of Hollywood. Errol Flynn in the leading role. Or was it Douglas Fairbanks?"

Pritchard nodded. "Flynn. The obvious choice. I imagine there are few people nowadays who know about things like that. But you do."

"I like the old black and whites."

"We have something in common."

Black bit his lip, uncertainty etched on his face. "We might have more than that in common."

"Tell me."

Black lowered his voice, to almost a whisper. "I know who you are. That's why I protected you."

Pritchard sat perfectly still, his face pale and smooth as alabaster. Then he said, "Who am I?"

Black met his dark gaze. "The Red Serpent."

"And what does that mean to you?"

"I understood, as soon as I saw it. The symbol scored into your face."

Pritchard narrowed his eyes. "And what does that mean?"

Black bowed his head. "I don't have the right to mention it."

Pritchard's eyes gleamed like snake skin in the bright light of the library. "Tell me."

Black took a deep breath, as if summoning up courage. "A circle. The serpent swallows its tail. I understand what you are."

"And what am I?"

Black met Pritchard's glittering gaze. "Eternal."

Pritchard leaned back on the chair. "You're a curious man. Why the need to protect me?"

Black faltered. "Because..." He dipped his eyes again.

"Yes?"

"Because I want to be like you."

Pritchard cocked his head. "You want to be like me," he echoed.

"That's wrong. I want to be you."

Pritchard fell silent. At length he spoke. "The serpent sheds its skin, and becomes anew. He is reborn."

"I understand. Reborn. My name is Adam Black."

"I know all about you, Mr Black. I know what you've done, and why you did it." The Red Serpent smiled.

Black had experienced many intense situations. He had seen death, dealt death. He was no stranger to man's brutality. He was a man of war, and as such, had borne witness to all the dread war brings. He saw something in that smile he had seen many times before.

Pure evil.

40

Black got the surprise of his life. It was 2pm on a cold, dreary afternoon, the day after his chat with Pritchard. He was in the exercise yard, getting some fresh air. Time was desperately short. He would need to seek out Pritchard again, hoping he might be in the library, where conversation could be conducted on a more intimate level, without interruption. Plus, it was safe, relatively. No way would there be a second attack in the same place. At least not until Hammer was discharged from his hospital bed. By which time Black would be gone. Such was the plan.

He was approached by Fletcher and two guards. Black braced himself. Fletcher meant bad news.

The three men stood square on, Fletcher in the middle. The other prisoners, instinctively, veered away, keeping their distance.

As ever, Fletcher stepped up close to Black, his face only inches away. Black detected the remnants of his lunch wedged between his teeth.

"You scared of me, Black?"

"Terrified."

"Terrified, Mr Fletcher, sir. Show some fucking respect when you address me. Say it."

"Say what?"

Fletcher's voice dropped, edged with menace. "Fucking smart arse. Say, 'I'm terrified of you, Mr Fletcher, sir.' Say it like a fucking dog."

"I don't know how to speak dog language."

Fletcher's face reddened. Black couldn't help himself. Fletcher was big, stupid, and a bully. If circumstances were different...

Still, Black knew Fletcher wouldn't try anything here, with witnesses. He would wait for his moment. And then, like Hammer, Fletcher would be left scratching his head. Because Black would be gone.

"You are such a fucking dead man, Black. When the time comes – and mark my words, it *will* come – I will be laughing so fucking hard. When you're on your arse, getting the bejesus kicked out of you. And there'll be a queue a mile long, I kid you not. I'll be at the front. Flattening your face into pulp with my steel-capped boots. What do you think of that, Adam fucking Black?"

Black wrinkled his face. "What do I think of what? You laughing so fucking hard? Me getting the *bejesus* kicked out of me? You at the front of a queue? Or your steel-capped boots? I'm not sure which section of your dialogue you want me to answer. If it's your boots, then I'm very impressed. Sir. Sorry – Mr Fletcher, sir."

Fletcher took a long deep breath. His hand brushed the clip of the baton at the side of his belt. Black cursed silently, at his own stupidity. Perhaps he had goaded him too much. He should learn to keep his mouth shut.

A sly smile crept across Fletcher's face. "That's good, Black. Keep it up. It will make it taste all the sweeter. Here, I'm fucking

God Almighty. You think the library was left unattended by accident? You think the video camera being switched off was some fucking coincidence. Pritchard had it coming. And I'm going to make sure he gets it. Just like you're going to get it. I control everything in this place. I can make things happen. I can make things disappear. What do you think of that, Black?"

"I think you know already what I'm thinking, seeing as you're God Almighty. Mr Fletcher, sir."

Fletcher nodded slowly, as if he were planning Black's fate then and there. He took a step back.

"Surprise, surprise. You have a friend, Black. Which I really don't understand. Someone wants to see you."

Black was dumbfounded.

"She's waiting for you in the visitor's room. So let's go. Fucking move it. Now!"

Arranging a meeting at Shotts prison was never easy, unless you were a relative or girlfriend. Or boyfriend. Rachel Hempworth telephoned admin, who then emailed her an application form, which she completed and sent back online – *reason for visit: I wish to interview Adam Black as part of a journalistic enquiry. Currently researching the rise of knife crime in the City of Glasgow.*

The application was vetted, considered, then given to the warden for approval. Within three days, she had her response. The visit was sanctioned.

She had visited Shotts prison once before, working on a piece about drug dependency and serious crime. And there was little doubt the crimes committed by those incarcerated in that particular prison were all serious. These men were dangerous. She had no illusions about Adam Black. He was a seriously dangerous man.

She was led into a waiting room. After ten minutes, her details were painstakingly recorded by a man at reception. Then down a corridor, to a man and woman in prison uniform. She was asked to empty her handbag and pockets into a plastic tray. She was swept by an electronic hand device. She was asked specifically if she carried drugs, alcohol, or any recording machines. She was not allowed to smoke. She had to relinquish her mobile phone. She could not offer the prisoner anything, nor physically give him anything. She could not touch him. If she breached any of the conditions, she committed a criminal act, proceedings would be brought against her, punishable by a fine and possible detention.

She was escorted by a prison guard down a long corridor. By now, she had lost any sense of direction. She was somewhere in the bowels of a state prison, full of murderers, rapists, arsonists and killers.

She was taken to a large room with high windows with bars, allowing wan sunlight to filter through. The place smelled of bleach. Laid out in neat rows were small square tables with metal chairs on each side. She was reminded of a classroom. Instead of a teacher, there were three guards, sitting at desks at the far wall.

The place was half full. The sound was the low drone of muted conversation. Intimate, secret exchanges. Husbands and wives; brothers; fathers and sons; mothers and sons; boyfriends and girlfriends. No children. Glances were given as she entered and was shown to an empty chair.

This was not the movies, she reflected. There was no glass barrier between prisoner and visitor. No special telephone. This was face to face. Real life. If things got rough, then the batons were out, people got hurt. Or so she imagined. She watched the guards and wondered if that was what they hoped for. Action. Violence. A justification for their presence.

She sat. She experienced a mixture of emotion. Excitement. She knew there was something here. Something bigger. Call it a hunch. An instinct. But also fear. She was about to meet a man capable of the most horrendous acts. He'd put two men in hospital, had mutilated one man's face with a hunting knife. A dangerous person. They had never met. He had never seen her before. How would he react?

She would find out.

Another door opened.

Adam Black entered the room.

41

It seemed to Rachel Hempworth that he dominated the place by his mere presence. Just as he seemed to dominate the court room, when she had first seen him. He was a big man, over six feet. Spare and strong. Coarse dark hair, cropped short. Harsh cheekbones. Narrow sky-blue eyes gleaming from a weathered face. Wearing jeans, faded grey T-shirt, white running shoes. His gaze swept the room, locking in on her.

She returned his gaze with a half-smile, raising her hand as if she were at school. His expression changed to puzzlement.

He walked over, and sat opposite.

"Hello," she said.

"Hello."

"My name is Rachel Hempworth. I work for the *Evening Standard*."

He waited a moment before he answered. "Good for you. My name is Adam Black. How can I help you?"

"I saw you at the High Court. I was covering the case. The paper asked me to try to do a follow-up story. I was wondering if you'd like to chat about it?"

"Chat?"

"That's all. Would you mind if I took some notes?"

She pulled out a lined notepad and pen from her bag. The prison officers watched her carefully.

Black also watched her.

"You were in the army, Adam. Do you mind if I call you Adam?"

"Yes and no."

"You fought with the SAS. You won the Military Cross. Do you miss military life?"

"Look around, Rachel. There's not a whole lot of difference between the two. Why are you here?"

She put the pen down, and met his eyes. "Because you're an unusual man. Uncommon. I know about your past. And what you did to these two men doesn't fit."

"You know nothing about me."

"I know you had a brother who died in Ireland. I know you left the army to work in a commercial law practice. I know that your wife and daughter were killed. Murdered in your house in Eaglesham. Then what? You dropped from view for months. Suddenly you're set up as a lawyer in Glasgow's southside. And then you're in the middle of some gang feud with the thug Danny Brogan, which to my simple, naïve mind, makes no sense. From lawyer to gangster. From conveyancing to cutting out tongues with a hunting knife." Her voice was raised. She swallowed, took a deep breath, tried to maintain a cool head.

"You've done your homework, Rachel," said Black, his voice quiet, level. "But I still don't know why you're here."

"You removed Brogan's tongue with a knife. You did that for a reason. What was the reason, Adam? Why were you involved at all?"

"Brogan was a money lender, extortionist, pimp, drug dealer. I'd say he got off lightly."

Rachel shook her head. "That's a glib answer, and I don't buy into it. What are you? A vigilante? You're more than that. I know about the prisoner. Beaten to death. Were you involved in that?"

"I think your journalistic imagination is in hyperdrive. I attacked two men. I'm serving my sentence."

She shook her head. "I saw you at court," she said quietly. "I've covered Sheriff and High Court cases a hundred times. I've seen men and women squirm, and cry, and scream in the dock. I've heard sob stories, and lies, and excuses, listened to social work reports, background reports, medical opinions. I've heard clever lawyers weave their tales, conjuring up bad luck stories for their clients. Making them out to be the victims. Painting them as poor souls, abandoned by the system. I've seen and heard everything. But you were different. I saw you at court. You're no poor soul. You're no victim. I saw something I haven't seen before."

The tremble of a smile seemed to flicker across his face. *Is he finding me amusing?* she wondered. She tried to read him. Tried to understand how he ticked. But it was like trying to understand a rock.

"And what was it that you hadn't seen before? Enlighten me, Rachel."

"I saw purpose."

"Really? A curious word in such a context."

"You did those things to these men in front of a dozen witnesses. I could call it up on YouTube right now if they hadn't taken my damned mobile phone. You pled guilty. You didn't ask for a lawyer to represent you. You made it easy for them. It was like you... contrived the situation. It was like you wanted to be here. Because you have a purpose. Tell me that's not true. What's going on, Adam?"

"You should write a book. This has all the hallmarks of a bestseller."

She held his stare.

Her pulse was racing, she realised. She found the man before her unquestionably attractive. Maybe that was the problem. Maybe she wanted to believe there was something more. That he wasn't the cruel, violent man his crimes suggested he was, that the press had made him out to be.

"Please speak to me," she whispered.

Black put both his elbows on the table, leaned forward slightly. His expression was cold, as distant as the ocean, his eyes blue and piercing, and when he spoke, his voice betrayed no emotion. "There is nothing to speak about. Write about other stories. This one is only bad news, I promise you."

He stood up. The visit was over.

"Take care, Rachel Hempworth." He nodded, giving her a quick smile, turned, and left through the door he had entered.

She watched him leave, and made a decision. Her mind was set.

She wouldn't let this go. For some reason this man called Adam Black had connected with her. He had a story to tell. She would keep pressing until she found the truth.

42

When it took hold of him, he lost track of time. Lost track of everything. Divers woke up in his living room, naked, sprawled on a large suede couch. The curtains were drawn, thankfully. He opened his eyes. The room was dark, but he sensed daylight outside.

He lay for several seconds, collecting his thoughts, reliving the scenes in his mind. The screams. The begging. The pleas. The savagery. And then blood. When the blood came, he orgasmed. He recalled every detail, moment by exquisite moment. He felt himself stiffen as he relived each second, over and over.

A noise penetrated his thoughts. A buzzing sound. Like the drone of a bumblebee. No bumblebee. His mobile phone, vibrating on the kitchen worktop. He groaned, got up slowly, wheezing for breath, padded his way to the phone. It had stopped. He picked it up. Seven missed calls. One from DI Vanessa Shaw. Three from the troublemaker Colonel Mackenzie. And a further three from the PM's office. Something was going down.

Still, his mind wandered. To the recent events. His thoughts flitted to DI Shaw. Her lithe body. He started to massage his dick, thinking about her. The things he would do. He snapped back, reining his thoughts in. He glanced at the clock on the kitchen wall. Two thirty. "Fuck," he said out loud. He pressed her number on speed dial. She answered immediately.

"What is it?" he said.

"Sir, thank God," she replied, her words rattling out. "The shit has hit the proverbial fan." There was hesitation in her voice. "Plus, we received another letter from our friend. Are you coming in?"

"Of course I'm coming in," he growled. His tone softened. "I've had a bug. Been in bed. Better now. Tell me about the shit and the fan."

When she told him, he listened, said he'd be at Pitt Street in forty-five minutes, then hung up.

"Fuck," he said aloud again.

Things just got a whole lot worse.

43

After his chat with Rachel Hempworth, Black went straight to the library, to join Pritchard. The meeting with her had surprised Black, for sure, and her questions doubly so. Was the Colonel's plan so transparent? Time was running out for Black. She was a distraction. He dismissed her from his mind. He had a bigger play to make.

Tick-tock.

They sat again, he and Pritchard, on the same seats, opposite each other, books open on the table before them. It was 2.45pm. There was no one else in the room, save a prison guard, who sat, arms folded, watching them.

Black had to bring it up a gear, hoping it wasn't too obvious.

"You have so much to teach me," he said, his voice in a reverential whisper.

Pritchard acknowledged the comment with a twitch of his lips. His eyes shone when he spoke.

"I can teach you everything you need. Provided you're prepared to be taught."

"I am."

"Then you'll need patience. To achieve what... eternal life?

You need to dig deep. You need to bare your soul to me, Adam. Can you do that?"

"I can try."

"Of course. I told you I knew about you, and what you had done. And why. Shall I show you something? Then you can begin to glimpse perhaps a little of my power. And what you can achieve."

"Please. Show me."

"Then I shall."

In the afternoon period, cell doors were open, or closed, depending on the mood of the inmate. To promote social interaction, prisoners were encouraged to wander, mingle. Always under the scrutiny of prison officers, who watched like sharp-eyed hawks, one stationed at the end of each corridor, ten roving the passageways and recreation rooms. And CCTV everywhere.

Black followed Pritchard back to his cell. He was aware of the dark glances as they passed, the mutterings, the threats. The price of fame, he thought grimly. He reckoned, at this moment in time, he and the Red Serpent were the two most hated men in the prison. He was surrounded by people who lived by the creed of violence. A wrong look, a wrong move, and that was it. A spark, and suddenly there was wildfire. Black followed, aware every second was crucial.

They got to the cell.

"Do you mind?" asked Pritchard, gesturing at the door. Black closed the door behind them.

Pritchard's room was neat, organised. He opened the only cupboard, and pulled out a book of A4-sized notepaper. A scrapbook.

"Look at this."

He placed the book on the bed. He opened the pages. Each contained newspaper clippings, carefully positioned. Each related to the rise of the Red Serpent, his victims, dates, places, descriptions, locations, photographs. A history of murder seen through the eyes of the media, over five years, ten young women, culminating in his capture, his guilty plea, his sentence.

"Look." He pointed to a photo of him being led from the court building, into a waiting van. "I had just been given life without parole. Look carefully, Adam. What can you see?"

Black scrutinised the picture, his face staring directly at the camera.

When he answered, he wasn't bullshitting. "Defiance."

"Correct. I am afraid of nothing. I will teach you that."

He continued turning the pages. More newspaper sections, less sensational – suggestions there were more victims, families still grieving. Pritchard had been in prison for six months. The news relating to his exploits dwindled.

Then another piece. Unrelated to the Red Serpent. All about Adam Black. His attack on two men. Photographed and filmed by witnesses in a main street in Glasgow. His court appearance. His sentence. The barbarism of the violence inflicted. Details of what he did.

"You sliced out a man's tongue," said Pritchard. "When you did that, I became interested in you."

"I did it to attract your attention."

"You copied me."

"I emulated you."

"A subtle difference," said Pritchard. "Do you know why I cut off their tongues?"

"I can only guess."

"Then guess."

"To avoid any... rude interruptions. When you worked on them, you needed full concentration."

Pritchard smiled. "We think alike. Good. Now see this."

He turned a page. A photographic image, similar to the one Pritchard had already shown him. Only it was Black being led from the court to a waiting police van. And similarly, Black was looking directly at the camera.

"Do you see?"

Black did. A similar look. Defiance.

A noise from outside disturbed them. Men talking rapidly, loudly. Footsteps. Black opened the cell door, to see prisoners herding towards the common room. He glanced round at Pritchard.

"I'll be back shortly."

He joined the throng, emerging into the room where prisoners played pool, sat about, talked, drank coffee. On one wall was a television, switched on every morning at the same time to Sky News.

The place was packed. The breaking news was incredible. Mind-blowing.

The Prime Minister's daughter had been kidnapped.

And it bore all the hallmarks of one of the most depraved serial killers in Great Britain.

The Red Serpent.

Which was impossible, of course.

Even for hardened prisoners, the effect was profound. A silence fell as every man there absorbed this piece of news.

Black absorbed it too.

It was maybe the edge he needed.

44

The old woman did not have the ability to walk far. But she still enjoyed fresh air. And when the sun was in the sky, even on a chill winter's afternoon, she made the effort to leave the house, steadied by a walking stick crafted from oak. Crafted for her. Sometimes she meandered through the woods. Sometimes, she walked the short distance to the cliff edge, only a hundred yards from the front door.

Today, the afternoon was bright, the sky blue. It was freezing, but with the cold came a wonderful clarity. On such days, she felt she could see to the other side of the world.

She stood at the cliff's edge, the sound of waves breaking against hard stone filling her senses. She liked to stand close to the precipice. How easy, she thought. How easy to put one foot forward, and let go. Seventy feet down into the sea, to drift on the waves, her lungs full of cold saltwater. She shivered. Her head would shatter on the rocks first, her legs and arms would break into odd angles. Her brittle spine would snap. Then the sea would sweep her away.

But her soul? What would happen to it, she wondered. Her soul was damned.

She turned away from the expanse of the sea, and made her way slowly back to the house, leaning heavily on her walking stick. She chose not to go back in. The thought repulsed her. Instead, she walked past it, to the edge of the wood at her back door. It was not a thick wood. But at night, there were no lights, and it spread out like a black stain. It stretched a mile or so, a barrier between her house and the village. The winter's sun chased away the shadows, dappling the leaves gold and bronze. The semblance of a path ran through it, like a single connecting artery between her and civilisation. The artery of a dying man, she thought, clogged with weeds and broken branches and spreading bushes.

She stopped at the trunk of a thick oak tree. It was from a branch of this tree that he had shaped and carved the walking stick. For her. His parting gift.

But he had never left. Here, he remained. She had seen to that. When the tree creaked in the mad winds from the sea, she thought it was him, groaning, restless. His soul searching, perhaps. For justice.

She thought back to that afternoon, as she did every day. It wormed into her brain, filled every corner of her mind. It had been cold and bright, like it was now. The sun had provided no warmth. She remembered every detail. Every word spoken. Every expression on his face. Every movement of his body.

And the colours. The blueness of the sky, the yellow glare of the sun, the stark paleness of his skin.

The rich red colour of his blood.

45

"The Prime Minister has resigned," said Chief Constable Divers, to no one in particular. More of a statement, thought the Colonel, confirming what everyone already knew.

They were seated in Divers' office – his massive figure squatting like a bespectacled Buddha behind his desk, the Colonel opposite, DI Shaw next to him.

It was breaking news. Huge. Monumental.

Spread across the desk were editions of each of the main newspapers. They each bore the same stunning, unequivocal headline – *The Prime Minister's Daughter Has Been Kidnapped*. No play on words. It was shocking. It was simple.

It had already been broadcast on television. Everyone was waiting on the Chief Constable's office to respond.

"Someone talked."

Again, a mind-boggling ability to state the obvious, thought the Colonel. But his thoughts were running in another direction.

"Someone was bound to talk," said the Colonel. "It was only a matter of time. It just happened sooner than we would have wanted. We take the blow, and keep running."

"That's fucking easy for you to say," snarled Divers suddenly, his face contorted in a spasm of fury. "It's us that get the flack. A thousand calls a day from fucking John O'Groats to Land's End. And every other fucking country. And it's me who's got to face the rabble, and give them some bullshit about the situation being under control, when the reality is, we do not have one fucking clue! It's easy to come away with glib pieces of advice, when you're sitting in the cheap seats, Mackenzie!"

The Colonel regarded Divers for a long moment. "We've been looking for you."

Divers blinked, taken off guard. "What?"

The Colonel's eyes furrowed in puzzlement. "Where were you?"

"Excuse me?"

"We were trying to contact you. Both DI Shaw and myself. I left messages on your mobile. But you were unobtainable."

The Chief Constable stood, slowly. He towered over the seated couple, a colossus. Over 240 pounds. Six-four. Mostly fat. *His heart would burst if he had to take the stairs*, the Colonel thought.

"That's my business," Divers said quietly. "I have a life outside the police force. I'm not answerable to you."

The Colonel shrugged. "You were needed."

"Well, I'm fucking here!" he roared. Vanessa visibly jumped. "The Prime Minister has resigned," he went on. "Right now, I wonder what authority you've got. And your fucking department." He leaned over the table, which creaked under the weight.

"With the PM gone, and without her backing, tell me, Colonel Mackenzie, what are you doing here?"

The Colonel was unperturbed by Divers' ranting. Shouting had never fazed him.

"Me personally? As much as I can, which I accept isn't much. But we still have hope. We have Adam Black. He might give us an answer."

Divers lip curled. His voice lowered to a hoarse whisper. "Fuck Adam Black."

46

Black had to do this right. Patience. But the tank was running low. Time was not on his side.

The news was profound. A real-life crime thriller was unfolding before the world's eyes. For once, the crimes committed by those incarcerated seemed almost miniscule, compared to the grandiose events in the outside world – *the Prime Minister's daughter has been kidnapped.*

Black wondered how his ally and friend the Colonel was coping with the sudden new set of parameters. Solving a crime with half the world's population watching over your shoulder wouldn't be easy.

But few people knew about Black. Which meant he still had the ability to complete his mission.

He waited a day. He did not return to Pritchard's cell that afternoon. He had to play this cool, and respond in the way Pritchard would expect him to respond. *To inhabit the mind of a monster*, he thought. Not easy.

The morning of the 27th February, following the usual routine, he collected his breakfast on a tray from the self-service canteen, and made his way over to a corner table, aware of the many eyes following him. He had no friends. No wonder. He had befriended a serial killer, and simultaneously cracked open the skull of the main prison crime lord, plus killed his friend with a library book. It couldn't get much worse. A thriller going on in the outside world, a fucking comedy sketch being played out inside. Ironic. A joke. But it was no joke. It was life and death. And death had always been loyal to Black. It had stuck with him since his service days with the SAS. Death was his real friend. It never left him. The day would come when death would betray him, and administer to him that which he had administered to his enemies. Black would get the final laugh, for when that day came, Black would not be scared. He would embrace it. Welcome it.

A man joined him. Black looked into the thin, weasel face of the man nicknamed Swifty.

"Hello, Adam," he said.

Black offered him the slightest nod.

"Good news," Swifty continued. "Hammer's making a good recovery."

Black gave him a cold smile. "When I hit someone with a weight, I really should do a better job."

"You're a funny man, Adam Black. But Hammer doesn't think so. You smashed his jaw. He's wearing some sort of face brace. He's looking forward to seeing you."

"Reminiscent of Frankenstein's monster. Can't wait."

"That's good. Because you won't be waiting long. He's coming back tomorrow. You got anything you want me to pass on?"

Black, who had been eating a bowl of muesli, stopped in mid-chew, as if thoughtful. Suddenly, he leaned forward, and spat the contents of his mouth onto Swifty's face.

Swifty recoiled, eyes wide in shock, pieces of Black's breakfast stuck to his skin.

Black stared at Swifty, eyes like lead. "Pass that on."

47

Black did not see Pritchard at the canteen. Nerves tingling, he sauntered past his cell, towards the common room. His door was closed. He made a U-turn, to the library. No sign of him. Clock was ticking. He wandered to the common room. Men playing pool, talking. The previous day's drama was still being discussed. He turned, to head back to his own cell, to stand square on with Pritchard.

"I've been looking for you," said Pritchard.

Black furrowed his forehead in a display of puzzlement. "I've been... thinking."

"Thinking? About what?"

"I'm confused."

Pritchard stared at Black for a long second. "I think I understand."

"I'm not certain you do."

"Don't underestimate me, Adam. You're a perceptive man. As am I."

Black said nothing.

"Let's meet. This afternoon. In the library. I think I owe you something."

149

"What?" asked Black.

"An explanation."

The wiretapping of each of the telephones in Shotts prison had remained in place, which meant the incident room at Pitt Street had to endure every conversation between inmates and their families, friends, lawyers, dealers, business associates. Some of the conversations could have added years onto existing sentences. All inadmissible in a court of law. Sometimes rules had to be broken. Exceptional times called for exceptional measures, mused the Colonel, who insisted that he hear each and every taped conversation. All done on the off-chance the Red Serpent broke his routine, and made further contact.

Which is what he did five minutes after his conversation with Black.

The Colonel had no office to call his own. He mingled with the others, in the main incident room. The Chief Constable had threatened to remove him entirely, for no logical reason the Colonel could think of, other than sheer bloody spitefulness.

When the young economics graduate, DC Chiltern, headphones still wrapped round his head, jumped up suddenly, and shouted, "He's just made a fucking call!" The Colonel thought maybe this might be the break he needed. The break everyone needed.

DI Vanessa Shaw, the Colonel, several others, circled round the table.

"Play it back," said DI Shaw.

They listened to the soft, clear, unmistakable voice of the man known as the Red Serpent.

"*Is it time?*"

The same deep, booming voice responded, rendered almost alien by a voice modulator. "*Yes.*"

"*Our brother is prepared?*"

Heavy breathing. Then, "*He is the death bringer. He is prepared. It is time.*"

The phone went dead.

DI Shaw ran her hands through her hair.

"What the hell does this shit mean?" She looked round her, at the suddenly silent room. "Please, somebody, give me a fucking answer."

No one responded, including the Colonel. He had no answer to give.

But something was going to happen, very soon. So much was obvious.

And it did. But in a way the Colonel could never have predicted.

No one could have predicted.

48

The Prime Minister had given a short, emotional speech outside Number 10. The crowd, consisting mainly of reporters, cameramen, and photographers, were silent, poised on every word. Her words were anguished, fragile, her voice breaking when she pleaded not as a leader, but as a mother – *please give my baby back.*

She withdrew behind the black door, ushered through, surrounded by a blanket of solemn, comforting people.

The Treasury Minister, a sombre individual called Nicholas Wetherby, took her place behind the set of microphones, and delivered a serious, measured speech. The nation listened. The nation was shocked. Galvanised against evil. Political boundaries were swept aside. This was a human story, striking the very heart of government, and by extension, the heart of the people.

The PM went straight to her private study. She had already packed, and would be out in a half hour. This was her last meeting held at Number 10. And it had nothing to do with politics.

Ernest Stanford followed her, along with her closest aides –

Katie Sykes, Tod Chalmers, who was the Police Commissioner of the Met, and Jack Ford, a friend and Cabinet Minister.

Here, in the bowels of Number 10, the silence was absolute, save the crackle and spark of flames from the hearth.

"What now?" was all she said, her voice distant, hollow. Stanford studied her. *How her face is ravaged*, he thought. Her cheekbones looked harsh and sharp, her eyes sunken in their sockets. *Dead eyes*, thought Stanford.

Chalmers cleared his throat. "She will be found, ma'am." He was small for a policeman, compact, a pugnacious build, solid chin. "I promise you. The met will work in conjunction with Police Scotland. It's nationwide now."

The PM gave a short harsh laugh. "The idea was to keep the whole thing low-key. I was told by the experts that was the best way to get Elspeth back. And now look at it." She took a long shuddering breath, fighting back tears, waving her hand as if she were swatting a fly. "It's like a carnival show." She bit her lip, voice breaking. "My daughter being the main attraction."

"More people involved gives us a better chance, Lynda." It was her friend Jack Ford who spoke. His voice was low, soothing, full of conviction. *There speaks the voice of a politician*, thought Stanford.

A silence fell. Then the PM spoke. Her voice was flat, lifeless.

"She's dead. I know she is. My little girl. I'm going to go now. I'm going to wait in the hall downstairs. I've packed a suitcase. Like a tourist leaving a hotel. Alone."

She turned to Katie Sykes, her Permanent Secretary, allowing her a small, sad smile.

"If you need anything, you know where to get me. I'll not be leaving my house."

Her house in the Cotswolds, thought Stanford. *More of a mansion.*

She got up to go. She fixed her gaze suddenly onto the Police Commissioner, and held it for several seconds.

"Find my fucking daughter."

She left the room. Chalmers and Ford both followed her. Katie Sykes and Stanford lingered behind.

Stanford was about to speak, but before he could open his mouth, Katie said, "You're a cunt."

Stanford, skin thick as a rhino's after years of navigating the choppy corridors of Whitehall, gave a silky response. "Your state school days never really left you."

"You wanted this. She's gone. Broken. For what? A fucking clarion call to the party troops. A new beginning? What did you say – a resurrection? The dead don't come back to life. Not in this world. You leaked it to the press, and guess what?"

Stanford shrugged.

"You signed Elspeth Owen's death warrant. How can you look so fucking smug?"

Stanford gave an easy, well-practised smile. "This is my natural look."

"I'll bet it is. Well, thank Christ we've still got people like the Colonel on board. He might find a way through this shitstorm."

"You're a fool, Katie. Did you see the PM? She's a spent force. Broken inside. A husk. Like our country. With her gone, the Colonel loses all his favours. He was an embarrassment to the government. For the PM to call for help from some shady, paramilitary department was a joke. He'll be gone too, by the end of the week. History. Never to be heard of again. New broom. And then we'll let the police do their job. And I have an admission."

"What?"

"It wasn't me. I didn't speak to the press. Though I had found the concept tempting."

"Liar."

He shrugged again.

"You're forgetting we have the soldier," said Katie. "The man called Adam Black. This is not a game. This man is risking everything to find Elspeth. What happens to him?"

Stanford reacted with a short, sarcastic laugh. "Adam who?"

49

They met in their usual place. The Red Serpent, killer of women, serial killer, and Adam Black, ex-officer of the Special Air Service, winner of the Military Cross. Also a killer, in his own way.

The prison library, as ever, was quiet. A few other inmates were at other tables, reading newspapers, books.

It was 4.45pm. They sat opposite each other, books open. Black had chosen one at random – *Catch-22*. Pritchard's book, he noted, was *Doctor Jekyll and Mr Hyde*. He wondered if there was some significance to that.

"You said you'd give me an explanation," said Black, his voice quiet, conspiratorial, as if he were plotting some big escape. "But you don't know about what. Unless you can read minds."

"I can do many things," replied Pritchard. "And I can guess. It's about her, isn't it? She worries you?"

"Her?"

"The daughter of the Prime Minister. Or should I say ex-Prime Minister."

Black averted his gaze, fixing his eyes on the open book in front of him. "It has your touch."

Pritchard remained silent.

Black looked up. "She's twenty-two. She has blonde hair. Done just the way you like it. Shoulder length. She looks like the others. In fact, the similarities are striking. And she just vanished, in a public place. In Edinburgh, which isn't a million miles from your hunting ground. Whoever did this was patient, methodical, clever. Do you see?"

Pritchard studied Black's face for several long seconds, as someone might consider an interesting picture on a wall. "And you require an explanation."

"You can see why. If you're here, and that's happening out there, then I can only think of three things."

"Tell me what you think."

Black furrowed his brow, as if measuring the right words to say. "First thought, there's a copycat killer out there. This is my hope. That there's a someone as impressed by you as I am, and carrying on what I can only describe as your legacy. I get that. But I have my doubts."

"Keep going."

"Thought two, and this is the hardest to bear. That you're not the Red Serpent. That you never committed those crimes. That you're stealing someone else's glory. But I don't buy that either. The evidence against you was so compelling. The mementos you collected, the body parts they found in your flat. So my thoughts are running to a third option."

"A third option," repeated Pritchard, staring hard at Black, eyes gleaming like shiny pebbles in the sun.

"That you didn't work alone. That you had a partner."

Black met his gaze, then suddenly lowered his head again.

"Please tell me. You understand why I need to know. If I am to believe in the Red Serpent, then I need the truth."

"We all need the truth," said Pritchard.

Black raised his head. "So what is it?"

Pritchard used his legs to push his chair back by a foot, the metal legs screeching on the tiled floor. The guard snapped a glance towards them, as did the other prisoners, then resumed back to their reading and quiet conversations.

Pritchard folded his arms, tilting his head to one side, lips twitching into a momentary half-smile. This was a different pose, thought Black. No longer the wise, all-knowing psychopath spouting bullshit non sequiturs to an eager apprentice. Rather, someone about to mock, to condescend. Black's heart raced. He might be close.

"You're a perceptive man, Adam Black. You're right. There was another. There *is* another."

Black waited.

"Don't you remember?" said Pritchard.

Black frowned, uncertain where this was going. What Pritchard said next made his blood freeze.

"It's you, Adam. We killed them all together. My brother. My blood brother. You and I – together we are the Red Serpent. Isn't it just fucking wonderful!"

50

The Colonel needed air. When DI Vanessa Shaw asked him if he could use a coffee, he gladly agreed.

They sat at a wooden table in a quaint, bohemian-style coffee shop in a narrow lane just off Byres Road, in the heart of Glasgow's trendy west end. A mile from police HQ. Vanessa drove, and said it was worth it, the coffee the best in the city.

"It's not cheap," she'd warned.

"That's why you're paying," replied the Colonel.

The place was small. Easily missed. The walls were simple white stucco, bedecked with old pictures of movie stars from the thirties and forties – Bette Davis, Judy Garland, David Niven. In one corner, a dramatic shot of a young Vincent Price, attired in dark robes, his face pale, dark eyes peering into some middle distance. False red ivy weaved across the walls, between the pictures. The floor was sanded wood, which creaked with every step. In one corner was a fire of smoking embers in a hearth of pale-blue stone. Beside it, on the floor and lying on its side, was a West Highland terrier, softly snoring. The place was suffused with the rich smell of fresh coffee.

It was 5pm, and it was empty. Which suited the Colonel fine.

They ordered – two regular coffees.

"Interesting place," said the Colonel. "You a fan?" He gestured to the pictures on the walls.

Vanessa shook her head. "To be honest, I don't recognise any of them. I don't seem to get the chance to watch any television. The job. It's all-consuming."

"If you let it. The trick is to give yourself a life. Before you know, it's too late. You wake up, and look in the mirror, and wonder where the time went. Too late for regrets."

Vanessa smiled. "Is that what you have, Colonel? Regrets?"

A middle-aged woman carrying a tray came over, bearing two cups and saucers and a small jug of warm milk. She placed them on the table. "Enjoy," she said.

The Colonel took a sip. He dispensed with the milk. He preferred it black and strong.

"Nice," he remarked, and he meant it. He was a coffee addict. This was, perhaps, the best he'd had for many years.

"You bet," said Vanessa. "So, regrets?"

The Colonel placed the cup back on the saucer, thinking about the past.

"My wife is dead," he said quietly. "She died of cancer. It was quick. There was no prolonged period of agony and torment. Before I knew it, she was gone. My daughter is dead too. She died in a car crash. A random event. She skidded in the snow. One minute she had her whole life to think about. Next, she was gone. She was twenty-one. My job took me all over the world. And it was everything. Like you said – it was all-consuming. I look back, and wish I had spent more time with them. The memories I have are few, and very precious. So yes, I have regrets. I guess what I'm saying is, don't let tragedy suddenly wake you up to what's important."

Vanessa was silent for a spell. "I am so sorry," she said. "Had I known, I wouldn't have..."

"Don't. I'm being maudlin. I guess knowing there's a young woman being held by some sick psychopath gives a different perspective on things."

"We're going to get the bastard."

"Tell me about you. A graduate? You could go far in the police."

"Politics degree. Honours. First class. Though I hate to mention it." She laughed. "Plus, an avid reader of crime novels. I thought – I can join the police and do good. Fight the fight against crime."

"It's not quite like that." The Colonel swirled his coffee with a teaspoon.

"It's nothing like that. It's swimming against the tide, non-stop. For every villain who goes down, five more pop up."

"Your parents must be proud."

"I hope so. They're both retired. Enjoying life. Living in the leafy Edinburgh suburbs. I try to see them every week." She frowned. "I'm sorry..."

"Forget it. It's as it should be."

Vanessa nodded. "And Adam Black? He's an exceptional man. To do what he did."

"He is," agreed the Colonel. "An interesting person. Ex-SAS. But you probably know that. His family murdered by a hired assassin. A man who has nothing to lose. He knew the risks, yet went ahead anyway. To try to save the girl. Like one of those old Hollywood films."

Vanessa stared at the Colonel.

"But to carry out that act? To Danny Brogan. Extreme, don't you think?"

The Colonel gave a cold smile. "Drastic measures. How else would he gain the Red Serpent's confidence? Danny Brogan got as much as he deserved. He was a means to an end."

"He cut out the man's tongue."

"He had to."

Vanessa narrowed her eyes, thoughtful. "It was part of the charade. I see now. Because Pritchard cut his victim's tongues out."

"It had to look good."

She hesitated, said, "Who can do that?"

"Adam Black." The Colonel gave a small fatalistic shrug. "He's a man who will do what it takes."

Vanessa took a careful sip of her coffee, placed it delicately on the saucer. She went to speak, thought better of it.

"Please," urged the Colonel. "Tell me what's on your mind."

Vanessa licked her lips, clearly uncomfortable. "I don't want to offend. He's your man, after all."

"Please."

"For Black to do what he did. To agree to doing what he's doing. Isn't he a little... unhinged? I'm putting this politely. I can think of other ways to describe him."

The Colonel looked at the young woman sitting opposite. It would seem to her that the world had gone mad, he thought. And perhaps it had. But sometimes a touch of madness was needed to save the world.

"Men like Captain Black are a rare breed. A man entered their house four years ago and put bullets into those he loved. It changed him. Such an act would change anyone. As I said before, he will do what it takes. He doesn't care about his own life. Which makes him unique, in many ways. An enemy can't cope with an adversary like that. He has a mission. To save a young girl's life. He will ensure he does everything he can to rescue her. Come hell or high water." He glanced at the pictures on the walls. "He's one of the good guys. The only difference is, he's the real deal."

"A knight in shining armour."

"Yes. In a way that's a good description. He is... how can I put it... chivalrous."

"Chivalrous," echoed Vanessa.

She had placed her mobile phone on the table beside her coffee cup. Suddenly it buzzed into life.

"Yes?"

The Colonel watched her expression as she listened, saw her eyes widen, the edge of her lips curling into a smile. She hung up.

"My God. That was DC Chiltern."

"Yes?"

"We've only had a fucking breakthrough. The numbers on the headstone? We know what they mean."

The Colonel waited.

"They're map co-ordinates. For a place close by."

"Where?"

Vanessa's eyes were bright with excitement.

"The village of Eaglesham."

51

Adam Black was a man rarely left speechless. On this occasion, he was dumbstruck. Pritchard sat, arms folded, and seemed to find the whole thing amusing. He lifted a hand to his mouth and giggled, like a school boy in a classroom trying to hide his laughter from a teacher.

"You just don't get it," said Pritchard. "Look at you, Captain Adam Black. Look at how you're trying to hide your puzzlement behind that macho image. Let me spell this out for you. You've been fucking played, my brother."

"I'm not your brother," was all Black could think of saying.

"Not in the literal sense. Now you're being obtuse, and that's disappointing."

"Then enlighten me, please."

Pritchard pulled his seat forward, and rested his elbows on the table, cupped his chin in his hands, and smiled a smile that stretched from ear to ear.

"Gladly. I know all about you. Everything. From your service days in the SAS, to the medal you won for being a good little toy soldier. Then the law firm you joined when you left the army. I know about your wife and kid, shot in the head in your front living room. Very careless of you, Adam. I know about your pathetic little office in Shawlands, trying to eke out an existence as a second-rate lawyer. I know about the crazy, stupid plan you hatched with your friend the Colonel." Pritchard giggled again. The guard snapped his head towards them, eyes narrowed, then looked away.

Keep talking, thought Black. *We're getting close.*

"What plan?"

"What plan?" repeated Pritchard. He sat, less than three feet from Black, across the table, gloating. Under the strip lights, his eyes flickered orange yellow, his skin glistening reptilian smooth. Is this the face his victims saw, wondered Black, in their final moments? How could anyone have been fooled? The veneer was gone. *This is his real face*, thought Black. *The face of a monster.*

"You cut the man's tongue out to impress me," continued Pritchard. "You knew you'd end up here, with me. And you had to make it real, because you knew I'd see through it if it were staged. But I did see through it. From the very beginning. We've turned the tables, Adam. The bullshit on the telephone. It was all done to confuse. It means nothing. Nothing at all."

"But you were talking to someone. That's not bullshit."

"Don't fuck with me. This is about you. It was always about you."

"About me? Why?" Black took a deep breath. He needed more. "You say you know all about me. You don't know a thing."

"Wrong! Every detail. I know your wife and kid's names. I know the house you lived in. I know the shithole flat you stay in Bolton Drive. A half mile from your office. I know the library you go to on a Wednesday night, the gym you go to what – four times a week? I know the name of your secretary. I know about the fucking fake silver-framed photograph you have on your desk of your wife and kid!"

Pritchard leaned forward. "I know all there is to know about Captain fucking Adam Black."

Black frowned. "It's not fake."

"What?"

"The silver-framed photograph. It's real silver. You should get your facts right."

"Fuck your photograph!"

Black shook his head, dismissively.

"You're confusing me. You say I'm your brother. That we killed them all, together. The ten girls? Is that what you meant? I think you're talking riddles, friend."

"You're in for the biggest shock of your life. But I've said too much already. You'll have to find the rest yourself – the hard way."

It was Black's turn to smile. Indeed, he was elated.

"You've said just enough, Pritchard. I'll have to take my chances with this big shock you've planned. Right now, I just want to thank you, for giving me the answer."

"What answer?"

"This is what's called a double bluff. You've just told me who your psycho partner is, on the outside, so thanks. I guess we've both been played, you dumb fuck."

Now it was Black's turn to lean forward, his face close to Pritchard's.

"Given our little game of charades is over, let me tell you something. You're a psychopath, who likes to murder young women. So here's my shock to you. You don't deserve to live. That's why I've decided to do one good deed before I leave this rathole."

Pritchard withdrew back into his chair, blinking, face leaden, eyes fixed on Black. He wiped a drop of sweat from under his nose. "A good deed?"

"A perfect deed. To break your fucking neck."

Pritchard's lips twitched into a smirk. "And that's the irony," he whispered. "Locked up in prison is about the safest place I can be from rogue vigilantes like you. So good luck with that, Captain Black."

Black regarded him for a further few seconds. How easy it would be to strike, lash out, snap his neck like a twig. But Pritchard was right. To kill him would complicate the situation, considerably. And the prospects of finding the girl would diminish to zero.

Black stood up, subjecting Pritchard to a smouldering gaze. "Your time will come."

"Maybe. But not before yours. Brace yourself, Adam. Buckle up. You have no idea what's about to hit you."

Black turned away, and left the library.

He wondered with a chill what Pritchard was getting at. He pushed it to the back of his mind. He had something. Information. He knew who the Red Serpent's accomplice was.

52

They left the rest of the coffee, and drove back to Pitt Street. They didn't speak, each consumed in their own thoughts. Something was harbouring in the Colonel's mind, like a dark shadow gliding just below the surface of the water. But it was too fantastical to give any credence. Or so he hoped.

It was after 5.30pm and already getting dark. The street lights were on. The air was thin and cold and clear. A faint glimmer of frost coated the pavements. The sky was a deep plumy red, just before true night set in.

They arrived at the main office, to be met by an exuberant DC Chiltern.

"They're map co-ordinates. We're sure of it. To the village of Eaglesham. Maybe our kidnapper friend is trying to tell us something?"

"Like what?" snapped the Colonel. "Lead us to the girl? Let's hope not, because if this is what this is, then she's dead already." The Colonel spoke in a flat monotone. He didn't like where this was going.

"Or maybe it's part of the game," suggested Vanessa.

"He's not the gaming type. This is different."

"There's only one way to find out," said Vanessa. "We need to go there. Now." She nodded to Chiltern. "You're with me." She flicked a glance at the Colonel. "You coming?"

"Wouldn't miss it for the world."

They took Vanessa's car. She placed a siren on the roof and hit the accelerator hard. Eaglesham was a village in an area twelve miles from Glasgow city centre called East Renfrewshire, nestled on the edge of the desolate Eaglesham Moors. A conservation village, quiet and respectable, with listed buildings and woody lanes, narrow streets and quaint shops.

The Colonel had never been to the place before. But he was well aware of its importance. For all the wrong reasons.

The young cop – DC Chiltern – was brimming with excitement. The chase was on.

"It might be nothing, of course," he was saying. "Maybe it's too obvious? I mean, why would he give us map co-ordinates? The whole thing could be a waste of time."

"I guess we won't know until we get there," replied Vanessa. The Colonel detected the edge in her voice. He was aware that he wasn't the only person in the car who knew the history.

They arrived in Eaglesham twenty minutes later, taking the M77. The traffic was surprisingly quiet for that time of the evening. They reached the main street of the village. It was as advertised – a picture-postcard haven. In the frosty early evening, with the sky darkening, it had a witchy feel.

"What now?" asked Chiltern.

Vanessa pointed to a small sign on some red copper railings – "Cemetery". An arrow pointed to a single lane to the right. "We look for the signs," she said. The Colonel remained tight-lipped, but his heart raced.

She drove down a narrow road, houses on either side, down a steep hill. The houses diminished, making way for fields and trees behind wire fences. Eventually, after a quarter of a mile, they reached a stone wall with open black gates.

Eaglesham cemetery.

She drove through slowly, and parked the car outside a small pavilion built of sombre grey granite. They got out. The place was maybe three acres, encircled by a wall six feet high. Vanessa retrieved a torch from the glove compartment. She brought up an image on her mobile phone. The picture of the headstone sent by the kidnapper.

She showed it to the others.

"Okay – it's by a wall, with trees close behind. There's a love heart engraved at the bottom."

The cemetery was built as a simple square. The lane at the front, fields on either side, and behind the back wall, a thin glade of silver birch and sycamore. They made their way to the back wall, down a narrow white-chipped path. It was darkening quickly. Despite wearing a heavy herringbone coat, the Colonel felt chilled. His lungs tingled with each breath. He had a woollen mountain hat in his pocket, which he put on.

Vanessa had the torch on. The light bobbed up and down with every step. Headstones flashed up, little wooden benches, new flowers, rotting flowers.

They reached the rear wall. The path ran parallel, headstones on either side. They concentrated on one side, Vanessa holding the torch, glancing at the picture on her phone every few seconds.

She stopped. "My God."

The three gazed at the headstone in the torch light. It fitted perfectly. The wall behind it, the trees. And a heart.

"This is it," gasped Chiltern.

She shone the light on to the inscription. The silver lettering was simple, touching. The Colonel read the words, though he didn't have to. He knew what they said.

Jennifer Black
1971–2010
My love, my heart
Merryn Black
2006–2010
A moonbeam,
Lighting up the dark

The three were silent for a short space. Then Vanessa spoke.

"This is Adam Black's family. They were murdered, weren't they? The assailant never caught?"

The Colonel nodded.

Chiltern spoke up. "Why send us here?"

Why indeed? wondered the Colonel.

Vanessa held up her phone, taking several photographs of the headstone.

"I'll get forensics here. We'll get this place cordoned off. You stay, Peter. As soon as the lab boys arrive, I want you to go speak to the people who live nearby. You never know – they might have seen something. Anything."

Chiltern nodded, his face pale in the cold, country darkness. He didn't look overly eager.

Vanessa turned her attention to the Colonel. "I think we should head back to HQ. I need to check something."

"Anything in particular?"

"I want to see that letter again. It didn't make any sense. You admitted as much yourself. But what if it did?"

"Please illuminate," said the Colonel in a dry voice.

"Not yet. It might be nothing. Call it a hunch."

They walked back up the white-chipped path, footsteps

crunching on the tiny stones. *How quickly the light vanishes*, thought the Colonel. He thought of Black's daughter. *A moonbeam, lighting up the dark*. As ever, his mind wandered back in time, to his own daughter, her smiling face, in a bright, sunlit field. Suddenly he felt old and incredibly tired.

DI Vanessa Shaw had a hunch.

And the Colonel had a bad feeling.

53

Mobile phones were banned in Shotts prison. They were still available, provided you had the right connections. Black had no such connections. He'd made too many enemies. To furnish Black with any help was akin to signing a death warrant. Which meant he had to use the public pay phones. But this was restricted. Only available for use between 11am and noon, and seven till 7.45 in the evening. He had to communicate with the Colonel. His information was crucial, vital, staggering. Plus, he had to get the hell out.

He made his way back to the common room, to kill time watching television. A voice stopped him. A voice he was hoping to avoid.

"Do you believe in justice, Black?"

He turned slowly. Fletcher stood three feet from him. Black took a deep calming breath.

"Sure do."

"Sure do, what?"

"Sure do believe in justice."

"That's not what I fucking meant," barked Fletcher. "It's – sure do, Mr Fletcher, sir."

"Got it."

Fletcher's lips curled into a smile.

"Be a smart arse all you want. I'm glad to hear you believe in justice. Because justice is what you're going to get. They say justice is a woman. If that's so, then justice can be a real fucking bitch. It's going to be a bitch to you, Black, make no mistake. Danny Brogan says hi." Fletcher took a step closer, lowering his voice. "Danny Brogan wants blood."

Black couldn't help himself. "I would have thought he'd want a tongue."

Slowly, deliberately, Fletcher unclipped the baton fastened to his waist belt. He drew it out, slowly. Black tensed. This was the last thing he wanted. He stared at Fletcher, ready to react.

Fletcher raised the baton, and gently rested it on Black's shoulder. "Marked man," he said quietly. The smile returned to his face. He replaced the baton back in its leather holder.

He brushed past him, another prison guard following, appraising Black with a smirk.

It looked like Black's time was running thin. He made his way to the common room, aware that every passing second was a wasted second. The news on the television played over and over. The Prime Minister's daughter had been kidnapped. He couldn't watch. He returned to his cell, and lay on his bed, and glanced at the clock on the wall, then got up, padded over to the small barred window, to gaze at the flat grey landscape. Elspeth was out there, somewhere.

And Black had the key.

54

The voice startled her. She'd been sitting on the edge of the bed, half asleep, a short blissful period of being unaware of the surreal nightmare world she was in. She jolted up with a start.

"Were you dreaming?" The same voice. Deep, resonant, unnatural. Amplified through hidden speakers.

"No," she replied thickly.

"I dream, Elspeth. Do you want to know what I dream about?"

"You know my name."

"I dream of you in that red dress," continued the voice, ignoring her. "Lying on the bed. Spread before me. In supplication. Waiting. Every breath tinged with fear. And excitement. In anticipation of the pain to come. The pain required."

She shook her head, groggily. She still felt half asleep. She thought perhaps she'd been drugged again.

"Why do you need pain? I don't want pain."

The voice fell silent. The sound of deep, slow breathing filled the air of her prison. That alone was more terrifying than the voice. Then it spoke.

"Don't you know?"

"No I fucking don't! I don't understand any of this!"

"Don't you remember?"

"What are you fucking talking about? Remember what?"

"I remember everything. You will too, when the time comes."

"Let me go!" she screamed. "Please! I promise I won't tell anyone!"

"Soon, you'll understand. Patience."

The voice disappeared.

Elspeth screamed at the bare walls, the only response her own echo.

55

The pretence was that he was still feeling lousy from a bug he'd caught. He knew it didn't look good, but he didn't care. DI Shaw and the Colonel were off on some fucking Sherlock Holmes wild goose chase in Eaglesham. He'd used the opportunity to slip out. He needed a couple of hours' kip in bed, to shake off the nausea. So he explained. Which was all bullshit. He needed something entirely different.

He was naked, standing at the top of the metal stairs of his basement. He punched in the digits of the keypad. The basement door opened. Behind him, below, her screams had diminished to short ragged moans. He didn't look back. The walls were perfectly soundproofed. He closed the door behind him, sealed shut, the sound of her existence instantly extinguished.

He would see to her later. Let the bitch think on this. Then, she would soon understand the true meaning of pain. Bad pain. And then the real screaming would begin.

Already, he felt his penis harden at the prospect.

Chief Constable Divers made his way to his bedroom, and

began the process of putting on his uniform, mind alive with thoughts of what he would do later. In the basement.

To the girl.

56

They arrived back at Pitt Street Police Station, DI Vanessa Shaw racing through red lights, overtaking everything in her path, siren blaring. The Colonel said not a word. Driving at over a hundred miles an hour on the motorway didn't faze him. The recent events troubled him far more. And what was to come.

"You know what the most important question is in a murder enquiry?" said Vanessa, as they waited for the elevator doors to open in the main foyer of Pitt Street Police Station.

"I didn't think this was a murder enquiry," replied the Colonel.

She turned, giving him a ghoulish grin. "Not yet. Do you know what the all-important question is?"

"Did the butler do it?"

"Not quite. I say to myself – what if?"

The Colonel remained silent, allowing her to finish.

"If I ask myself that, then sometimes an answer pops up. It might not be the right one. It might be ludicrous, far-fetched. But it's a start. And I can build from that start. So that's what I'm asking myself right now – what if?"

"Okay, so what if what? What are you getting at?"

The elevator chimed; the doors slid open.

"I'll tell you upstairs. I need to check something. Then maybe I'll ask what if. And just maybe I'll get an answer."

They got to level 4. The doors opened. They went through a long corridor, Vanessa half running. A door to the left opened into the incident room. The room hadn't changed any since the Colonel had left it an hour earlier. Full of bodies, policemen and women, civilians, manning the phones, studying computer screens, pouring over files, information, data. The low drone of conversation permeated the air like summer insects. The place smelled of human sweat. The Red Serpent made them work for their money.

On one wall, enlarged and shining bright and clear, was a photograph of the most recent letter. Vanessa marched up to stand facing it, gazing at it with eyes bright from its reflection.

The Colonel stood next to her, wondering where this was going.

"Look at it," she murmured. "What do you see?"

The Colonel wasn't sure if she was talking to him, or herself. He chose to answer anyway.

"Nothing. It's designed to confuse. Counterproductive. My belief is that we should ignore this. It will waste time."

She darted him a side glance, impossible to interpret.

She read it aloud.

Art imitates life.

Odd that few believe this to be true. It's there. All you have to do is look.

Transcending. It's a process, you understand. Open your eyes.

Tremble in excitement. And anticipation. And fear.

Don't believe me? Open your eyes. She looks magnificent. But that magnificence is nothing, a speck.

You're liars. You hide from truth. When she becomes, then you cannot hide. Look. Open your eyes.

Behold all of you, for what she will be, for when she emerges. To become eternal.

I will pick the place, the time. Open your eyes. Look, and everything is revealed.

Liars. Tick-tock. Tick-tock.

"What if he's trying to tell us something. 'Open your eyes'. He uses this phrase three times. 'All you have to do is look.'"

She took a step back, cocked her head, frowned.

The Colonel watched her closely. "What do you see?"

"My God," she breathed. "It's a fucking code."

57

R achel Hempworth was good. But she wasn't that good. She was held in high esteem by her editor – a little grey-faced man called Billy Cosgrove – and as a crime reporter, there were few better. But she still didn't get her own office. She sat with the general ruckus in the main office, amid the clamour and frenzy associated with the running of a busy newspaper.

Sometimes it got so bad, she barely managed a few lines a day. But now she was fixed on something, and she wanted to write, and suddenly the distractions disappeared.

The man called Adam Black was a mystery. A war hero turned lawyer turned vigilante. With a tragic past. His family murdered. She'd dug deep. A man, supposedly a hired assassin, had entered his house in the village of Eaglesham, and shot his wife and four-year-old daughter, and then left. No trace. Professional hit. The police had been worse than useless. No one was ever brought to justice. Rumour – and it was exactly that – spoke of a revenge killing by a mafia-style boss.

Black was left to pick up the pieces. Her journalist nose twitched. She smelled police cover-up. The man had been to hell and back. And now he was languishing in Shotts prison, the last stop for the worst criminals in Scotland. But she had met him. Face to face. He didn't look the type to languish. The opposite. He looked like a man who... what? She wrestled with her thoughts.

"Give it up," said Cosgrove. He had summoned her into his spacious office. They were one storey up, in a glossy black-panelled building in the centre of Glasgow, near Strathclyde University. The paper rented the entire floor. He had his window open, and was sitting on the ledge, smoking a Capstan, blowing clouds into the freezing air. He only smoked unfiltered cigarettes. Rachel was amazed shops still sold them. He gave a sharp, racking cough, flicked the cigarette into the open air, but kept the window open.

"It's minus two," she remarked. "It seems pointless to have the heating on and the window open. But what do I know?"

He moved from the window, and sat behind his over-large desk, giving her a long, withering look. His face was the colour of grey paste, his eyes regarded her from deep sockets. In a certain light, and from a certain angle, he resembled a ferret.

"I like the cold. And the heat. All at the same time. That way I get the best of both worlds. What I don't like is my chief reporter hooked up on old news."

"You mean Adam Black?"

"Damn right. He's a *has-been*. He's all washed out, with a washed-out story. There's other stuff out there. Why are we not dealing with the *here and now*? And right now, the whole fucking island is in uproar. The Prime Minister's daughter has been kidnapped, in case you missed that one. But you're hung up on a nobody called Adam Black. You're better than this, Rachel."

She twitched her shoulders in the slightest shrug. She didn't argue with him. But that didn't mean she agreed. "He's an interesting man," was all she said.

"By fuck!" Cosgrove raised his hands, as if praising God

above. "Front fucking page news. Hold the press. I can see it now. Rachel Hempworth, winner of the fucking Pulitzer Prize. Why, I hear you ask? Because of her groundbreaking piece on the man called Adam Black. And what's so special about this individual? Don't you know? Rachel Hempworth found him interesting!" Cosgrove leaned back on his leather office chair. "Here's the real news. No one else finds him interesting. No one gives a shit about a psycho who went to prison for getting into a gang fight."

"He cut the man's tongue out."

"Damned unsociable of him."

"And I went to prison to meet him, in case you didn't know."

"Actually, I did. What's he like? I speak only from casual interest."

She wanted to say, he's remarkably handsome, but chose not to. Her boss wasn't in the mood. He was more irascible than usual. "He's a man with a past."

"We all have pasts."

"SAS, medal winner, family murdered. It's all there."

"One big cliché. He's in prison, doing his time. Where he belongs."

"Perhaps."

"Now that's a peculiar thing to say. Surely you don't believe he's innocent. He pled guilty. I can google it right now, and watch his surgical expertise on my mobile phone."

"I didn't mean that." She hesitated. "I don't know what I mean. I have this feeling he intended to be there. Does that make sense?"

"Not one bit."

"He committed a horrible act on a known villain. But it was a most specific act. And Adam Black's not a careless man. He allowed his crime to be witnessed by a dozen people."

"He was in a mad-dog rage. Psychos don't care about things like that."

"Sorry to contradict, that's where you're wrong. Psychopaths are extremely careful. They don't want to be caught."

"So what's your point?"

"Adam Black wanted to be caught."

Cosgrove gave a barking laugh, culminating in a coughing fit. He reached over to a plastic litre bottle of mineral water, unscrewed the top, and drank it straight.

"You really need to think about cutting back," Rachel said. "At least smoke cigarettes with a filter."

He turned her an acid look. "When you get your medical degree, I'll be sure to look you up. And I have cut back, for your information."

"Really?"

"Down to thirty a day. I'm rather pleased with myself."

"Did you know the Red Serpent cut out all his victims' tongues?" she said suddenly.

Cosgrove wiped his mouth with the back of his hand, and settled his cavernous gaze on Rachel. "So?"

"The Red Serpent is serving several life sentences in Shotts prison."

"And again, I repeat – so? A man like that will be ensconced in some secure unit with all the comforts. Safely cocooned away, in a private ward. Bet your bottom dollar on it. If you think Black did all this to get to the Red Serpent, then that's a conspiracy theory in overdrive. Drop it, Rachel. For your own sanity."

"And did you know the Red Serpent's been moved?"

"Moved?"

"From his private cocoon. He's with the general population. And Adam Black is the brand-new guest."

Cosgrove took a deep, wheezy breath. "It sounds compelling. But it's still the stuff of fairy tales. Too many questions."

"That's why you employ me."

"What?"

"To find answers to the questions."

Cosgrove tapped the side of the plastic water bottle with one nicotine stained index finger. "You know, I think I've established the problem."

"Which is?"

"You need a life. A life outside this place. You overthink things, because you've got nothing else going on. If you did what normal people do, like go to restaurants, or the cinema. Or get pissed in a pub somewhere, then you might get some..."

"Grounding?" Rachel finished.

"Good word. Grounding. And less time to dream up conspiracy theories where none exist."

Rachel placed both hands on the table, gave her boss her best intense, serious look. "There's a story here," she said quietly. "You know when you can feel something? You know it's there, waiting to be cracked? I just can't put my finger on it. Call it a gut feeling."

"You know what I feel right now, Rachel?"

"What?"

"Despair. You wear me down by your youthful, and immensely irritating, enthusiasm."

"Which means...?"

"Which means... If you really think it's worth it, then keep digging. But can I be honest?"

She arched an eyebrow. "I would expect nothing less."

"I have a feeling about this. And it's not good. Call it an old hack's instinct. What I'm saying is – be careful. This man Adam Black. He's dangerous. I don't like the sound of him. Don't get too close."

Rachel gave him a mock salute. "Understood."

She left his office, returning to her desk, and it came to her. Cosgrove had mentioned the word cliché. Here was the perfect cliché, yet her instinct told her it was true.

Adam Black. He looked like a man who was on a mission.

58

A number of people had congregated round DI Vanessa Shaw. The Colonel found a seat and decided to watch, almost as a spectator. He was intrigued.

"Look carefully," she said. "That's what he's asking us to do. He's telling us it's here. In the letter."

She approached the blown-up picture of the letter, and traced her hand down the lines, whispering to herself, took a step back.

"Goddammit. Go to the first letter of the first line, the second on the second line, the third on the third, and so forth. What do you get?"

The Colonel followed her instruction, as doubtless everyone else did. He studied the lettering.

Art
Odd
Transcending
Tremble
Don't believe
You're liars
Behold all

I will pick

Liars. Tick-tock.

"Adam Black," she said softly. Those around her repeated the name, wondering. They had no idea of his involvement. Except the Colonel. She spun round, to face him. Her eyes shone with a fierce bright light. "I can get a warrant in half an hour."

"A warrant for what?" he asked. His heart thumped in his chest. This made no sense.

"A warrant to search Black's flat. He's up to his neck in this."

"In what? A photograph of his family's headstone? An obscure reference in a letter? We're being played."

"I don't know." She faltered, hesitation in her voice. "I don't understand it either. But it's a lead. We've got nothing else. I'll run it by the Chief." She caught the attention of a colleague. "Is he about?"

The woman responded by a shake of her head. "He left a couple of hours ago. Said he wasn't feeling well. But I think he's on his way in."

Vanessa started to press digits in her phone, presumably to contact him, for his authority to seek a search warrant.

And it was at that precise moment, it struck the Colonel. Struck him like lightning. A flash of genuine insight.

The Red Serpent had always worked with someone. And he knew, in that moment, exactly who it was.

His phone buzzed. He glanced at the screen, answered. A voice responded, low and urgent. *Nice timing*, he thought. The man of the moment.

It was Adam Black.

59

The seconds dragged by. The waiting was almost exquisite, worse than any torture. The phones weren't available until 7pm. Another forty-five minutes. He checked his watch, checked again, rechecked. Black had wandered back out of his cell, and back to the common room, to kill more time. He sat on one of the plastic chairs. Everyone avoided him. Like a leper. Black didn't give a shit. He had more important things on his mind.

He stared at the television mounted on the wall, but was only vaguely aware of what was being shown. More news about the Prime Minister's resignation, the procedures for appointing a new one, the sympathy of the nation as it tried to cope with the abduction of her daughter. Again and again. Political commentators droned on. The head of the Met was interviewed. The media was waiting for a statement from the Chief Constable of Police Scotland. Chief Constable Divers. His silence was debated, judged. There was speculation. Police Scotland were way out their depth. Experts on criminal psychology were hauled in, giving bloated expositions on the mind of a kidnapper.

And the one person who can really help is waiting on the phones to open, he thought sardonically. The whole thing was a sick joke. But it was no joke at all. A young woman's life depended on his actions. He checked his watch. Even time was against him. He wondered what Pritchard was thinking. His words echoed in Black's mind. *You have no idea what's about to hit you.* What did he mean? Black felt powerless. He had a sensation matters were conspiring against him. The quicker he got out of Shotts prison, the better, for his own sanity.

Perhaps he should saunter to Pritchard's cell and put a pillow over his face. The idea had merit, for a whole range of reasons. One less psychopath was a benefit. And of course, he would get immense personal satisfaction. But the notion was unthinkable. Another death, another lockdown. And, of course, he might get caught.

He got to his feet, paced up and down the room. Other prisoners watched him warily. He was a pariah. An outcast in a world of outcasts.

Five minutes. He headed for the corridor which housed the row of telephones. A short queue had formed behind locked double glass doors. Black waited in line, nerves stretched. An alarm sounded, ringing through the building. Like a fire alarm. It was time. The doors automatically unlocked. Behind them, waiting, was a prison guard. He ushered them through.

Black got to the phone. He inserted a token, giving him ten minutes. More than enough. He got through to the Colonel almost instantly.

The Colonel said, "Have you got something to tell me?"

"Blue. Number 2."

"Say again?"

"Blue. Number 2"

The Colonel was silent.

"What are you talking about?" the Colonel said eventually. "You'd better think again."

Black stared into space, thoughts suddenly in overdrive. He'd delivered the message. The Colonel too had responded. But not what Black was expecting. They'd rehearsed for every contingency.

The Colonel hung up.

Black did likewise. He knew the phones were tapped. The last thing they wanted was to warn the enemy.

He turned. Fletcher was waiting at the double doors, with two guards.

Fletcher was grinning.

"Watch your back, Black," said Fletcher.

Black didn't respond. He met Fletcher with a thin-lipped smile, but kept walking, mind racing.

The message had been delivered. The plan now was simple. In theory. Strings pulled, orders issued from above, and Black gets freedom.

That was the plan.

You'd better think again, the Colonel had said.

Which was the Colonel's message back, signifying one thing.

Trouble.

A chill ran down the length of Black's spine. A thought sprang into his mind, uninvited, but one which he had to consider.

Maybe, just maybe, he was on his own.

60

Divers arrived at Pitt Street Police Station, to find DI Vanessa Shaw and several police officers waiting for him at the main entrance, hunched in the cold.

He'd been appraised of the situation by Vanessa Shaw as he drove in, on his hands-free. She sounded breathless, excited. He listened, absorbing the details. The photograph, the cryptic message. The reference to the man called Adam Black. All very mysterious. Not what he was expecting. And when she requested his consent for a search warrant on his flat, his heart sang. Divers had a different set of priorities from most people on the case.

One hundred per cent, he had said to her. *Get the goddam warrant. Looks like you're really onto something.*

Divers parked his Jaguar in his designated space in the station car park, and watched as the group, headed by Shaw, hurriedly approached.

All this commotion, he thought. For a fucking whore. Good would come of this. He felt it in his bones, his soul. Anything which crushed the Colonel, and Adam Black, was good. More than good. Blissful.

But he had one stipulation. He wanted to be there. He wanted to be at the scene. Bear witness to what might unfold.

If Adam Black was a part of the Red Serpent killings, then Divers wanted the glory.

61

Black lay on top of the covers on the single bed in his cell, staring at the ceiling. All doors were locked, prisoners accounted for and secured away. This would have been Black's last night, supposedly. The process was meant to be simple and clean, supervised by the Colonel himself, who Black trusted implicitly. A call to the warden first thing tomorrow morning, release papers emailed, authorising a transfer to another prison.

Black, escorted, would be placed in the back of a van, and depart Shotts prison. But the van would never arrive. Black then had a choice – to start a new life, new papers. Start afresh. Or resume his old life, having been granted immunity from any further prosecution, his initial crime erased from the public record. The Colonel, and the government, would prefer he take the first option. That way, less questions were asked. Nice and neat.

Now Black wondered. He had no way to communicate with the Colonel. At the present moment, he was just another con serving a stretch for a violent crime. Only a handful of people knew the strategy, the motive behind Black's actions.

Something was badly amiss. The Colonel's response on the

telephone was a warning. Trouble afoot. Was this what Pritchard was alluding to? *Buckle up for a rollercoaster ride.* Up until the conversation with the Colonel, despite being incarcerated in Shotts prison, Black had never actually felt trapped. There had always been an exit plan. Now however, Black had a hollow feeling in his bones, a pinch of dread in his stomach. If he were left here to rot, the rotting process wouldn't last long. Inevitably, someone, somehow, would get him. A razor blade shiv sliding across his throat in some quiet corner. In the shadows of his cell, his world was all darkness, and Black, at that moment, did all he could to press back a sudden tsunami of panic.

His thoughts were interrupted. The grate of his cell door being unlocked. Black sat up. The large, unmistakable shape of Fletcher filled the doorway. Behind him were two guards. The same stupid grin was glued to Fletcher's face.

"Up, Black."

Black stood.

"Looks like you're a special man," said Fletcher. "The warden wants a chat."

Black was wary. "Why does he want to see me?"

"What did you just fucking say to me?"

Black didn't speak. He gave Fletcher a smouldering look.

"No more of your lip. Or else you get a taste of this." Fletcher slapped one hand on the baton clipped to his waist. "You clear on this, Black?"

"Crystal. Sir."

"That's more like it. Respect your betters. Remember, Black, I am fucking God in this establishment, so what I say goes. Now – out."

Black still wore his clothes – dark pullover, dark jeans, running shoes. Fletcher backed out of the door, watching with a hard, glittering gaze. Black moved slowly, carefully, conscious that Fletcher would use the slightest excuse to unleash random violence.

Black emerged into the corridor outside his cell. Fletcher and two guards stood in a line. Fletcher gestured with his arm, pointing.

"You first."

Black began to walk, hairs on the back of his neck standing on end, senses notched up to a heightened awareness. His soft footfall was virtually silent on the metal corridor floor. The footsteps of the guards behind him clanged. They weren't talking. There was no chat. He waited, ready for the sudden swish of movement, the song of the baton swinging.

"Down the stairs," said Fletcher. The four men made their way down to ground level, to the main hall where prisoners often congregated. It was eerily empty.

"Keep moving," said Fletcher.

They passed rows of locked doors.

They reached a wide single door with a little glass window at head height.

"Stand to one side, back against the wall," directed Fletcher.

Black did as he was told, the two others standing on either side.

Fletcher had a large ring of keys attached by an elastic cord to his belt. He stretched it up, selecting a particular key, used it to unlock the door.

"Through," said Fletcher.

Black went first, followed by the others. He knew the corridor well enough. It served as the connection between B Hall and another building, part of which was the gym. Like an umbilical cord. It was constructed of thick glass, a snake of light cutting through the dark outside.

They reached the end. Another door. Same procedure, Fletcher unlocking. To the right, the gym. To the left, more corridors and stairs, possibly leading to admin and ultimately the warden's office, or so Black imagined.

"Stop."

Fletcher faced him, flanked by the two guards. Black was outnumbered. They had weapons. Black had his bare hands. He waited for Fletcher to speak.

Fletcher sighed. Black smelled beer from his breath.

"This job, you know? Sometimes it can be a real pain in the arse. All the fucking paperwork, the reports, the memos, the rules. It gets me down, Black."

Where the fuck's this going?

Fletcher's face suddenly brightened. His big blunt face broke into an almost boyish grin.

"But sometimes, every now and again, that rare moment of sunshine comes along, and makes all the shit worth it. It's like seeing a fucking rainbow on a crap day."

"You should have been a poet, Mr Fletcher."

"That I fucking should. And here's the good part. For me anyway. You are that piece of sunshine, Black. You are about to cheer me up."

"Glad to hear that, Mr Fletcher."

Fletcher nodded, scrutinising Black's face as if he were considering a crossword puzzle – trying to find the sarcasm, thought Black.

"I'm sure you are. This way." He pointed, towards a door at the end of a short corridor. The door to the gymnasium. Black tensed. Fletcher sensed it.

"Move it," he hissed.

"That's not the warden's office."

"A detour. Let's call it a reunion."

"I don't understand." But Black understood perfectly.

"You will. Move it." Now he unclipped his baton and had it out in one swift movement. The other two, as if on cue, followed suit. Fletcher was a big man, about the same height as Black, but any athleticism he'd possessed had departed a long time ago. Too many days wandering about prison corridors and filling out forms and drinking lager, thought Black. The other two were smaller, regular. Men who were used to getting their own way, and had grown complacent with it.

Black debated. He did as he was told, and walked slowly toward the gym. He'd let this play out. See where it took him.

The door wasn't locked.

"Open it," said Fletcher.

Black turned the handle, opened the door.

There, on one side, in rows, were the machines. Running, cycling, cross-training, rowing. At the far end, the area devoted to free weights. The place where Black had broken Hammer's jaw. To one side, a guards' station, which was empty. Black heard laughter.

Five men meandered round from the back area. Leading them was Hammer, dressed in a tracksuit, wearing a neck brace and a skin-hugging wrap around his head. Behind him, with the others, was the man called Swifty. Black noted each held a dumbbell bar – a solid cylindrical piece of metal twelve inches long. To be used for something other than weight training, he assumed.

They stopped, all facing Black. Black made his way in slowly, turned, and faced them.

"Wait five minutes," said Fletcher. He glanced round at one of the guards. "Bring him now."

The guard nodded at the instruction, left the gym.

Fletcher continued, addressing the five men. "You'll have fifteen minutes with Black. The CCTV is switched off. Work him over good. For Danny Brogan. Break some bones. But you don't kill him, understand? I can't have any deaths. Not tonight. That's for later. Plus, you'll clean up the fucking mess. There's mops and buckets in the back. Not one drop of blood do I want to see in the morning. You understand me, Hammer?"

Hammer signified he understood by a slight nod. It was Swifty who spoke on his behalf.

"We understand, Mr Fletcher," he said. "Hammer can't talk right now, but we get the picture. Fifteen minutes. Plenty of time."

"Good," Fletcher said. "Plus, there's a bonus."

Fletcher turned his attention back to Black.

"Payback time. Like I say, I am God in this fucking paradise. And this is called retribution."

Black ignored him, concentrating on the five men before him.

"You scared, tough guy?" shouted Swifty.

"No," replied Black softly. "But you should be."

This caused a ripple of laughter. The only person not laughing was Hammer, either because he couldn't, or else he didn't find the situation amusing. Perhaps both.

"Five of us. One of you. Don't like your odds."

Black responded, apparently unperturbed. "You can't really count Hammer, face all trussed up like something from a horror movie, and very stupid. Which means there's only four of you. And you're not exactly a born fighter, Swifty. More of a faggot type, for pleasure purposes. So that leaves only three. Which I can handle."

Hammer made a grunting sound. He tightened his grip on the metal bar, his face reddened.

The door opened. A guard pushed a man into the room. He seemed dazed, disorientated. He looked around him, blinked.

It was Oliver Pritchard, aka The Red Serpent.

"What's happening?" he murmured.

"There's your bonus," said Fletcher. He snapped his head towards his two colleagues. "You two make some rounds. I'll meet up with you later." The two guards left. Fletcher locked the door behind them and faced Black.

"Danny Brogan wishes he was here to see this. We go way back, from school days. Seeing as he can't be present, I'm going to give him the next best thing. A fucking ringside seat." He took a step back, pulled out his mobile phone, and started to video.

"Remember – break as many bones as you want, Hammer. But no kills. Not today."

Hammer nodded. Black wasn't entirely convinced the instruction got through.

The five approached. Pritchard retreated until his back hit the wall. He whimpered. A high-pitched moan. Not very godlike, thought Black.

Black faced his enemy.

The Colonel had given him a dire message. The mission, possibly, had been compromised. Black had to assume Plan A, which was his imminent release, was in jeopardy.

Black needed a Plan B.

Black allowed a small, cold smile, as he weighed up the five approaching men, each with extreme violence on their minds.

This could be the angle he needed.

This could be his Plan B.

62

The water and food were laced with a powerful sedative. She had been given precise instructions as to how to apply it, the quantities to use, and when. The instructions as to application and quantity had been written down for her on notepaper, which she had pinned on a wooden message board on her kitchen wall. The timing of the administration of the drugs was relayed by telephone. Not the mobile phone which had been a gift from her son. But *they* had confiscated it. Any verbal contact was through the landline.

Her visitor arrived every two weeks, barely talking, going immediately downstairs to change the girl into specific clothing, arrange her hair, apply make-up.

The old woman always made sure she was out when it happened. She would stand at the cliff edge, her back to the house, and look out on to the endless reach of the sea. She could stand like that for what seemed an age, and forget time. But always, in those moments, when her dreaded visitor was in the house, she thought back to how it began, and wondered despairingly how it would all end.

Her house had been occupied that morning, briefly, the

visitor appearing for a short visit in the early hours, descending to the basement to make further preparations. Such was the routine. Checking up on the prisoner, and then finally removing her. To a different location, was the explanation. The old woman didn't ask any questions, didn't dare to. She had no idea what happened to them when they left – when they were *moved on*. She knew in the marrow of her bones it was bad. But she'd made a choice. She refused to think about it. She didn't own a television, radio, and she shunned others from the village. She chose never to know.

But there were things her mind could not refuse. Her memories. They reared up in her mind, like grotesque phantoms. And as she'd gazed out on to the flat darkness of the ocean while her visitor had been busy below, so they had reared up again, unbidden.

The child. From the village. Found in the woods behind her house. Found wandering, crying, dazed. Naked. The police arrived, with questions. She had two sons, she had explained. One was working in London. The other, the younger, working in Glasgow. Her husband had died years back. She was living by herself in the big rambling house. All alone.

Which was a lie.

The police went away, and never came back. The little girl – only three years old – was too traumatised to remember anything. The conclusion reached was that her abuser was probably from the mainland. A tourist. The investigation moved from the island to elsewhere. She never heard anything about it again.

But she had lied.

Her son had come back that weekend. From Glasgow. Or wherever he was working. He drifted, from job to job. He'd arrived with a stack of American sightseers on an early morning ferry crossing. He'd walked to their house by hidden paths. No one knew he'd come. He was invisible, a faceless stranger. He was good at that.

Morphing into the background, becoming non-existent. A loner. A boy who had never really fitted in. A troubled young man.

He'd done things to the little girl. He'd admitted as much. She thought back – more than just admitted. Announced it. Almost with pride. He'd found her in the woods. Crying and lost. He knew how to comfort little girls. In his special way. She remembered those words. She would never forget them. Each letter of each word branded into her soul. In his special way. And his voice. Not contrite, not regretful. No remorse. Laughing. How he laughed, when he told her what he'd done. And what he'd done to others. And how he would keep on and on.

He'd told her all this as he was leaving. He was going back to Glasgow. It was safe for him to go there now. Get a job. He'd told her all this, casually. Conversationally.

He had left her. He was at the verge of the woods. At the foot of a big oak tree. He'd made a walking stick from one of its branches the year before. She'd told him he couldn't leave. He'd said she couldn't stop him. Nothing could stop him.

She'd grabbed a carving knife from the kitchen. Why she'd picked it up, she didn't know. She supposed blood was on her mind. She supposed, deep down, she knew what she had to do.

He had turned to face her, and the smile still played on his lips when she sank the blade through his body. It entered so easily, she remembered. Slid in, like his substance was soft butter.

He'd dropped to his knees. He'd tried to speak. A bubbling rattle was all he'd managed, then blood. Blood everywhere. On the ground, on her dress, her hands, in her hair. Rich and red and flowing.

She looked up at the sky. It was pale and mottled with broken clouds, the colour of grey gauze. She remembered the tears she'd shed that afternoon.

And she remembered the two people looking at her from the darkness of the woods.

And thus the next chapter of her life began.

63

Two police vans, a forensic unit, two police cars. Parked outside Black's one-bedroomed flat in Bolton Drive, in the south side of Glasgow. A blazing convoy. Curtains twitched, faces suddenly appeared at windows, people congregated on the street. The scene was given added gravitas because of the presence of Chief Constable Divers.

They pressed all the buttons on the front voice entry system, and a second later someone buzzed the door open. They made their way up the communal stairs. Black's flat was on the first floor. They hovered outside, changing into the papery plastic all-in-one suits, peeling on the skin tight rubber gloves, all to avoid contamination.

Divers, DI Shaw, and two other detectives were to enter first, together with a photographer. The forensics would follow.

"How are you feeling, sir?" asked DI Shaw.

Divers looked at her, askance. He had to think. It took him a second to reply.

"Much better, thanks. Must have been a bug. Or maybe food poisoning. Thanks for asking."

His thoughts, as ever, strayed back to the young woman, waiting in his *special place*.

His dungeon.

He switched his mind to the present. He couldn't afford to be distracted.

They had their gear on. Divers took a step back, letting Vanessa Shaw take control.

This should be fun, he thought.

Vanessa nodded at a uniformed cop. He carried a portable battering ram. He swung it into Adam Black's front door. Once, twice. The door shuddered open. The cop stood back. Vanessa entered first, then Divers. The rest followed.

Divers looked about. The flat was small and simple. A narrow hall. Bedroom on one side, and on the other, living room, bathroom, kitchen. They went immediately to the living room.

The place was a mess. Photographs filled the walls, strewn on the floor. Photographs of the victims, following various stages of their lives, culminating in final death poses. Stacks of police files. Forensic and post-mortem reports on shelves. Groups of names written on paper and tacked to the walls.

"Lookee here," said Divers. He was studying a list of names – those in the police task force who had been assigned to each of the Red Serpent murders. Divers name was top of the list. Then working down, rank and file.

"He's a thorough man," said Divers.

Vanessa stood beside him. "What's he doing?" she murmured.

"Christ only knows."

Cupboards were being opened, drawers pulled, everything owned by Black exposed, studied, photographed. The kitchen was bare.

"He knew he was going to prison," suggested Vanessa. "No point in buying food."

An officer shouted from the bedroom. "Something here, sir."

They made their way along the corridor to the bedroom. The room was devoid of anything other than a single bed, a wardrobe, chest of drawers and a mirror.

"A monk lives better," observed Divers.

The wardrobe had been opened, then pulled out. Behind it, a section of the skirting board looked as if it had been cut away and then replaced.

"It's loose," said the policeman who'd discovered it.

"Open it up," said Vanessa. "Careful now."

He knelt down and gently dislodged it. It came away easily in his hands, to reveal a space in the wall. "Looks like it's been hollowed out." He put his hand inside. "I've got something." Delicately, he pulled out a narrow, grey metal box, three inches high, ten inches long.

"Open it," said Divers.

The box wasn't locked. It was a simple lid with hinges. He opened it.

Divers peered into the contents, and took a few seconds before he spoke.

"Looks like we've got the bastard."

64

Fletcher held his mobile phone before him, hoping to catch the moment of Black's destruction, a wide grin filling his face, rendering his features pinched and squeezed, like a plump white pillow being compressed.

Black gave him only a cursory glance, more wary of the five approaching men.

"You don't want anyone dying on your watch, Fletcher," Black said quickly. "How would you explain that to the warden?"

"Shut the fuck up," said Fletcher.

"Try this then," and Black did something no one could have anticipated.

Pritchard was behind him, face pale and drawn in stark fear. Black turned, took four long strides, to stand looming over him. For a fleeting second, their eyes locked.

"Here's my good deed," said Black, his voice low, serious. "As promised."

He flashed a hand forward, pulled Pritchard's head down into his waist, caught the back of his neck in the crook of his arm. Pritchard gasped. The gasp was cut short, as Black leant in, levering his body weight, and snapped his neck. Pritchard slumped to the ground.

Black stepped away. "That's one!" he shouted.

Fletcher stood, motionless. He lowered his mobile, no longer interested in catching the moment.

"What the fuck have you done?"

The five men stopped. Black's display of violence was shocking. He'd just killed a man, before their eyes, in cold blood. It was the hesitation Black needed. He did the second thing no one could have anticipated.

He attacked.

The five men were in a loose group. Black ran, crouching forward. The first was Hammer, who drew back a step, raising the barbell. Black seized the upraised wrist. At the same time, he kicked at Hammer's knee, thrust an elbow up under his padded jaw. Hammer's teeth rattled at the impact. He stumbled to the ground. Another man lunged towards Black, swinging the bar. Black ducked, moved in, jabbing the man's throat once, twice, in rapid succession. The man lurched away, spluttering, his breathing tubes ruptured.

Black finished with a lethal blow, using the heel of his hand, striking the area between upper lip and nose, driving a spike of bone into his brain. Black was conscious of a looming figure at his side. A fist lashed out, punching him in the face. Black shook away the pain, and responded instantly with a thunderous blow to the side of the man's head, to his temple. The blow was perfect. He collapsed to the ground. Black stamped on his neck for good measure, crushing the windpipe, breaking the bone.

The entire episode took less than ten seconds.

The odds were looking considerably better. Five, reduced to two. Hammer groaned, tried to clamber to his feet. Black seized a dropped barbell, brought down a vicious blow to the top of his head and then two more. His skull rippled open. Blood, bone, brain leaked onto the gymnasium floor in a canvas of bright colour.

Black squared up to the remaining two. One was Swifty, in the act of backing off, fear stamped in the whites of his eyes. The other – a burly man with a shock of white hair and long rangy arms – ran towards him, howling, brandishing his weapon. He brought it down, hoping to crack open Black's forehead. Black tensed his legs, raised his own barbell with two hands, and blocked. He swivelled, spinning on one foot, and lashed the man's ribs with a powerful side kick. The man reeled back, into a desk used by the guards. Black rounded on him, striking him with the barbell, first on the neck, then another to his face. The man clattered to the ground, onto his stomach. Black sank his knee into the middle of his back, cupped his hands under his chin, thrust up, and snapped his neck.

Swifty darted past him. Black leapt out, tackling his legs. Swifty fell heavily to the ground. Black worked quickly, first breaking his wrist, then his collarbone. Swifty screamed, half dragging himself towards the door. Black casually picked up the dropped barbell, and struck the back of Swifty's head. Swifty dropped at the feet of Fletcher, who stood, riven to the ground, still as marble, clutching his mobile phone, blood drained from his face.

Black regarded him. "That's several dead men already. All on your watch, including the prison celebrity, our friend the Red Serpent."

Black glanced down at the figure of Swifty, who shifted feebly, blood pouring from a gaping wound.

"What do you say Fletcher? Does he live, or does he die? Seeing as you're God in this fucking shithole, you decide."

Swifty groaned. "Please."

Fletcher gaped at Black. "I... I..."

"Lost for words? I'll take that as a negative. Sorry, Swifty."

Black struck the barbell down hard, then again. Swifty convulsed. Black brought down a third blow. Swifty stopped moving. Black brought it down a final time. To be sure.

Black straightened, surveying the scene behind him. Bodies littered on the floor, blood spreading on the blue-grey tiles, seeping round the gym equipment, the machines, the weights. A lake of blood.

He turned his attention back to Fletcher.

"You've killed them all," Fletcher gasped.

"They started it." He took a step forward. Fletcher shrank back.

"You started it," said Black.

Fletcher fumbled for his keys, hands shaking. "Fuck..." he mumbled.

Black loomed in. Fletcher was concentrating on finding the right key. His face took on a new sheen. No longer smug, sneering. A different expression entirely. Fear, desperation.

Black slapped him hard across the face. Fletcher staggered back.

"Please!" he cried and sank to his knees.

Black looked down at him, and felt nothing. "Please what?"

Fletcher started to sob into his hands. "Don't kill me."

Black grabbed him by his collar and hauled him up. They stood, only inches apart.

"Look at me, Fletcher," said Black.

Fletcher raised his head.

"You brought this on yourself. You designed your own downfall. You understand this?"

"This wasn't meant to happen," he mumbled.

"Shit happens, friend. You keep telling me you're fucking God. Guess what I am."

A tremor seemed to pass across Fletcher's face – fear, a premonition of what was to happen? Black would never know.

Black looked into Fletcher's eyes, close up. "I am the fucking devil."

Fletcher took a step back. Black made a sudden lethal motion. As he had been trained. And Black had been trained by the very best. Fletcher slumped to the ground. Black stooped down, going through each of the keys attached to a ring on Fletcher's trouser belt. He found the one he was looking for. The smallest one, but to Black's mind, the most important. He tucked it into the back pocket of his jeans.

He straightened, took a deep, calming breath.

Clock was ticking.

The other guards would be here soon.

Black had work to do.

Blood work.

65

The Colonel hadn't joined the posse to Black's flat. Instead, he stayed in the main incident room. Phones were still buzzing, police officers still at their stations, hunched over phones, taking calls. It was constant. Lots of leads, from all over the country. Possible sightings, suspicions, theories. Most of it bullshit. In fact, all of it, he mused. The story had been leaked, Pandora's box well and truly opened.

But there was something else in the wind; the Colonel's bloodhound nose sensed it. Anticipation. A general feeling that perhaps, at last, they were on the verge of something. A breakthrough. It was a feeling the Colonel couldn't share. In fact, if anything, he was inclined towards the opposite sentiment. Dread. And bewilderment. He had no idea where this was going. But wherever it was headed, it was in the wrong direction.

Just under two hours later, a car emerged into the car park. The Colonel watched from a window three levels up. The place was illuminated by a yellow glimmer from lights set in the walls, giving an almost dreamlike cast to the place. The unmistakable bulk of the Chief Constable filled the passenger seat, and driving, DI Shaw. They got out, and made their way through the bitter cold, to the front entrance. The Colonel could see the little puffs of cloud forming in the amber light, as they talked. They looked like two people with a purpose. The Colonel's mood blackened. He sensed something very bad was about to come crashing down.

He waited, sitting in a chair in the main corridor, sipping a polystyrene cup of something described as coffee. Two minutes later, the swing doors opened, and the two came bustling through. The Colonel stood, and spoke immediately. "What's happening?"

They stopped. It was Chief Constable Divers who answered him. His small eyes seemed to glow.

"You still here, Mackenzie?" he said. "Why? You're not needed. Not now." He flicked a knowing look at Vanessa Shaw. "I don't have time for this. I'll brief the team." The edges of Divers' mouth curled up into something approaching the semblance of a smile. Cold, thought the Colonel. Gloating.

Divers waddled off, towards the incident room.

The Colonel took a deep breath, regarding Vanessa, and waited for her to speak.

"We found something at Black's flat. The truth is, we found a hell of a lot."

The Colonel nodded. "Of course you did. He'd been working on this case for over a week before he went to prison. We both had. Our remit was simple. Direct from the top. Get as much information as possible on the Red Serpent. There were no limits to the information we were given. Do whatever had to be done."

"He had photographs on the walls. The place was crammed with files."

"So? Let's go to my room right now, and you'll see an identical scene. What the hell did you find, Vanessa?"

She hesitated, and wouldn't look him in the eye.

"What the fuck is going on?" he said, his voice cracking, the words firing like bullets.

"The forensic guys will be bringing it later. They're still there. They'll probably be there for the entire night."

"What?"

"It doesn't make sense," she stammered. "But the Chief has it in his mind that it's enough."

"What's enough?" The Colonel was at breaking point. If she didn't tell him in the next three seconds, he'd shake it out of her.

She met his eyes, fixed him a long look.

"We found a box concealed in his bedroom."

The Colonel waited, breath held. *Where the hell was this going*? "And?"

"We opened it." She swallowed. She sat on one of several blue hard-plastic chairs lining the corridor. The Colonel sat down next to her.

"And?" he urged, his voice softer.

She paused, turning her head to look at him. "We found things in it."

Her face was pale, weary. "Mementos. From each of the victims."

She held the Colonel's intense stare.

"Trophies."

66

The Colonel absorbed the data, for all of one second. "Bullshit, and you know it."

Vanessa Shaw blew out her cheeks, shaking her head. "It makes no sense. None of it."

"Of course it doesn't. Why would it? It raises more questions than answers."

"The Chief doesn't want to know. He thinks we've made real progress. It wouldn't surprise me if he called a press conference tonight."

The Colonel sighed. Suddenly he was bone weary.

"We know Pritchard was talking to someone on the telephone. That certainly couldn't have been Adam Black, given he was in a prison cell in the same block."

Vanessa shrugged. "Unless the conversations were pre-recorded?"

"Seriously? We got the second letter, remember? How did that happen? Black didn't send it – how could he? He was in prison. And if he were involved, why would the letter implicate him? And the fucking photograph of his wife and daughter's headstone? Surely you can see this is crazy."

Vanessa responded in a carefully neutral voice.

"Everything's crazy in this. But we have to look at the facts. That's what we're trained to do. Remember the *what if?* What if Black was always involved. What if there were three of them all along? What if the third got scared, panicked. Or there was some kind of grudge between him and Black, and this is revenge, payback. "

"That's a lot of what ifs."

"I could keep going. They abducted the Prime Minister's daughter. Perhaps it's got too hot for them to handle."

"I thought you dealt in facts," said the Colonel, his face expressionless. "All I hear is wild suppositions."

"Not quite. What we found in that metal box in Black's flat was not supposition."

The Colonel lowered his voice. "What did you find?"

"Items of jewellery. Plus..." Her voice wavered.

"Plus?"

"Body parts. More specifically, fingers. Wrapped in little air-tight plastic pouches. You remember..."

The Colonel finished the sentence for her. "Of course I remember. Each girl had her right index finger removed. A clean cut. This is fucking mixed up, and you know it."

"At this moment, I don't know anything. Except your star man Adam Black is in the frame, and it doesn't look good. However you see this, Colonel, however you want to back your boy up, these are the facts. In a couple of hours, we're going to pick him up at Shotts prison, and bring him back here, where he will be interviewed as a suspected accomplice to the Red Serpent. Full stop. Adam Black has a lot of explaining to do. And he might just lead us to Elspeth Owen."

The door at the end of the corridor opened, and Divers appeared. He glanced down the hallway, saw them both sitting.

"DI Shaw!" he shouted. "My office. We have things to

discuss. We don't need you anymore, Colonel Mackenzie. You can go home now."

Vanessa stood. "Sorry it didn't work out, Colonel. Sometimes it's the people closest to you who hurt us most."

The Colonel grabbed her hand. "We need to talk. You and I. Not here. The coffee place. It's open late, yes? Let's meet in an hour."

She frowned, uncertain. "I've got a lot on. I want to be here when Black arrives."

"We should meet. It's important. Please. There are things I need to tell you. It won't take long. It has a bearing on the case."

She gave a reluctant nod. "Okay. One hour. But it has to be short. And it had better be important, Colonel."

"It is. I promise you."

She hurried away. He watched her go, through the swing doors at the end of the corridor.

The most important news, he thought.

Mind-blowing.

She disappeared from sight, as she headed towards the office of Chief Constable Frank Divers.

67

His mobile phone vibrated. Ernest Stanford felt it drum against his chest. He reached into his inside jacket pocket. He was walking at the same time. The name illuminated on the screen was not a caller he was expecting.

Chief Constable Frank Divers. Stanford took the call.

"Imagine hearing from you," he said. "How goes it in lovely Glasgow?"

"Glasgow is not lovely. It's freezing. And depressing. There's been a development. Are you in London?"

Development? It had to be something significant. Divers would not be calling on his mobile if it were anything other.

"Has she been found?" asked Stanford, his voice heavy with irony.

"It's not about Elspeth Owen. Not directly."

"Now you're being cryptic, Chief Constable."

"I'd rather we talk, face to face. Can you get a flight up?"

"No need. I'm in Edinburgh, as it happens."

"Edinburgh?"

"Liaising with some people from your Scottish government. I'm staying the night here. I can be in Glasgow in an hour."

"That's good. Come to my office."

"Seeing as you're asking so politely. But I need a clue. A hint."

"It's about Adam Black."

"Adam Black? Has something happened?"

"Very much. It's sensitive."

"Another clue, perhaps? It's a freezing night, and I have a rather splendid room booked in the Princess Hotel."

A silence. When Divers answered, impatience edged his voice. "It's important, dammit. It's something I need. It's something we both need."

"Which is?"

A pause, then Divers said, "Our silence."

68

Black groaned, shifted a fraction, raising an arm an inch from the ground. He witnessed, through half-shut eyes, the shocked, frozen faces, heard the panic, the raised voices, the shouts and urgent screams into mobile phones.

He had lain down in the middle of it all. Seven still bodies, strewn on the hard gymnasium floor like discarded mannequins. He was the eighth. He'd smothered himself in their blood, his head, face, hands, his clothes. At initial glance, just another dead man. First, he'd heard the rattle of keys, as prison guards entered, to check, probably wondering why the lights were still on. Black heard their gasps of shock, horror, fear.

Then urgent voices, firing out calls on their walkie-talkies. Black waited. He sensed their presence, as they went from man to man, probably not knowing what to check for. Signs of life, perhaps. But they'd do nothing until the paramedics and doctors arrived at the scene, too nervous about making things worse, contaminating a crime scene. Footsteps, then more bedlam, as men in green uniforms with stretchers and medical equipment arrived. Emergency services. They buzzed about, like flies round shit.

And that's when he groaned, and raised his hand an inch from the ground.

"Christ!" someone shouted. "We have a live one."

Black made an attempt to speak. He performed a low, incoherent mumble.

A man crouched over him. "It's okay, buddy. I'm going to raise you slightly, and get you into a neck brace."

Another man appeared. Gently, they lifted Black a little off the ground. He was aware of something being fitted round his neck, under his chin, then he was gently lowered back.

He detected another voice. The warden. He was close by, voice pitched to an almost feverish falsetto.

"There's how many?"

"Eight down, sir. Looks like seven dead. Including an officer."

"Who?"

"Walter Fletcher."

"Christ! What the hell happened here?"

There was of course no response, because there was none to give. Only Black knew the answer.

"One breathing, sir. The medics are taking him now."

Black didn't hear the answer, nor did he care. He was lifted again, by three people, only inches off the ground, and then placed on a stretcher. The last thing he saw as he was being carried out the door was the warden, sitting on a low bench, head cupped in his hands, staring into oblivion. His job was finished, reckoned Black, ending on a dramatic note. He gave him no more thought.

He was taken along corridors, groaning intermittently to maintain the act. Two prison guards escorted them. A blanket was placed over him, and suddenly he was out of the front entrance, and in the freezing cold February evening. The front area to Shotts prison, normally designed for staff and visitors parking, was ablaze with lights and noise, almost like a funfair.

Flashing lightbars, sirens, headlights. A clamour of noise. Black was placed in the back of an ambulance with a waiting paramedic and both prison guards. He was immediately handcuffed to a side railing, while one sat next to him, the other sitting on a fixed chair opposite.

"Is that really necessary?" asked the paramedic. "The guys hurt, and going nowhere fast."

"Protocol," replied the guard. "We're dealing with murderers and rapists, and a whole lot worse. So you can't to be too careful."

"You'll just get in the way." The paramedic leaned over Black. "We're taking you to the Queen Elizabeth Hospital in Glasgow. Can you tell me your name?"

Black cracked open one eyelid and gave a groan in response. The paramedic carefully cut away his clothing.

"I can't see any puncture wounds," he said. "Nor any deep wounds. Probably sustained a head knock. Maybe suffering from concussion. Looks like he was the lucky one."

Black felt movement. The ambulance pulled out of Shotts prison, and sped towards the M8, the main route between Edinburgh and Glasgow. With the siren blaring and lights flashing, Black estimated he'd be in Glasgow in a half hour.

What then, he had no clear idea.

But Plan B had worked, miraculously. He'd got out of Shotts prison.

And Black was seriously hoping never to return.

69

Divers got the call direct from the warden, whose name was Gordon Price. His voice shook when he spoke. Carnage. Murder. Mayhem. The man was hysterical. Divers told him to calm the hell down, and eventually the message was conveyed. Seven men dead. One prison officer, six inmates. One man still alive, being taken to hospital. The place was a madhouse. Nothing like this had ever happened before. Worse than prison riots. Worse than anything he'd ever experienced blah... blah. It was obvious the only thing the warden cared about was covering his own arse, which was now well and truly shredded. Divers didn't give a shit about the warden. He was more interested in names.

The warden had been given a list. He rhymed off the dead men. Divers listened with rapt attention.

"And the man taken to hospital?"

"Black. First name Adam."

Divers took a long portentous breath. *What was Black's game?* Whatever it was, it was over.

"Thanks for keeping me briefed, Gordon. Sounds like you've got a big clean-up operation. We're here to assist you."

"Clean-up operation?" retorted the warden. "That's the understatement of the year. This could close us down! And where does that leave me?"

Up shit creek without a proverbial paddle, thought Divers.

"Tricky situation," he said, his voice emotionless. "Keep me posted."

He hung up before Price had a chance to continue whining.

Divers focused on the dapper figure sitting opposite. Slim, immaculately dressed in a dark-blue three-piece suit, a tailored camel cashmere coat, silver-grey hair oiled back, the room suffused in expensive aftershave. Sitting cross-legged, arms folded, looking like he didn't have a care in the world.

Ernest Stanford. The prick from Whitehall. He had the ear of the Prime Minister, so it was believed. The previous one, the one about to be appointed, and no doubt the one after that. A useful man to have on his side. And at that moment, Divers needed his co-operation.

"Black's on his way to the Queen Elizabeth, as we speak," Divers said. "Chaos in Shotts prison. Seven men dead, apparently. Sounds like the place went mad. And trust Black to be involved. He's up to something. I feel it in my blood."

Stanford reacted by raising one sceptical eyebrow. "I think that's a little far-fetched, Chief Constable. Maybe it's exactly what it sounds like. He got embroiled in trouble, got hurt in the process, and now he's on his way to hospital. Don't create when there's no need."

"He's a dangerous man," grumbled Divers. "Perhaps better if he'd died."

"Who for?"

"For us."

"And Elspeth Owen? If you've uncovered evidence in his flat, then don't we need him alive? What's the expression – to help with your enquiries."

Divers took a deep breath. He had his own set of priorities.

"We need him buried. Depending on his condition, we intend to interview him. We'll see what he has to say for himself. And then we throw away the key. Good for everybody." He decided he'd turn the screw just a little more, to ensure he had Stanford's compliance. "Imagine the reaction, if it got out that the government was behind this. Behind getting Black into prison, to get the Red Serpent talking. And it turns out Black's the bad guy all along. What do you imagine the fallout will be like?"

Stanford gave a languid smile. He seemed to be imperturbable. Divers was reminded of a lizard in the sun.

"I like that expression – *buried*," Stanford said. "I think we agree, on this at least. Adam Black is serving a lengthy sentence for terrible crimes. I think we leave him to it. He becomes... disavowed. Disowned."

"There's no other way."

"But what of the others who know of Black's involvement? The Colonel will fight tooth and nail for his man. He won't abandon him. And there's Katie Sykes. She knows about Black. Though I think I can control her. She has morals, but they're outweighed by ambition. If I suggest that if she forgets about Black her career prospects improve exponentially, then I think that should buy her silence."

"A regular Judas."

"I don't know what the female equivalent of a Judas is."

"Bitch," said Divers.

Stanford shrugged. "And you? Anyone on your side of the fence?"

"Only one of the team knows about Black's true purpose. But I suspect that's been shattered now, with the stuff found in his flat. DI Shaw. She's a good cop, and tough. But after what she saw, I think she won't give a fucking shit about Adam Black."

"Fair enough," replied Stanford. "That might do. Which takes us back to the Colonel. The fly in the ointment."

"A crushed fly. He's lost all credibility. He should have retired years ago. Who would believe his crackpot plan? His own 'number one' man could end up being the Red Serpent's accomplice. Where does that leave him? Broken and finished. He came in, and started throwing his weight around. Like he owned this fucking place. Like he owned me! Well, fuck the Colonel. And fuck his department. He's a dead man walking."

"Fierce talk. I sense you don't like him. Which leaves one other person."

Divers frowned. "Who?"

"Adam Black."

Divers gave a derisory laugh. "He's a con, a prisoner. He's nothing. Less than nothing. A piece of shit on the heel of my police boot."

"He may have a different view on the matter. I mentioned the words disavowed, disowned. These are strong words. Black may reply with another word. Even stronger."

"And what word would that be?"

"Betrayed."

70

The conversation in the back of the ambulance was sparse. The prison guards didn't talk. Black knew too well the symptoms. Shock. They had witnessed something they had never seen before, and probably never would again. Violent death, on a large scale. Men lying in their own blood, eyes wide and staring. Life gone, replaced by vacancy. The guards were in no mood for idle chat, faces tight and shiny with sweat, each deep in their own thoughts. Black had witnessed death on many occasions. He was usually the perpetrator, he thought grimly. During active service with the SAS, he'd hunted behind enemy lines countless times. His job – to kill, pure and simple. Dispose of the enemy. With a C8 assault rifle, with a Glock, with a knife, with his bare hands. An assassin.

Shock had never been a major problem for Black.

He had killed seven men. To Black, there was a degree of justification. They had tried to kill him, after all. It wasn't his fault if he was dealing with amateurs. Too bad. He dismissed them from his mind. More pressing was how he could take advantage of his new set of circumstances.

The paramedic attending him worked with a silent

competence. He'd cleaned away the blood from Black's face, took a reading of his pulse, and hooked him up to a saline drip, the procedure awkward, with two other men in the back.

The siren blared. Black had a sense of hurtling speed. He checked the time on the prison guard's watch – 8.30pm. Black had to get free, and time was running out. For him and Elspeth Owen.

The ambulance slowed, then lurched up and down. Speed bumps. He reckoned they were in the hospital grounds. It stopped. Doors opened. Black watched through half-shut eyes. He was taken out, still in his stretcher bed, helped down by two hospital orderlies. He was transferred to a trolley bed. One of the guards re-handcuffed him to a metal side bar. The bed was pushed through the main hospital doors, and straight into the Accident and Emergency ward, past staring patients sitting on rows of blue plastic chairs. All the while, the paramedic was describing Black's condition to a young doctor, stethoscope dangling round his neck, black-framed spectacles dominating his face, attired in green hospital overalls.

"How are you feeling?" asked the doctor.

Black shook his head, groaned.

"We'll get him up to Ward 11. We're going to monitor you, Mr..." He snapped his head towards one of the guards. "What's this man's name?"

"Black. Adam Black."

They entered a lift. A sensation of movement. Black watched the lights shift to level 11. The doors slid open. The trolley was pushed through more doors, along corridors, until they arrived at a private room. The trolley bed, along with saline drip, was wheeled up to a wall.

"Are you feeling pain in any particular place?" asked the doctor.

"Everywhere," mumbled Black. He lifted his hand, but it

jarred against the handcuffs, allowing him to raise it by only a matter of inches.

The doctor turned to the prison guards. "Can't you take those bloody things off?"

They looked at him, as if he were mad. "Protocol," said one. "They stay on. That's the way it is."

The doctor raised his arms in exasperation. He turned his attention back to Black.

"The consultant will be here soon. He might recommend a CT scan to check for internal bleeding. If you need anything, press the red button, and a nurse will come." He placed a small plastic switch next to Black's hand. "You understand?"

Black nodded. The doctor left. Seconds passed. The door opened. Black turned his head a fraction. A policeman entered the room, then another. Dressed in body armour, each holding a semi-automatic carbine.

A figure loomed in. Large, adorned in full police regalia.

Chief Constable Divers.

He stood at the bottom of Black's trolley bed. Two more armed men followed. Suddenly the room was full.

Divers barked out a command to the prison guards, voice sharp in the small room.

"You're both relieved. This is a police matter. This man is now in our custody."

The men glanced at each other, and very quickly came to a decision. Almost by telepathy, thought Black. They had been given orders by the highest-ranking policeman in the land. Who were they to argue?

Silently, they both left the room.

Divers scrutinised Black with eyes set deep in the folds of his face. "You can all leave us, for now," he said. "I need to talk to this man."

The four armed police left, filing out the room, and stationed themselves outside. Divers closed the door and pulled up a chair, to sit alongside Black.

"What bullshit is this?" said Divers.

Black sat up, restricted somewhat by his wrist handcuffed to the side rail. "Good question, Chief Constable. What bullshit are you referring to, exactly?"

"You, here. With seven dead men in Shotts prison. Including a prison guard."

Black dismissed the question with a fractional shake of his head. "That's a distraction. The prison guard you refer to was corrupt and arranged for five guys with dumbbells to rough me up. They would have killed me. We can talk about that later. Right now, get me the hell out of here."

"So, you killed them. Is that it?"

"It doesn't matter, Divers. What does matter is that I spoke to the Colonel. The message I got was that I was on my own, which I really don't understand. So I guess, going back to your original question, I did kill them all, because otherwise I'd still be in Shotts prison, and not out, talking to you. Perhaps you could explain what the fuck is going on?"

"One of the men you killed was the Red Serpent. Lucky for you. Dead men don't talk."

Black gazed at Divers. "He was there. Collateral damage. Anyway, he's irrelevant. He gave me information."

Divers carried on as if he hadn't heard. "We've been to your flat."

Black remained motionless, trying to understand the logic of the conversation. "Good. Don't blame me for the interior décor. I got it like that. Can you remove these handcuffs?"

"You're a funny man, Black. We found your little hiding place. And guess what we also found?"

Black didn't respond.

"We found your box of goodies, you sick fuck."

"Good for you. I have no idea what you're talking about."

"Sure you don't. You psychopaths like your trophies – but fingers? That takes it to a new level."

Black absorbed this, trying to process.

Divers continued, his cheeks taking a reddish hue, eyes shining. This was enjoyment for him, thought Black. "In about half an hour, DI Shaw will be walking through that door, to ask you some questions."

"That's nice," said Black, an edge to his voice.

"And then, when you're all back to fighting fitness, you're taking a trip down to Pitt Street Police Station. To be charged. For the murders of ten young women. And in the process, you might tell us where Elspeth Owen is."

Black met Divers gaze. He spoke, a metallic undertone in his voice. "That's convenient. We had a plan. Sanctioned by you, and others like you. To gain the confidence of Pritchard, and get information from him. Whatever you found was put there to confuse. To mislead. Get me out of here, Divers. You promised me that."

Divers leaned forward, his bulk momentarily blocking the light of the ceiling strip light, two hands resting on the bed. "What promise? All deals are off, Black. You're going to rot in prison, my friend. For the rest of your miserable life. Doors locked, keys well and truly thrown away."

He edged closer, the bed creaking under his weight.

"And what did you actually achieve, Black? What information did you prise out of our celebrity serial killer? The one you conveniently murdered."

He glared at Black, eyes burning into him. But Black trusted only one person.

"Bring the Colonel here. He knows. Bring him here, and then you'll find out."

Divers straightened, pulled his chair back, stood. His round, fleshy face crumpled into a broad grin. "The Colonel." Suddenly the grin dissolved to a sad frown, like a fat clown. Divers shook his head solemnly, put a hand to his heart in mock melodrama. "The Colonel." He sighed.

"What the fuck is wrong with you, Divers? If you don't want to bring him, then he'll bring himself. It's only him I'll speak to."

"And therein lies the problem."

Black waited. Divers looked down at him, tilting his head, as if he felt sorry for him.

"What problem?" said Black quietly.

Divers resumed his grin.

"The Colonel is dead."

71

"The body bags keep coming."

Seven dead men. The prison officer sounded breathless as he relayed the events to Rachel Hempworth. She was in no mood to give him sympathy. He got well paid for the information.

"Names," she said bluntly.

He wasn't aware of who the dead men were, except the chief prison guard – Walter Fletcher. The whole place was in a state of shock. No one knew the facts. Not yet. Nothing made sense. Nothing had ever happened like this before.

"But we do know some facts." Rachel was rapidly losing patience with her informant. "We know there are seven dead men. And you mentioned one was still alive."

"He's been rushed to the Queen Elizabeth. In a bad way, it seems. Christ knows what the hell is going on."

"That's why I'm paying you," she said slowly, keeping her voice neutral. "So you can tell me what the hell is going on. Who was the man taken to hospital?"

"The new guy," stammered the prison officer. She heard a babble of voices in the background. A general melee of noise.

Sounded like World War Three had erupted. If this wasn't major news, she didn't know what was.

"The new guy?" Her heart skipped a beat. "I need a name."

More noise, sounding like a fire alarm. She could barely hear him.

"What did you say?" she shouted.

"I think his name is Black. Adam Black."

She hung up, ears still ringing.

She was at her desk in the office. Her boss, Cosgrove, had left for the evening, his departure marked by a cavalcade of sharp, barking coughs. There were a handful of colleagues at their computers, all jerking their heads up simultaneously when she shouted down the phone. She ignored them. She dropped her mobile into her handbag, snatched it up, grabbed her coat and scarf.

Instinct told her that what she was doing was wrong, stupid. Dangerous even. But sometimes she had to trust something else. Her instinct.

She ran out of the office. She knew where she had to go.

To the hospital. To the man called Adam Black.

72

Black lay on his back, staring at the ceiling. The world around him was collapsing. The Colonel was dead. Divers had taken gleeful delight in providing the details – a hit and run, apparently. Poor street lighting. He was leaving his hotel. No one saw anything. The ambulance got there, but the Colonel was dead, every bone in his body crushed. Flattened like a fucking pancake. The Chief Constable's exact words.

"You're fucked, Black," were his parting shot as he left the room.

Maybe he was. Black had seen desperate times before. He had faced death square in the face. It had faced him back, and Black had always won. So far. But this wasn't death. This was worse.

He'd lost his friend. His *ally*. The man he could trust. The angel on his shoulder. Of course, Divers could be lying, but Black knew he spoke the truth, because of the sheer enjoyment in his tone. And Divers had made his position plain. He'd turned his back on Black. The Establishment had turned its back on him. Left to rot, like a carcass in the sun. The objective side of his mind argued, *who can blame them*? Divers revealed they'd found trophies of dead women in his flat. A rather compelling argument to throw away the key, he thought ruefully.

Black had been on his own before. And he'd survived. And to survive this he had to keep going. He had the girl to save. There was still time. To do that he had to escape. He pulled at the handcuffs attaching his wrist to the side bar of the bed. They rattled against the metal. The irony didn't escape him – he got out of a maximum-security prison, but was struggling to get out of a hospital bed. Divers had left, leaving four armed cops outside Black's door. No doubt more would be arriving. The situation appeared bleak.

But Black had a knack for turning bleak situations around. And now he knew he was on his own, everything was simpler. He had to escape. Pure and simple. And he knew what he had to do.

He pressed the red button.

Within ten seconds, a nurse entered, followed by one of the armed police, semi-automatic rifle resting in his hands.

Black was sitting up. He looked directly at the cop.

"I want to make a confession," he said. "To all the murders. But not here. At Pitt Street. Take me there now, and I'll tell you everything. Plus, I'll take you to Elspeth Owen."

73

DC Chiltern had made his rounds, but the residents who lived near Eaglesham cemetery knew nothing. He'd drawn a blank, and hitched a ride in a police car back to HQ at Pitt Street.

He'd been working thirteen hours straight, but wasn't tired. This was the biggest case of his career – possibly the biggest case in anyone's career – and his mind and body were fuelled by adrenalin overload. It seemed that every five minutes, something was happening. And when he arrived back at Pitt Street, the rollercoaster kept on rolling.

He joined the team in the incident room. He encountered a muted, low-key atmosphere. Men and women still working, taking calls, eyes stuck to computer screens, but something was wrong. The place was subdued. He spied DI Shaw in a corner, sitting alone, hands cradled round a plastic coffee cup, staring at the floor. She looked up when he entered. Their eyes met briefly. She was pale, her skin tight and harsh in the raw light of the room.

He made his way across to her. "What's up?"

She shrugged, and sipped her coffee.

He wheeled a chair up beside her. "What's happened, boss?"

She gazed into her coffee cup when she replied. "The obvious answer is that the fucking world is falling apart." She regarded him with a side glance. "Where the fuck have you been?"

"You asked me to speak to the people who lived near the cemetery. I had to get a lift back."

"And?"

He shook his head. "Nothing. No one saw anything. Nothing suspicious."

She drew a deep breath. "I could murder a cigarette."

Chiltern licked his lips, not certain what to say next. He didn't have to say anything.

She ran her hands through her hair. Normally, it was scraped back to a ponytail. She'd let it hang free, dark curls falling loosely to her shoulders. "I'm sorry," she said. Another sip. "I don't mean to sound... waspish."

"What's happening?"

"There's been some sort of prison riot at Shotts. Guess who's in the middle of it all?"

"I don't know."

"Adam Black."

Chiltern weighed this in his mind.

"I didn't know he was in Shotts prison."

Vanessa sighed. "Of course you didn't. Why would you? He's been taken to the Queen Elizabeth. He's left behind a fucking maelstrom of dead bodies."

"Is he okay?"

"Don't know. The Chief is over there now with armed police. We'll go across shortly to question him. If he's able."

Chiltern swallowed. He didn't like to sound stupid. But sometimes that was the only way. "If you don't mind me asking, why are we questioning him?"

She looked at him again, and gave a grim, cold smile. "I forgot. You've been having a vacation in Eaglesham while the rest of us have been working. We got a warrant to search Black's flat. We found a whole lot of shit there. Incriminating shit. He's our number one suspect."

"Fucking hell," he muttered. "I was only gone a couple of hours." He frowned. Another stupid question formed on his lips. But DI Shaw answered before he could speak.

"I know what you're about to ask. If Black was in prison, then who was the Red Serpent talking to on the phone, and who wrote those charming letters and sent the fucking photograph of Black's family's headstone."

It was Chiltern's turn to finish. "Unless there are three," he said.

"Unless there are three," she repeated in a hollow voice. "It's the only explanation. And still none of it makes much sense. And every minute we spend trying to figure our way through this maze, those words keep repeating themselves."

"What words?"

"Tick-tock. Time's running out."

Chiltern sat back, blew through his cheeks. Then he looked at her, inquisitively. "But that's not it."

"No. it's not." When she spoke, she didn't raise her eyes from her coffee cup. Her eyes were faraway. "We got a call. A man was killed only three streets from here. Hit and run. Traffic division got his name from his credit card. They ran it, then contacted us." She looked at him. "Colonel Mackenzie is dead."

Chiltern gasped.

Vanessa seemed suddenly more remote than ever. "None of it makes sense," she muttered. She stood up, tossed the cup in a wastepaper basket. "You can come with me. We need to interview our number one suspect. You up for this?"

Chiltern nodded, unable to think of anything to say, his mind numb.

"Good," said Vanessa.

Her phone buzzed. She answered. Her expression altered as she listened – from expressionless to frown, to amazement. She disconnected, and turned to Chiltern. He wasn't entirely sure if she was looking at him or some inward space. "We need to get a hold of Chief Constable Divers."

Chiltern raised his shoulders, spread his hands – *what just happened?*

"That was one of our men at the hospital. Adam Black wants to confess."

Confess, echoed Chiltern, mouthing the word, not saying it.

"He wants to come here." Vanessa took a deep, shuddering breath. "There's something bigger going on. I just don't know what it is. But what I do know is that Black is clever and dangerous."

Chiltern waited for her to finish.

"It's a game, Chiltern. And Black's playing us. Playing all of us."

74

Divers' excuse was simple – he had a late meeting to attend to. He did something he knew he shouldn't, but he had more compelling matters on his mind. He switched off his mobile phone. Events were moving forward. Positive things. Black was in the frame. Which meant the heat was off Divers, for a while. The press and Whitehall and all the other fuckers had another scapegoat to crucify. So why not a piece of self-indulgence. *Me time,* he thought. That was how his wife had described it, when she was justifying her extravagances, her extra-marital liaisons.

The thought of his wife triggered the usual reaction. He squeezed the steering wheel until his knuckles turned white. He sensed the red mist descending, when the skies darkened, and everything around him was tinged with the colour of blood.

The drive from the Queen Elizabeth Hospital to his house in the leafy suburbs of Kilmacolm took thirty mins. Traffic was quiet. It was 9pm. He switched the radio on, then switched it off. He wanted his own thoughts. In fact, he was thinking of only one thing. Fixated on it. The girl.

It had been several hours. Her screams would eventually

have drained away to a whimper, to nothing. What would she be feeling? He tried to picture himself in her position. Fear? Dread? Anticipation? He dismissed the notion. Divers was incapable of feeling empathy.

He approached his house, and stopped the car a hundred yards away. He could see its shadowy silhouette through the trees, through the glimmer of the street light. His heart was racing. He swallowed, trying to even his breathing. She was in there now, trapped. Waiting for his return. Manacled. Waiting for him to do his worst. That's all she could do. Wait. And live every second, wondering what would happen to her, what he would inflict upon her.

His dick was rock hard. This was the best moment of all. The anticipation. He took another long, deep breath, quelling the urge to cum right there, in the car.

He started the car up, and drove on, past the house. Let her wait a bit longer, he thought. Let her agonise. Like the meat of the beast – a frightened animal was much sweeter after the slaughter.

He would return. In a little while.

And when he did, she would feel the pain, and all that came with it.

When the red mist descended.

75

Under the watchful eyes of four armed policemen, Black was allowed to change back into the jeans, socks and trainers he had arrived in. His sweat top had been cut away and discarded. The hospital had provided him with a fresh vest and pullover. Two of the guards had their weapons out, trained on him. They weren't taking any chances. One trigger-happy cop was all it would take. Suddenly Adam Black becomes Adam Black deceased. More police had arrived and were waiting outside. All armoured up and carrying rifles.

He was told to raise his hands. He was patted down, then spun round, his back to them. His arms were forced behind, handcuffs locked round his wrists. He was spun back again.

"You go out that door, Black. Don't do anything stupid. You get outside, and you stop."

Black nodded. The door was open. He left the room, the four cops following, into a corridor of a general ward, to be met by another six policemen, all carrying semi-automatic carbine rifles. In particular, SIG MCXs. Counterterrorism weapons. Good for their low recoil, and supreme accuracy. People shredders. One-shot killers.

"Okay, Black," spoke the same man. "You follow the men in front of you. We will be behind you. I repeat, try anything stupid, then we have orders to shoot. You understand?"

"What if I need the toilet?"

"Fuck the toilet, you fucking lippy bastard. You shit and piss in your pants. Now move forward."

He moved, as instructed. They all moved together. Four in front, one on each side, four behind. A convoy of men, body armour, helmets, and loaded weapons. With him in the middle. They passed rooms. Patients watched, stunned at the procession. They passed waiting nurses, doctors, staff who stared, wide-eyed. No one said a word. The scene passing before their eyes was beyond words.

"We don't take the lift," barked the police officer. "The stairs." *Damn right*, thought Black. In a confined space, how easy it would be for a firearm to discharge. Whether accidentally, or not.

They passed through heavy fire exit doors, and down the stairs, wide enough to keep to the same formation. There was no conversation, the only sound booted feet on the steps, the creak and rustle of body armour. Occasionally a voice coming through someone's radio, which was ignored. Black's thoughts were in overdrive. He was surrounded, handcuffed. A millimetre twitch of a finger, and he was a dead man. What he had originally surmised as bleak, was graduating to impossible.

They got to the ground level. Through more doors. Now they were in the main foyer. Seating space for three hundred, two restaurants, a coffee and sandwich shop. The restaurants were closed. The place was half full. This was the biggest hospital in Scotland. Never would it be empty. People stared. The men marched through. The usual buzz of conversation dropped to zero.

"Move aside!" commanded one of the officers. Men, women,

kids, scurried out the way. Like Moses, commanding the Red Sea. Only Moses didn't possess a semi-automatic killing machine. He only had God on his side.

They reached the far end, through more doors, which swished open as they approached. Past more bemused people, some in wheelchairs. Along a corridor, past Accident and Emergency, until they reached the exit. They emerged into the night. It was freezing. Several stairs led down to a wide road – an internal road, forming part of the massive hospital campus. Parked on the opposite side was a fleet of vehicles. The place was illuminated by strong white lights from sconces fitted into the hospital walls.

"I had no idea I was this popular," remarked Black. Every breath created a little plume of smoke.

"Shut it. You speak only when I tell you."

Black counted. A police van, six police cars, six motorbikes. Traffic cones placed across the road.

The policeman who had done the talking was speaking into his radio.

"We're taking him across now," he said.

A voice responded through the static.

Car doors opened. More uniformed police poured out into the frosty evening. They waited. All of them waiting for Adam Black.

"Move it!"

They made their way down the stairs, across the road, all in unison, like a black beetle, with Black in its stomach.

The back doors of the police van were open.

"Inside!"

Black stepped up and into the van. There was a row seats fixed along each side, facing each other.

He was gestured to a seat farthest from the back doors. He sat. A policeman loomed over him, buckling him in a seat belt.

"Can't be too careful," said Black. He was ignored.

Four more police entered and sat on the seats opposite. They each held their weapons, barrels pointed downwards, to the floor. Safety catches were *off*, noted Black. They each stared at Black, faces flat and hard.

The door shut behind them. Black heard voices outside. Instructions. The engine rumbled into life. Sirens started up. The windows on each side were darkened; lights flashed and flickered. The van moved off, into the Glasgow darkness.

Black smiled. The four faces opposite were expressionless. They hadn't removed their helmets, and wouldn't until Black was safely in custody, but they had lifted their face visors, and Black read their eyes. He saw complacency. He was no threat, not against four of them with guns, and Black alone and handcuffed. Black's smile widened.

The van bumped up and down, as it negotiated speed bumps. Black used the motion to lean slightly to one side, and fish into his back pocket with index and middle finger, feeling for the key. The key he had taken from Fletcher in the gym, as he lay in his own blood.

He found it, and with the delicacy of a surgeon, manoeuvred it from his pocket. He edged forward three inches, and let it drop on the seat behind him. He needed to distract.

"You ever killed anyone?" he asked suddenly, directing his stare to the man sitting on the far right.

The man looked at him and through him. Black continued.

"It's not an easy thing. To kill another human being." He looked at the next man. "To squeeze that trigger, knowing that the tiniest motion of your finger has such profound consequences."

He contorted his hand, twisting it round, trying to guide the key into the locking mechanism. The van sped up. They had left the hospital and were on the public roads. The sirens blared, the lights blazed. Street lights glimmered by. Going at speed, and disregarding traffic lights, Black estimated the journey would take no longer than fifteen minutes. He flicked his gaze to the third man.

"You shoot someone, and you shoot to kill. There are no half measures. I've shot and killed, when I was in the army. I was trained to do nothing but kill. You could say, I'm an expert in it."

The van turned a corner. Black compensated, as did the others, by swaying his body in the opposite direction. The movement allowed him to twist his hand and fingers round more fully, without drawing attention. He carried on, focusing on the fourth policeman.

"I fought with the SAS, all over the world, including the badlands of Afghanistan, where life's cheaper than a bullet. I've killed more men than I care to remember." He locked eyes on the cop. "The question I have to ask is – could you kill me?"

He found it! The key slid into its miniscule keyhole. With exquisite care, he turned it, one full revolution. He sensed a click against his skin, as the handcuffs loosened free. He tried not to laugh out loud. He shifted slightly, hands still behind his back, drawing his wrists slowly apart.

The fourth policeman decided to reply. "I could kill you in a heartbeat, Black. No problem. Now shut the fuck up. Or I might be tempted to blow your brains out right now in this van."

Black responded with a cold smile. "You understand the problem, don't you?"

The policeman gave a crooked grin. "The only problem is you, so shut the fuck up."

"The problem is space," said Black. "Or lack of. Four men, all suited up in body armour carrying semi-automatic rifles. In the back of this van, even if there's a hint of a struggle, the chances are you'll end up shooting each other. So your guns are useless, because you won't dare use them. You've picked the wrong place for a firefight."

The fourth policeman suddenly appeared uncomfortable, glancing at the men next to him. Another one spoke up. "There's going to be no struggle, Black. No firefight. You're going nowhere, unless we let you." He grinned, showing white teeth. "But if you're keen to try it, then make no mistake, I'm not scared to fire a bullet into your skull. There's one right here with your name on it." He patted the magazine clip of his rifle.

Black's smile widened. "Shall we?"

"Shall we what?"

"Try it." Black's smile dissolved. "Let's see if I'm right."

"Fuck you, Black."

"No, fuck you."

He brought his hands round, and with almost contemptuous ease, unbuckled the seat belt, and stared at the four men, letting the situation sink in. They sat, each of them, and could only stare back, slack-jawed.

Two seconds passed. Black leapt forward.

And then all hell broke loose.

76

Rachel Hempworth passed the side road to Accident and Emergency, on her way to the Queen Elizabeth's main entrance, and spied the line of police vehicles, parked in a row on one side of the road. Traffic cones prevented access. Lights were flashing. Something was happening. She didn't have to be Einstein to figure that, nor that it had something to do with the man called Adam Black.

She stopped, pulled up, turned her headlights off and parked hard onto a walkway, a hundred yards from the entrance. And watched. She saw a van, several cars, a flotilla of motorbikes. She saw silhouettes of men in the cars, waiting, and more sitting on the motorbikes, all waiting. Two more stood in the middle of the road, either end, to divert traffic away.

Figures emerged from the building. *Armed police.* They came out as a unit. She counted ten. Bulked up in their black body armour, carrying weapons, like monstrous two-legged insects. There! Cocooned in the centre, she glimpsed a man, dressed in a pullover and jeans. Tall, casual, almost languid movements. Could have been strolling in the park.

Adam Black. They guided him to the cars parked on the

opposite side of the road, in particular to the back of the police van. Men got out to meet them. Suddenly, Black disappeared from view, hidden by bodies swarming round him. The back doors of the police van opened. She caught sight of Black's dark hair as he disappeared inside, followed by several of the armed police. The doors shut, the noise echoing in the still, freezing night. The men were milling about, talking, giving instructions, taking instructions. The cones were removed, and bundled in a boot. They got back in their cars. The motorbikes headed off first, slowly, the cars and van following, more motorbikes taking up the rear guard. The sound of sirens filled the air. A procession of sound and light.

She had a choice. Go back and let the whole thing go. Concentrate on other stuff, as suggested by her chain-smoking boss.

But something told her, maybe something as simple as instinct, that Adam Black was connected to everything. That maybe Adam Black *was* the story. That if she followed this to the end, she'd uncover a greater truth. She took a deep breath. She'd met Black in prison. She'd looked into his eyes. She'd glimpsed adventure, danger, darkness.

She had a choice, but knew what she'd do even before she'd asked the question.

She started up the engine, and followed the police convoy, keeping a cautious distance. Down the path of danger.

Rachel Hempworth could not have predicted then just how dangerous her choice would be.

Nor the incredible events about to unfold.

77

The four men sat in a row, clumsy looking, pressed together because of their body armour. Like sardines crammed in a tin. Black leapt forward. He grabbed the rifle of the man closest to him. The jolt caused a round to go off, into the floor. The noise was deafening, heightened by the metal walls, the close space. The man kept his grip, refusing to let go. The miraculous freedom of Black, the ensuing struggle, and the noise of the discharge, created exactly what Black needed. Hesitation.

None of them had been trained for this. Not fighting at close quarters, where one wrong move meant a head blown off. These men were snipers, killing from range. Black, on the other hand, was trained to be a killer, a fighter, a street brawler, if need be. Able to deal in any situation. And when it came to killing, Black had experienced every situation imaginable.

Instinct kicked in. The cop jumped to his feet, Black with him, both grappling for control of the rifle. Black simultaneously swivelled, spun, kicked the face of the next man. A perfect connection, the heel of his shoe on the bridge of the man's nose. The impact knocked him into the third man, knocking him to the floor. Skittles in a bowling alley. Another round cracked off, like a firework. The fourth got to his feet. He aimed, but Black and his opponent were weaving back and forth in an awkward frantic dance, each clinging to the rifle.

The man could fire, but this was no clean shot. He could kill his friend as easily as Black. Instead, he grabbed his radio. Black thrust forward, using all his weight, the man he was grappling with staggering back, both of them colliding into the fourth cop. They all clattered to the floor. Another round thundered, catching one direct to the body armour on his chest at close range, propelling him into the two back doors. He lay in a daze, semi-conscious.

Black had wrestled away the rifle. He leapt to his feet. The two men were slower, hampered by the bulk of the armour. Black flicked a glance to the side, to the man he'd kicked in the face. He'd slumped to his side on the chairs, out cold. Two down. He pointed the rifle at the two men standing, their faces pale, shocked, scared. All complacency blown away. They were now introduced to a new world. Black's world.

The van had stopped. Black had no way of knowing where they were. But he did know that there would be at least twenty policemen waiting for him, some with rifles and itchy trigger fingers.

Better out there than in here, he thought. When you have no fucking place to go, you bring it to them. Drummed into him from day one in the 22nd Regiment.

He focused on the two men facing him.

"Drop your weapons!" he shouted.

They did as instructed, the guns making a tinny echo when they hit the floor.

"Open the doors!"

One of the men pulled an internal lever, the door slid open.

The two men stood at the edge of the van. Black looked

beyond, at the army of uniforms massed outside. He recognised where they were. They had crossed the King George V Bridge, and were stationary on Oswald Street. A two-lane one-way street leading into the centre.

The van had stopped in the middle of the two lanes. Police vehicles and motorbikes surrounded it. They had effectively snarled up the traffic flow. If it kept up, Glasgow city centre would stop in ten minutes. Already people were congregating on pavements, only to be hustled along by police, barking out commands. Black saw all this, a knot of dismay in his chest. He was trapped. He'd reached the end. If he wasn't picked off by a bullet, he'd be captured. It was a fool's plan.

Then he had an idea. Crazy. A long shot, but he had nothing to lose.

"Shut the fucking door!" he bellowed. One of the policemen looked at him over his shoulder.

"You're going nowhere, Black. Give yourself up. We'll make sure nothing happens to you."

"Thanks for the concern. Appreciated. But just shut the fucking door, or I swear to Christ I'll blow the back of your head wide open. And at this range, your helmet's as soft as butter. So please, humour me."

They slid the door shut. They faced him. One spoke. "There's twenty guys out there. In five minutes, there'll be fifty more. With a fucking arsenal. Where's this going, Black? You're not going to kill cops. That's not your style."

Black raised the rifle.

"You don't know my style."

78

Chiltern was sitting in the incident room when the news came through, the likes of which he'd never heard before, and would probably never hear again. Vanessa Shaw was hovering at a large poster board, where pictures of the victims had been placed, along with notes, time frames. And in the centre was a photograph of Elspeth Owen, daughter of the Prime Minister. Chiltern corrected himself – *ex-Prime Minister*.

The news came through. General alert. Major incident at Oswald Street. Only five minutes from their office. Hostages. Man armed and dangerous. The hostages were fellow police. The man who had taken them, the man described as armed and dangerous, was none other than Adam Black.

Chiltern's breath caught in his throat. He looked at Vanessa Shaw. She stood, rigid.

"Fuck!" she screamed. "Fuck! Fuck!"

Everybody stopped what they were doing.

She swivelled her gaze around the room, not focusing on anyone in particular.

"If Black gets shot, then we've lost!" She stabbed a finger at the photograph of Elspeth Owen. "And this woman dies!"

She fixed her eyes on Chiltern, and was moving for the door as she spoke.

"You can drive."

"Where are we going?" Chiltern scurried after her.

"Where the fuck do you think? And where the hell is the fucking Chief!"

She was running now, along the corridor, towards the elevator.

"We're going there?" said Chiltern, still following her. "To Oswald Street?"

The elevator door opened. They got in. It was cramped, and to Chiltern, always smelled of stale smoke and old sweat.

"Who the hell is this man?" muttered Vanessa.

"A psychopath?" ventured Chiltern.

"Maybe. The Colonel trusted him." She turned to Chiltern. "And I trusted the Colonel."

A soft chime. They'd reached the ground floor.

"But do we trust Black?" he asked.

"Black is what I'd describe as a fucking conundrum."

The door opened. They got out, to a wide waiting area, and a counter behind which two admin staff were sitting.

They ran past them and out though the main exit doors, and into the bitter cold Glasgow evening, heading for a row of parked cars.

"A conundrum?"

"You heard me," replied Vanessa. "A conundrum. With fucking attitude."

79

Rachel Hempworth followed the procession of cars. They were travelling at speed. The feeling was exhilarating. She was immersed in the moment. They reached the King George V Bridge, spanning the River Clyde, and one of the arterial routes into the centre, from the south side.

The van Black was in suddenly cut across the adjacent lane, then weaved like a dodgem, until braking to a stop, its entourage forming round it.

She parked full onto a pavement, got out her car, tossed her heels onto the passenger's seat, and climbed the bonnet and onto the roof. Her view was clear. The van was only about a hundred yards distant, in the middle of the road, encircled by vehicles. Police were crouched behind car doors, some armed, poised.

She saw all this, and like everyone else there, she waited, heart in mouth. The van door opened. Two policemen, suited up in body armour, stood in the door frame, silhouettes. They stood for a matter of seconds, then disappeared back into the interior, and the door slid shut.

Time seemed as frozen as the winter evening. A stillness

settled. Others were watching – pedestrians, people looking out from tenement windows. A crowd had gathered outside a pub, bemused, awed.

Then, shots. From the inside of the van. Sharp, whip-crack sounds. Like fireworks. She jumped. The air seemed to quiver. Four, in quick succession. Then silence. Thirty seconds. A minute. Then another shot.

What the hell was happening?

The ensuing silence was something real, tangible. She could feel it, almost touch it.

The door of the van slid open again. Two policemen stood on the edge, still in full body armour, shielded pads on their arms and legs, around their midriff, black helmets, visors down, concealing their faces.

One was propping the other up, holding him round the waist, taking his weight. The guy was slumped into his shoulder. *Unconscious.*

The other one raised his free hand. When he shouted, his voice sounded muffled, blanketed by the visor. But Rachel made out every word.

"It's over!" he shouted. The response was sheer silence. "Adam Black is dead!"

80

As soon as the van doors slid shut, Black had ordered the two men to remove their helmets, which they obligingly did. Black, using the butt of the rifle, rendered quick sharp blows. The men had dropped to the ground, barely conscious. Four bodies lay sprawled, incapacitated, but alive. He'd then fired several rounds into the floor of the van, and one through the ceiling for good measure. Then, he'd stripped one man of his clothes, his protective armour, his ballistic helmet and visor, which he'd quickly put on over his own pullover and jeans. The boots were tight, but manageable.

He'd heaved one of the men up onto his feet, propping him up with one arm, the man leaning against him, head slumped forward.

Black stood, confronting the posse of police, the cars, the lights. Strangely, a silence had fallen on the place. Surreal. He was in a dream. A fucking nightmare. He had brought all this about, he thought ruefully. His own creation. Confusion, carnage. Seek to bewilder the enemy. If in a tight spot, kill, kill, kill. Shock and awe. SAS training. But none of the men before him deserved to die. Black would try to escape, and keep the wet-work to a minimum, if he could.

He reckoned he had all of ten seconds before his little ruse was discovered. Then a million cops would be on top of him. But he spied what he needed. And if luck was with him, he could still escape the shitstorm.

"Adam Black is dead!" he shouted. Nothing like a bit of theatrics. With visor down and helmet on, his voice and face were disguised. Ten seconds. It was maybe all he needed.

The van had a single metal step between the back edge and the ground. Black manoeuvred himself and the man he was holding, down to ground level, the man's boots dragging.

"Stay where you are!" someone shouted.

"He needs medical attention!" Black shouted back. He sensed hesitation. Two armed police approached, slowly. Others held back, rifles poised and ready.

"Stay!"

"He needs medical attention!" repeated Black. He moved towards them, half holding, half dragging the unconscious man. He had to get up close. When he did that, all the rifles in the world were useless. They wouldn't dare shoot into a crowd.

"Stay back!"

Black ignored them. He was now only ten yards from the nearest police car. Suddenly he sank to his knees, and let the cop he was holding sink with him. More theatrics.

"Help them!"

Hesitation dissolved. Men rushed towards him. It was all he needed. He surged to his feet, pushed one man away, kicked another hard in the crotch, whipped his helmet off and battered a third across the face. He sprinted past more bewildered cops. The armed response unit could only watch. They wouldn't, and couldn't, shoot a moving target in a crowd. He leapt onto the bonnet of a BMW, slid across, hit the ground running, and reached his destination. The policeman on the motorbike stared at Black, open-mouthed, until Black's foot propelled him off. He and his motorbike clattered to the ground. Black kicked him again, then hauled the motorbike back up, sat astride, started it up, and within a second, was moving. He felt its power – a BMW, 1170cc. A beast. He leaned forward. He had no helmet, but at that moment its absence was not a priority.

It roared past men, women. He weaved past cars blocking the road, and mounted the pavement. People leapt out of his way. He stayed on the pavement until he passed the last police car, then back onto the road. He flicked a glance over his shoulder. Police were pouring into vehicles, but they were in a jam, all cluttered together. By the time they'd got moving Black would be well out of their reach. But not the motorcycle cops. They were gunning after him. Three of them. Plus, they'd radio ahead, obviously, try to predict his route, and head him off. Plus maybe net the road with tyre shredders. Dangerous, but they would be desperate, and Black had to anticipate the worst. But they had to predict his route. Black had to make it difficult for them.

He was still on Oswald Street, one-way. He reached a crossroads, had to swerve round a bus, cutting across at right angles, almost toppling. He righted himself, and travelled straight through on to Hope Street. Three lanes, one-way. The traffic was congested. The city centre was in confusion. Caused by Black. He dodged between cars, overtaking, bobbing in and out. A police car was parked at an angle in the centre of the road, siren on. A man and woman were getting out. Black slowed. The woman held up both her hands.

"Please, Adam! I'm Detective Inspector Vanessa Shaw! Come with me. We'll bring you in quietly. Please. Just get into the car."

Black stopped, the engine of his powerhouse still thrumming. "DI Shaw?" he shouted.

Shaw nodded.

"And you'll take me in quietly? I have your word."

She nodded again.

He regarded her coldly. The noise of approaching motorcycles drew louder. They were only fifty yards behind, slowed by traffic. They'd be on him in seconds.

For a fleeting second, their eyes locked.

"You know I'm innocent, DI Shaw. So, fuck your word."

He gave full throttle, and sped the motorcycle past and beyond them, hurtling up Hope Street. In an instant, the three motorcycle cops were there, following.

Central Station was now to his right. He veered sharply onto the pavement, the bike lurching over the kerb, and up two sets of stairs.

"Out the way! Out the fucking way!"

People dived to one side, startled, uncomprehending. Disbelieving.

Black was now in the main pedestrian area of Glasgow Central Station.

And he wasn't slowing.

81

"What do we do now?" Chiltern was way out of his depth. They had never trained him for this at the police college. He suspected they'd never trained anyone for this.

DI Shaw compressed her lips. Whether it was anger, frustration, or puzzlement, he couldn't determine. Maybe a combination of all three. He thought, in the dull amber glow of the street lights, she looked fragile as glass. One gust of wind, and she would break.

"He's on a motorbike, and he's escaping. He'll ditch it and disappear. Melt into the crowd. And what does that mean?"

Chiltern gave her a blank expression.

"He's escaped." She had her radio in her hand, calling it in, looking for backup. The problem was, by the time other vehicles arrived, Black would have moved on to a new location.

"What do we now?" he repeated.

"I have to make some calls. Where the fuck is Divers when you need him!"

Chiltern wondered at that. He wondered a lot about this case, but that was the biggest mystification. Chief Constable

Divers, the top man in Police Scotland, was absent. He'd been absent a lot.

Which didn't make sense.

But then nothing about this case did.

82

Black was in the huge meeting area of Glasgow Central Station. Rows of designer shops lined the high red-brick walls; the usual conglomeration of coffee shops; burger joints. On one corner, a pub. In another, the grand entrance to the Central Hotel. The place was bright and busy. Above him, a complex patchwork of metal beams and girders, laced beneath an immense roof of glass. Suspended in the middle, a hundred-year-old gilt-framed box clock with four faces. Commuters sat, stood, walked, ate, chatted, did everything waiting commuters did. Along one end, a massive electronic display showing train arrivals, departures, delays.

The last thing anyone expected was a man on a speeding motorcycle. Followed by three others. People dodged, leapt aside. Black kept going. His aim was to reach the other side – a distance of a about two hundred yards – to the opposite exit, then down a flight of stairs, and on to Union Street. After that, he had no clear plan. A woman screamed. A trolley with suitcases suddenly loomed before him. Black hit the brakes, skidded on the glossy marble floor. The motorbike skittered away, and Black was flung off. He rolled, absorbing the impact.

Two transport policemen rushed towards him. He got to his feet. One grabbed his shoulder, endeavouring an armlock. Black twisted free, stepped back, kicked him in the groin. The other lunged towards him. Black stepped in to meet him, caught his arm, and by adjusting his weight, performed a one-arm shoulder throw, slamming him onto the marble. The other fumbled for his baton, in obvious pain. Black swivelled, striking him in the face with a roundhouse kick. He fell back, on his backside, and sat in a daze.

Black sprinted for the motorbike. By now, the place had stopped. Talking had ceased. The world was caught in a frozen moment. The only noise was the incoherent announcement over loudspeakers of arrivals and departures. Black reached the bike. He turned. Two of the motorcycle cops were on him. They both stopped, kicked out the side stands, dismounted.

"Stay where you are!"

They both had batons out. Black didn't have time to raise his bike. He faced them. He was conscious of a third approaching.

"No thanks," he said, and ran towards them. They were caught off guard. They had expected Black to run, not to fight. One swung his baton down, aiming for the top of Black's head. Black blocked with his forearm, brought his knee up into the base of the cop's stomach, and sliced down onto the side of his neck with a knife-hand strike. All carried out in one smooth movement. Exactly as he had been trained. The cop fell to the ground. The other used the baton for a body blow, catching Black on the chest. Black still had the body armour on, and barely felt it. Black reacted instantly, trapping the baton against his body with his arms, bringing the man in, and then kicking away his legs. The cop flipped over and landed on his stomach. Black fell with him, performed a manoeuvre, snapping the man's ulna.

He got to his feet. The third cop remained on his bike,

talking frantically into his radio. Black nodded politely, mounted one of the motorbikes standing, started it up, and raced off. The other cop immediately followed. He would keep track of him, and radio his position.

Black reached the far side, slowing down, negotiating the steps. Shocked people backed off, pressing against the wall. He reached the bottom, glanced back. The motorcycle cop was twenty yards behind, bumping down the stone stairs. Black needed him gone, and fast. He guided his motorbike using his legs, pointing back up the stairs. He turned the throttle. The bike sped into movement. He accelerated, faster. The cop tried to avoid his path. Black adjusted his direction. The bikes collided. Black leapt off. The cop was flung backwards. Black found his feet, strode across. Part of the standard equipment issued to armed police was a Glock 17 handgun, holstered and strapped round the thigh. Black had dispensed with the rifle on his exit from the police van. The Glock, he had kept. He unclipped it, aimed, and fired a shot into the bike's engine.

He turned to the cop, groaning on the ground.

"No hard feelings."

He returned to his own motorbike, righted it, and sped down and into Union Street. Buses and cars jammed the road. A helicopter buzzed high above. Black flitted through traffic, went through a red, carried straight on, hitting the throttle hard. In two minutes, he'd reached the Clyde side, to an area called the Broomielaw. He turned sharp left, then left again, up a narrow lane. There was no one about. He ditched the bike, tore off the body armour, the police uniform. Underneath, he still had his jeans and pullover. He tossed the stuff in a vacant shop entrance. Except the Glock. The night was not yet over. He might require its fire power.

Suddenly he was just Joe Normal. He jogged back onto the main thoroughfare, and became another pedestrian. The street was quiet. Everybody's attention was diverted to the police stand-off only three hundred yards away. He tried to walk as casually as possible, nerves tingling.

A car pulled up. Black tried to ignore it, ready to run. The passenger window slid down.

"Get in!"

A woman's voice. One he recognised.

He looked round. A face, leaning over. The woman who had come to the prison.

Rachel Hempworth.

83

The text was simple, and all the more dramatic for it.

I need you here, now. Please come. It's urgent. I love you.

She had never texted before. If she needed to speak, it was usually done from her landline, the old-fashioned way. Actual dialogue. It sounded desperate.

He double-checked the number. It was definitely her. He'd bought her a mobile phone years back. He had to. She would never buy one herself. She avoided technology like it was the plague.

The message shook him. He'd phoned her mobile immediately he'd received her message. The phone was switched off. He'd phoned the landline. It rang out.

Ernest Stanford hadn't spoken to her for months. Now he got this.

A message from his mother.

And it shook him to the core.

He had no choice. He had to drop everything, and get to her.

To his mother.
To the Isle of Jura.

84

"Why?"

Rachel Hempworth drove, not entirely sure how she could answer this question.

"I followed the police convoy, from the hospital. I saw the whole thing. I reckoned that you'd double on yourself, if you could. The last thing the police would suspect. It was luck I saw you."

"That's how," replied Black. "It's the *why* I'm interested in."

"I have no idea where I'm going," she said, eyes fixed ahead. "I've never done this sort of thing before, you understand."

"What thing?"

"Aiding a fugitive."

"I'd be a little surprised if you had. Let's get a little distance between us and half the Scottish police force. He'd rented an apartment in Giffnock. Hopefully, the lease hasn't run out. Do you know how to get there?"

She nodded. "Who's he?"

"A friend. A dead friend. One of the very few people I could trust. Answer my question, Rachel. Why the hell are you doing this?"

She took a long breath, composing herself.

"I'm a journalist. I seek out stories for a living. I suppose I have a knack for it. I don't know what you call it. Maybe instinct, though I know that's a cliché. But there it is. I guess I have this antennae for a story. I believe you're a whole story to yourself. I watched you back at the High Court, when you were sentenced. That didn't fit. It got my antennae twitching. When I met you in prison, you looked like a man who didn't belong there."

Black gave a sardonic smile. "I think you'll find all the prisoners at Shotts would argue that they don't belong there."

"You were different. I heard the Red Serpent was introduced into the general population, after only six months of segregation. That didn't fit either. And then the biggest piece of the jigsaw."

"Which is?"

"The Prime Minister's daughter being abducted. A twenty-two-year-old. Blonde hair. Kidnapped not a million miles from the Red Serpent's old stomping ground. Six months after his last victim. So perhaps you're beginning to see the *why*."

"Not quite. You're not in the periphery anymore. You've opted for a ringside seat. You said it yourself. You're assisting a fugitive. I reckon right now I'll be the most wanted man in the United Kingdom. And here you are, driving me away from the long arm of the law. For what? A story?"

"Not just any story. *The* story. Tell me I'm right. Tell me there's a connection. You had to get to Pritchard – the fucking Red Serpent – because you thought he might have information. That perhaps he had an accomplice. That cutting out Brogan's tongue was a way in. A way to get his confidence. Tell me it's true!"

"Pull over," said Black, his voice harsh.

They had crossed back over the Clyde, and were heading south, on a long road called Pollokshaws Road, one of the major routes to and from the city centre. The traffic in the lanes going into the centre was already log-jammed. Police cars and ambulances raced past them, sirens blaring, lights blazing, cutting on to the opposite lanes. She did as instructed, pulled into a bus lane, and stopped.

A fearful thought entered her mind. One which had never occurred to her, triggered by the ambulances.

"Did you kill anyone?" she asked, still looking straight ahead, not daring to meet his eyes, scared to see what she might find there.

Black drew out the Glock he'd tucked in his belt, hidden under his pullover. She held her breath.

"What are you going to do?"

"Look at it, Rachel."

She glanced, looked away. Her voice seemed to catch in her throat.

"What are you doing?"

"This is a Glock. A powerful handgun. Standard issue for the Tactical Response Unit. It's also favoured by British Special Forces. You're asking me if I killed anyone. I've killed lots of people. Men who have tried to kill me. Men who delight in killing others. Bad people. One might describe them as evil. I kill men like that without compunction. But I don't kill police officers."

"And me? Where do I fit in?"

"You have a choice. You can drop me off here, and we'll go our separate ways. Or, you can keep going, and enter my world. The world of evil men. The world of Glocks and bloodshed and death. The dark path, Rachel."

"You're... you're giving me a choice?" she stammered. She turned to him, looked into his sky-blue eyes. The edges of his mouth lifted into a cold smile.

"To be perfectly blunt, you'd be useful. No one's looking for a couple. But then there's the other end of the spectrum."

"Which is?"

"That you get killed. Or you go to prison."

"Tell me I was right!" she said fiercely. "Tell me it wasn't all in my imagination."

Black held her gaze.

"You were right. I work for a section of the government you might describe as niche. To be deployed in special circumstances. People like me are used because they have certain... abilities. My mission was to get convicted for a particularly barbaric crime, to catch the attention of the Red Serpent. I was to obtain information from him, and pass it to my contact. We believe the Red Serpent did not act alone. Once I had anything useful, I was to be released, and start a new life."

She swallowed, trying to grasp the sheer audacity of such a plan. "So..."

"So – my contact was killed." He paused. He continued, his voice flat, emotionless. "And I was betrayed. Someone wanted me to spend the rest of my life in prison. Maybe the same person who abducted Elspeth Owen. Someone who was close to the Red Serpent."

"Do you know who it is?"

"I believe I do."

"Who?"

Black didn't respond. Rachel perceived it was a question he would never answer. At least, not yet.

"So what now?"

"Elspeth Owen could still be alive. I need to find her. I owe her that. And I'll move heaven and earth to do it. I'll ask once more, Rachel. Do you drop me off here, and forget you ever saw me? Or do you come with me? The choice is yours. But you need to make it right now."

Rachel didn't hesitate. "I'm with you," she said, breathless. This was the story of a lifetime. And she was right smack in the middle. And she had no intention of moving from what Black had described as *her ringside seat.* "All the way."

"You're sure?"

"Yes. What now?"

"Time to hunt."

85

"He's gone. Into the fucking mist."

Both Vanessa Shaw and Chiltern were back at HQ. The phones still droned on. People still worked. Black, miraculously, had escaped the clutches of fifty cops and an armed response unit, putting nine men in hospital. No deaths, thank Christ. Out there, in the streets of Glasgow, a huge manhunt was underway. In here, thought Chiltern ruefully, life went on. The day job continued. The Prime Minister's daughter was still missing. And they were no further forward.

"What are we not getting?" said Vanessa, her voice almost a whisper. She was staring at the large board on the wall, pinned with photographs, notes, arrows pointing from picture to picture, names, trying to create a link. A theory. In the centre was a picture of Pritchard, aka The Red Serpent. Placed beside it was a mugshot of Adam Black, taken when he was arrested for the assault on Danny Brogan, a life time ago. Two polar opposites, thought Chiltern. Pritchard was pale, sunken-eyed, gaunt, wispy blond hair curling over his ears. Black was dark, harsh cheekbones, brooding good-looks. Piercing eyes. He looked at the camera, daring it, as if he didn't give a damn.

She took her mobile, texted. "Where the hell is he? The fucking Chief Constable better not be sleeping through this shitstorm."

"He wasn't well," replied Chiltern. "Said he had some sort of bug."

"Fucking fat bug," she muttered. "Black was the key. Now he's gone. Pritchard's dead, probably killed by Black. We have nothing. Fucking nothing!"

"And the Colonel's dead as well, remember."

She nodded. "A nice coincidence. He wanted to speak to me. To tell me something. Think back. When Pritchard was making his phone calls from prison, he alluded to three. Three perpetrators, working in conjunction. If Adam Black was one, then maybe there's another, and maybe that's what the Colonel knew."

"But the Colonel's gone. Whatever he knew is gone with him."

"We can't give up, Chiltern. Are you coming?"

"Where?" he asked, as he was getting his coat.

"To visit the dead."

86

Giffnock was only a twenty-minute drive from the city centre. Wedged between upmarket Whitecraigs and rundown Shawlands. A sort of halfway house, Black had always thought. Ordinary houses for inflated prices. A cluster of shops, a couple of restaurants, a pub and a supermarket. Then you were through it, and on to the next place. Anonymous. Unremarkable.

Which was why the Colonel had chosen it.

Black had asked Rachel to key in the address in the satnav. Twenty-eight Church Street. A secluded block of flats two hundred yards from the main road. Four storeys, two apartments on each level, each with its own balconied window.

"No one knows he stayed here," said Black. "Except for me. Colonel Mackenzie was careful with his secrets. We planned it this way from the beginning. For everybody else, he booked a room in the Premier Inn in the city centre. This was the only way we could keep the affair... clandestine."

"You really don't trust anyone."

"Not in this game."

"Does that include me?"

He gave her a steely smile. "Especially you. One of the golden rules – never trust strange women who pick up desperate men."

They parked a hundred yards from the building, and walked. Like any other couple, enjoying an evening stroll on a still winter's evening. The building was set in the middle of neat lawns behind a low stone wall, illuminated by subtle lighting set in shrubbery and on sconces on the walls. The front entrance was communal. And locked. Black sauntered to the side of the building, to a wooden bench looking on to the gardens. He bent down, using his fingers to feel under the wooden frame. He stood up, and sauntered back. He held up a small polythene bag which had been stuck under the bench with strong tape. He opened it, to produce two keys.

"You really thought of everything," remarked Rachel.

"Almost."

He put one of the keys in the lock, turned. The door opened.

"Top floor."

There was no lift. The stairs were tidy, clean, decorated with baskets of plastic flowers hanging from metal brackets. They reached the third floor, to the flat – 3A.

Black used the other key, turned the lock. They were in.

The rooms were neat, of regular dimensions. The kitchen was open-plan, merging into the living room. The furniture was simple. No television. No ornamentation. On the walls were pictures, photographs. Crime scenes. Faces. Bodies. On a dining room table was a laptop, surrounded by sheets of paper, files, case notes. One wall was shelved, dedicated to rows of books.

The first thing Black did was go to the kitchen. He opened a cupboard, and allowed himself a wry chuckle.

"As promised." He took out a bottle of Glenfiddich whisky.

He opened other cupboards until he found what he was looking for. Two glasses. He poured a generous quantity into each, and handed one to Rachel in the living room, as she studied the pictures on the wall.

"The victims," explained Black. He lifted the glass, let the whisky flow over his tongue. He was back in the human race. It tasted like liquid honey. He let it sit for a second at the back of his mouth before he swallowed, savouring every exquisite drop. "Thank you, Colonel," he whispered.

He finished it off, poured himself another. "Make yourself at home. I'm going to shower and get a change of clothes."

"You have clothes here?" she asked.

"This was supposed to be the safe house. When I got out of Shotts, I was to be taken here. Rest up for a couple of days, while we decided what to do next. Such was the plan. The plan has gone a little off course. Only one thing has remained constant throughout."

"Which is?"

"That the Prime Minister's daughter is in the hands of a fucking psychopath."

Black showered, shaved, changed into dark jeans, running shoes, T-shirt, black woollen round-necked sweater. When he went back into the living room, Rachel was sitting on the carpet, surrounded by a sea of papers and photographs.

"You're busy," said Black.

"There are pictures of all the victims." Rachel pointed to a line of photographs on the floor. Photographs of naked young women lying mutilated, dead.

Black nodded grimly. "The Red Serpent had a flair for the grotesque." Black padded through to the kitchen, and looked in the fridge. He was famished. The Colonel was clearly not one for domestic bliss. A loaf of bread and a packet of thin-sliced ham. Marginally out of date. Otherwise the fridge was bare. Black shrugged. It would do. He'd consumed a whole lot worse.

He made some sandwiches, brought them through. Rachel accepted the food without actually looking at it, which Black found faintly amusing.

"Ten victims," she said. "Ten young women. All roughly the same age. Same colour hair. Look at their faces."

Black knelt down beside her. He looked at the photographs arranged before him. He'd done this a thousand times. The empty eyes, skin white as cool marble, fear still etched on their frozen expressions. And for the thousandth time, he wondered what depth of terror they had endured in those last moments, when they knew they had reached the end.

"What do you see?" she asked.

"Death."

"The mark. Look at the mark on their faces."

Black scrutinised them again. The Red Serpent had left his calling card. Beneath the right eye of each of his victims, he had carved a serpent swallowing its tail, forming a circle, stained with red ink. Performed with some skill, and while they were still alive, but probably unconscious.

"I've seen them, Rachel. The circle of life. Or not, in this case. A closed infinity, or whatever else goes through a psychopath's mind."

"But the pattern's been broken."

Black regarded her, curious.

"Victim number eight. Look, Adam. What do you see?"

Black flicked through the photos. Victim number eight. A dental student. Patricia Fleming. Used, abused, murdered. Tongue excised. Fingers amputated. Left to rot in a metal bin behind a restaurant in the west end of Glasgow.

"The carving into the skin isn't as careful. We looked at that, and dismissed it. Maybe Pritchard was feeling less fastidious that day."

"There's more. Look."

Adam took a bite of his ham sandwich. He had viewed the photographs so many times, they no longer turned his stomach.

He stopped chewing, stunned by the minor revelation.

"Jesus, you're right. The pattern's been broken. Number eight doesn't fit."

87

The world had turned upside down, inside out. The world was fucked. Reality replaced by a nightmare. But it was no dream. No waking up, no return to his cosy life. He stumbled back to his car, blood on his shirt, his hands. Confused. Disorientated. What he had confronted did not make sense. Beyond his comprehension, and the more he tried to figure it out, the greater the panic. Run. Flee. Hide.

He had to get away, as far as possible from his house, from what was there. He needed refuge, to think, regroup, work it out. But there was nothing to work out. The whole thing was fucked.

Chief Constable Divers drove out of his white-chipped driveway, tyres scrunching on the stones, speeding past the wrought iron gates, blood on the steering wheel, and away into the chill winter's night.

To the place he went to when he had to think. To work it out. Sanctuary.

To his lodge on the shores of Loch Laggan, in the Scottish Highlands.

88

The drive to the Premier Inn took all of five minutes from Pitt Street Police Station.

"It was close enough for him to come quickly," said DI Shaw. "The Colonel wanted to be available 24/7. At a moment's notice."

Chiltern nodded, but said nothing. The events of the day were mind-numbing, from a cemetery in Eaglesham, to a race to a Glasgow hotel. And in between, the escape of a dangerous prisoner. And the sudden death of the man he knew simply as the Colonel. He had to pinch himself to believe it was really happening. There were so many twists and turns, his brain felt frazzled. Plus, he was exhausted. He hadn't slept in twenty-four hours. And he had a gut feeling there were a few twists left.

They got to the hotel on the corner of George Street, overlooking George Square. A glass-fronted block of six floors, with economy rooms, the place reflecting a glossy shimmer in the glow of the street lights. A building no different from a million hotels anywhere. Blink, and you'd miss it. Simple, cheap, clean.

It was 10pm. The foyer comprised a few seats, couches, and to one side a small bar. The place was empty. They got to a reception desk manned by a young man and woman, dressed in matching company uniforms. DI Shaw explained the situation, that they were police, and that one of the guests had died, and that they were following up enquiries. The receptionist, shocked, punched in the name, told them the room number, gave them an entry card, and told them, somewhat irrelevantly, that he had paid in advance, up until the end of the month.

They got to his room, opened the door. The place was basic, utilitarian. Single bed, wardrobe, dressing table, desk, and an en suite. The view was of a wall of the adjacent building. The room was neat. Too neat.

On the desk was a file.

"Check what's in it," said Shaw, as she looked in the bathroom.

He opened it. Inside, treasury tagged, was a sheaf of papers and photographs.

"What the hell is this?" said Chiltern.

Shaw was back in the bedroom, looking in the wardrobe, in the small bedside cabinet. "What?"

He showed her. The topmost item was an A4-sized black and white photograph of a man, dressed in a suit, sitting at a table in a restaurant, smiling a dazzling smile, toasting the camera.

Around his head, a circle had been drawn in black ink, with an arrow pointing from it. At the tip of the arrow, the words – *the third man?* Chiltern studied the picture. "What does this mean?"

Shaw took a deep breath. "Maybe the Colonel was onto something, after all. What else do you notice, Chiltern?"

Chiltern stammered. "Nothing?"

"Exactly. There's no toothpaste or toothbrush in the bathroom. No shaving foam. There's nothing in the wardrobe. The bed hasn't been slept in. And I'll wager..." She pulled open the drawers in the desk, "...that they're empty. He's never slept here. He really didn't trust anyone. Yet he left this file."

"He knew he was in danger," suggested Chiltern. "He left this for whoever. You, perhaps?"

"Perhaps. Maybe he found a connection between Black and this man. Take the file. We'll look at it back at HQ."

Chiltern tucked it under his arm. "Who is he?"

"I don't know. But if the Colonel was interested in him, then so am I."

89

The serpent was facing the wrong way. On all the other victims, the serpents open mouth was facing clockwise. On number eight, it was counterclockwise.

"Perhaps it doesn't mean anything," said Rachel.

Black gazed at the picture, cursing inwardly at his incompetence. Something he should have seen. "It means everything. Pritchard was obsessed. For him, that mark was the most important thing in his life. It empowered him. It *made* him. Never would he get that wrong. It was his *raison d'être*. My view is that he killed his victims precisely because he wanted to mark them. They were a means to an end."

"Maybe Pritchard should be questioned again. I could go to the authorities, explain this... anomaly. Maybe the case could get re-opened."

"Don't waste your energy. Pritchard would never talk. It's academic, in any event. Unless you know a good clairvoyant."

"He's dead?"

"Wrong place, wrong time. I mentioned earlier, I don't get a guilt complex over extinguishing evil men. Does that worry you?"

"No. Not a bit."

Black got up, and made his way to a laptop on the dining room table, which he opened and powered up. He knew the password to get in. He and the Colonel had tried to plan for most eventualities. The Colonel had emailed anything of interest from his mobile phone to a private email address, and then immediately deleted the message on his phone. Since Black's internment in prison, the Colonel had sent dozens of emails to himself, firing into the ether little vignettes of choice information he had picked up. Only Black had access. Black typed in the password, and suddenly he was in.

"A top-up?" asked Rachel, going to the kitchen.

"A shame for Glenfiddich to go to waste."

Reading the emails from his friend sent a pang through Black's heart. He scrolled to the last one, sent only three hours ago. His last message. The information disclosed probably got him killed, he thought grimly. As usual, it was concise, clear, unambiguous. He read it.

The Colonel had come to the same conclusion as Black, but for a completely different reason. But put both reasons together, he thought, and the answer was damning.

They had both come up with the same name. The Red Serpent's accomplice.

Which, according to the Colonel's emails, didn't make sense, unless there was a third.

Rachel returned with a glass of whisky, and placed it on the table. "Anything interesting?"

Black logged out, and closed the laptop. There was a plastic container with pens and pencils next to the computer, along with a notepad. Black pulled out a black biro, scribbled something down, ripped a page out, folded it, put it in his trouser pocket.

A name.

"An epitaph," he replied. "The last words of an old friend before he died. It's nothing." Black, trained in a world of secrecy, where loose lips usually brought about death, chose not to divulge the information to Rachel. He didn't trust anyone. Especially a journalist.

On a wall above a grey-veined marble fire surround, a painting had been removed, and left to one side. In its place was a large whiteboard screwed into the plaster, and on it, the Colonel had used a dry wipe marker to write lists of names.

"Are these suspects?" asked Rachel.

Black studied the list. "Everyone's a suspect. These are people who were involved in some way in the murders. University staff, friends, family, police, lawyers. Most of them peripheral. Anyone who had some bearing in the case, no matter how small. We gave each section a colour code. University staff were red, friends green, police blue, and so on."

She nodded slowly. There were about a hundred names, in five columns, and at the head of the first was the name of the man Black wanted to meet very badly. The man who'd turned his back on him. Chief Constable Divers.

"Divers headed up the Red Serpent case," said Rachel. "I interviewed him. I found him particularly loathsome."

Black was interested. "How so?"

She sat on a black leather sofa.

"Do you know him?" she asked.

Black gave a cold grin. "I do. He was one of the very few who was aware of our plan. I've met him several times. The last was less than two hours ago, in a hospital ward. It did not go well. I'm hoping to resume that conversation with him very soon."

"You know, there were rumours being bandied about the newspaper. Rumours involving the Chief Constable and his... peccadillos."

"Yes?"

"We couldn't substantiate anything. We started asking questions, but in a millisecond, we were locked down. He got wind of it, and suddenly there were threats. Court action. Defamation. Litigation."

"You were onto something," said Black.

"But the editor baulked. He's old, and tired, and doesn't want to fight anymore. We let it go."

"What did you let go?"

"Our dear Chief Constable, according to street chat, likes prostitutes. I spoke to one of them. She was scared. He has very unique requirements."

Black nodded. "He likes to inflict pain."

"You know this?"

"We've known from the beginning. He's a sadist. The Colonel had a skill for uncovering people's secrets. But I get why you might find Divers loathsome. Others might have used the word 'repulsive'."

He paused. A sudden thought blossomed in his mind. Ridiculous? Perhaps.

There were files of each of the victims on the dining room table. He got up, and rummaged through them until he found a manila folder containing details of Patricia Fleming – No. 8.

He flicked through the pages, found what he was looking for, read the typed paragraphs. "Pass me the photograph."

Rachel picked it up from the floor, handed it to him.

He gazed at the picture. Blood had congealed around the edges of the mouth. A broken tooth. Broken nose. Purple bruising. Swollen eyes. Beaten to a pulp.

"What is it?" Rachel asked.

"Maybe nothing," whispered Black. "Maybe everything." He took a deep breath. "The Red Serpent was never alone. There may have been three, working in concert. A little coterie of death. I believe I know the identity of one of them. So did the

Colonel. We arrived at the same conclusion, but by different methods. My guess is, the Colonel was killed because of that knowledge. Which means that one of the Red Serpent's fellow conspirators is ready, prepared. A difficult target. Which doesn't get us any closer to finding the Prime Minister's daughter. But the third might be easier. The third might think nothing can touch him."

Rachel looked confused. "And who are we talking about?"

Black walked across the living room and pointed to the whiteboard, to the name at the head of the first column.

"You can't really be serious!"

"I don't know what I am. Except that I have to save that young girl's life. And my gut tells me this bastard holds the key. You ready to start hunting?"

Rachel nodded. Black glanced at a clock on the wall. It was 11pm.

"Then we go now."

He went through to the bedroom, retrieved the Glock, tucked it under his belt. When he returned, he noted the look of bewilderment hadn't left her face.

"Where are we going?"

"To pay a visit to Chief Constable Divers. About time we had a real chat. Man to man. You can drive."

90

The old woman got the call. It was late evening. She had drifted into a light sleep, as she sat by the fire in her living room. The only sounds were the crackling of the embers, and the low moan of the wind outside. Her telephone was the old-fashioned type, pale cream, chunky, with a round finger dial, and a receiver kept on a cradle on top. It rang suddenly, jarring, cutting the air. It sat on a little table at her side. It rang four times, stopped. For ten seconds. Then rang again. The code. With a dismal heart, she picked it up. She rarely spoke. She was only required to listen and follow the instructions. If she complied, then there would be no trouble.

She placed the receiver back. The instruction was clear. The girl was to be sedated. For something special the following day. There was a shelf in her kitchen dedicated entirely to drugs – sedatives; tranquilisers. Amytal; Butisol; Pentothal. Trazodone. Others. Her visitor brought fresh supplies every while. She didn't know anything about drugs. But she was told precisely how to mix them, when to use certain types. They were secreted in the girl's food and drinking water. The old woman was to give her a concoction in the morning, crushed and sprinkled in some muesli. The girl was sleeping now. Like the wind, she would moan in her sleep. And when she woke, she would scream.

The old woman got up, and shuffled out the room, and into the kitchen. It was big, and old, and square. Above, a pulley was fastened to the ceiling, from which her clothes hung to dry. Her cooker was forty years old. Her fridge was older. She used to own a radio. She'd destroyed it when the nightmare began, refusing to listen to the outside world.

She opened a cupboard, and looked at the bottles on the shelf. Big bottles, little stubby bottles, different-sized boxes. All containing drugs. All clearly marked.

She closed the cupboard. She left the kitchen, and sat back on her chair, and stared at the dying embers.

The phone suddenly rang again. No code this time. She let it ring out. It had been ringing throughout the evening. Someone was trying to reach her, but it was too late to care. She had made her decision.

No more, she thought. She couldn't go on. Her soul was damned. Maybe there could be redemption.

The girl would wake in the morning. The old woman would unlock her prison door.

She would give the girl her freedom.

Then she would walk to the cliffs.

And kill herself.

91

Getting to the Isle of Jura was not easy. At night, it was impossible. Stanford's intention was to catch the only flight from Glasgow Airport the following day. It was winter, and flights were reduced. There was only one in the afternoon, at 2pm, landing at Islay Airport an hour later. Then a taxi to Port Askaig, covering the fifteen-mile stretch. Then the ferry across the Sound of Jura to Feolin, the main port in Jura. Then a bus trip to Craighouse, the capital of the island. A desolate place, especially in winter, when everything was stripped down to the bare bones, and the occupants totalled about a hundred and fifty. In the summer, a different story, when tourists visited in their thousands.

But there was still more, thought Stanford glumly, as he planned his journey. The bus dropped him off in Craighouse, and then a mile's hike through rain-soaked woods, along an overgrown path, and all other kinds of shit. He'd have to leave his Armani suits, and buy jeans and mountain boots. Then, and only then, would he reach his destination.

He was in his hotel room – The Princess Hotel in the centre of Edinburgh, a short walk from the trendy 'Old Town' – and booking a flight on his laptop. He hadn't thought about his mother for months. He initially sent her texts, to which she never responded. Why he'd given her a mobile phone, he couldn't work out. He knew she'd never use it. Perhaps it went someway to salve his conscience, his mother alone in a big rambling house in the middle of nowhere. But it was what she said she wanted. She would never leave. Born and bred there. She'd met her husband, his father, on Islay. She'd inherited the big house when her mother had died, and they'd both moved there after they got married.

His father had been a terse, solemn-faced man, who wore dark suits and sombre ties. He'd died an abrupt death when Stanford was fifteen. A heart attack on the ferry to Islay, where he'd worked in a bank. He'd left three behind – his wife, himself. And his brother.

They struggled along, his mother taking up jobs here and there. His brother was twelve years younger. He barely knew him. Stanford won a scholarship at Cambridge, arguably the most prestigious university in Britain, and couldn't leave the island quickly enough. He never looked back. Why would he? He went on to greater glory, a first-class honours degree, a gilt-edged job in the Civil Service, and on to Westminster.

He hadn't spoken to his brother in years. He thought back – maybe twenty, maybe more. On those rare moments when he phoned his mother on the landline, they never spoke of him. He never asked, she never volunteered any information.

The truth was, he didn't care.

He phoned his mother's landline again. It rang out. His mother could be wilful. And spiteful, sending him a dramatic text, then refusing to answer the phone.

Fucking bitch, he thought. But the text frightened him. He detected trouble. His mother needed him. He had no option.

But he was glad he had an excuse to go. Adam Black was a

fugitive, and no doubt gunning for blood. Stanford had no desire to be in his firing line.

But if Black were to die, then one less fly in the ointment. The other fly was already dead.

The Colonel.

And one thing Stanford knew for certain. The dead couldn't talk.

92

Divers' home address was in the Colonel's files. A forty-minute drive from where they were. Rachel logged in the details in her satnav.

"What do you expect to find there?" she asked.

"I really don't know. I'm hoping he'll be in. He won't be expecting me. If he's out, then it doesn't matter – we'll gain entry, and have a look about. Who knows what we'll find."

She remained silent for a while, taking the turn off on to the motorway, the M8.

"You're suggesting we break into the dwelling house of the Chief Constable of Police Scotland?"

"That's correct. I might as well add a few more crimes to my long list. You're free to stop anytime."

"In for a penny." She sighed. "But I don't get why we're doing this. You don't make it easy for me, Adam."

"I don't think I make it easy for anyone. I'll tell you soon, once I understand. It could be a complete wild goose chase. In which case, I've achieved nothing, except waste valuable time."

They remained in silence. Black's mind was racing. There

were three. Of that he was sure. The Red Serpent was dead. Two left. Black had a gut feeling about Divers. Black knew in his bones he was connected, but couldn't understand why. The connection was fragile. Tenuous. Still, it was all he had, and he had to pursue it to its end.

Then there was the third, who for now was beyond his reach. For now.

Clock was ticking. *Tick-tock.*

The traffic was quiet. They got to the sleepy village of Kilmacolm. Houses worth a million plus peeped out from leafy gardens. Driveways were filled with expensive cars. Silhouettes in the dark, of large, sombre mansions.

They arrived at the house. Set back from the main road, concealed behind trees and shrubs. In the cold winter's evening a stillness had settled. The metal gates were open.

"Drive in," said Black. "Otherwise it looks suspicious."

"This should be interesting – let's see how the Chief Constable reacts when he sees Adam Black, fugitive and outlaw get out the car."

Black shrugged. "We'll see."

The entrance was narrow. She drove through slowly. The driveway was chipped stone. After fifty yards, they reached the front of the house. Black was alert. He had no idea what to expect. His senses heightened, he got out of the car. The house had a country feel, white walls laced with ivy the colour of blood, stained-glass windows framed in red brick, a red high-peaked roof. Lights were on, inside.

Black tensed. The front door was solid dark wood, arched in Gothic style. It was wide open. Black was staring into the man's hallway.

"Is he in?" whispered Rachel, at his side.

"No car. Unless it's in the garage." Something wasn't right. He pulled out the Glock. "You'd better get in the car."

"No fucking way. This is one creepy place. And you're the one holding the gun."

Black couldn't argue with that.

They crept to the door, and entered into a broad hallway. The lights were on.

Black closed the door quietly behind him. The house felt empty.

He crept along the corridor. Handcrafted wood panelling on the walls, subtle downlighters on the ceiling. Rachel followed. They passed closed doors, got to a kitchen at the back, opening up to a split-level living room, the entire back wall comprising glass bi-folding doors. The place was bright with light. Outside, darkness. The back garden, assumed Black. He felt exposed. He pressed a switch, the drape closed.

"There's no one here," said Rachel, her voice still in a whisper.

Black nodded. He pointed to the side of a white leather settee. It was smeared in blood.

"Let's follow the trail."

With Glock poised, he made his way slowly to a door at the other side of the room. There was blood on the wall beside it. He opened it, emerging into another corridor. There was a red imprint of a hand on white paint. Another door at the end of the corridor. Open. Hardly daring to breathe, he made his way towards it, expecting anything. He reached it, and pointed to where the handle had once been. It had been blown apart.

"Gunshot," he whispered. He raised his finger to his lips, indicating silence. Rachel nodded. Stairs, going down. At the bottom, another door. Hanging open. More gun blasts.

He made his way down, through the open door, and emerged onto a small landing. He was looking down into a basement. The place was illuminated by harsh white strip lights.

Rachel stood at his shoulder. He heard her sharp intake of breath.

No fucking wonder, he thought. The scene below was like something from a horror show.

93

Their footsteps echoed on the metal steps as they descended. They reached the bottom, and stared. The scene before them could not be articulated.

This was the basement. There were no windows. In the centre of the room was a long table. On it, lined neatly, were various items. Black was reminded of the precision of an operating table. Whips, of differing size and colour. A mace, complete with short chain and spiked ball. Knotted rope. Nylon cord attached to weights. Leather masks. Knives, ranging from a thin stiletto blade to a broad hunting knife. Handcuffs. Other stuff designed to render pain. The knives glistened red.

A metal frame had been constructed against one wall. On each corner were manacles – iron rings, to which were attached heavy linked chains, which in turn were attached to manacles on the wrists and ankles of a young woman.

She was dead. Black had seen death in many forms, and saw it now. She hung limp, her head lolling forward on her collarbone. Her long blonde hair fell over her breasts. Beneath her spread legs, a large blue plastic bucket had been placed. To collect the blood and innards. She had been gutted. The perpetrator had not been idle. The walls were decorated in her blood. More specifically, two words. Written in block capitals. Over and over.

ADAM BLACK

"Jesus Christ," muttered Rachel.

"He wasn't about when this happened."

Still holding the Glock, he approached the dead woman, facing her. With one hand, he lifted back her head. Her face was drained white, her skin almost translucent. Her eyes had rolled round, two pearl orbs. Carved on her forehead was the number 8. Carved on her chest, above her breasts, were more numbers.

"What the hell does this mean?" said Rachel.

"I think our friendly serial killer wants a chat."

94

Chief Constable Divers wasn't picking up, and what had started as anger, was changing to concern.

"He said he was unwell," said Chiltern. He and Vanessa Shaw were in the canteen, sipping coffee. It was officially closed, given it was 11pm, but it was a change of scenery from the incident room. Chiltern had forgotten when he'd last slept, he needed a shave, and undoubtedly a change of shirt. But he was still buzzing. There was too much happening to feel tired. He studied DI Vanessa Shaw, and wondered if he looked that exhausted. Like him, she'd been working round the clock. Fatigue etched the bones on her face, her eyes were dark, sunken.

"What the hell are we supposed to do?" she said quietly. "I'm all out of answers."

They'd discovered the identity of the man in the photograph within ten minutes of arriving back at Pitt Street. One of the team had recognised him. A high-powered civil servant working in Whitehall no less, who reputedly had the ear of the PM. The photograph had been scanned and emailed to London, a response was emailed back. A name. Ernest Stanford.

"We should be able to pick Stanford up," said Chiltern. "A guy like that can't become invisible."

She tutted, shrugged. "I'm not even sure he had anything to do with it. Maybe someone wanted us to think that. Maybe we're wrong about Adam Black. Maybe the whole thing is one big fucking incomprehensible riddle. And we're lost somewhere in the middle of this shitstorm."

Chiltern couldn't help twitching his mouth into a half-smile. Lately, his boss had resorted to swearing with alarming regularity. She was human after all.

"Maybe you need some kip."

She arched one eyebrow at him.

"And what's the punchline?"

"Just a suggestion."

"We all need to sleep. But it won't help. So I guess we need to press on."

"You can't have doubts about Adam Black," said Chiltern. "Look at the stuff found in his flat. And he confessed!"

"You ever heard of a glut of evidence? Too much, too obvious? And he did confess – but he was trapped in a hospital. A ruse?"

A silence fell. Each sipped their coffee.

"We need to get a hold of the Chief. He needs to be here, and not... wherever the hell he is."

"We can go round to his house," suggested Chiltern. "Make sure everything's okay?"

Shaw's phone buzzed suddenly. She picked it up, listened.

She snapped her attention back to Chiltern, getting up from her chair. "Good idea. We go right now. A member of the public's just phoned in. Possible intruders. Guess whose house."

"You must be kidding."

"You couldn't make this fucking up, I swear."

95

The drive to Loch Laggan would, under normal circumstances, have been a leisurely one. Two and a half hours, taking in the view. But Divers was driving at night, and he was hitting the accelerator hard. He had really no idea why he was going there. Sanctuary. Flight. He needed to think, regroup. Few people knew about his lodge – his *boathouse*, as he liked to describe it.

Sitting back forty yards from the lochside, shrouded by tall trees, and on a good day, a view from his porch of the blue-grey water as flat as glass, and beyond, the Cairngorm mountain range sawing the skyline. But he wasn't going up for the scenery. He needed to think, clear his head. And plan. Plan how the fuck to get out of the mess he'd found himself in. A dread thought niggled the back of his mind, one he tried to shut down, but wouldn't go away. Like an itch. Perhaps there was no way out. Perhaps he was well and truly fucked. A wave of fear surfed up into his mind, which he pressed back. If he were sent to prison...

His mobile phone was on the passenger seat next to him. It was buzzing continually. For a brief moment, he felt like lowering the window and tossing it into the darkness. Fuck it.

Fuck them all. He drove north, driving over ninety miles an hour, then slowed. Ironic if the Chief Constable got caught speeding. With blood on his hands, on his shirt, on his steering wheel.

But a far greater fear was that someone knew. His terrible secret was no secret at all. His wife? He'd rip her guts out. Maybe she talked? It didn't matter.

Someone knew. He was being taunted. Played like a fool.

A terrified fool.

Chief Constable Divers drove through the night, a haunted man, the realisation dawning on him that perhaps there was no way out. That this was the end. That his sins had at last caught up.

96

"We need to go," said Black. "Now."

"We leave her here? Like this? Shouldn't we at least call the police?"

"You're forgetting. This is the police. This is the house of the Chief Constable. My name is all over his walls, written in this young woman's blood. The police are the last people I would trust. I imagine they've already had a call, and are on their way here as we speak. So I really think we need to get the hell out."

Rachel turned to him, stony-faced, expressionless. "What are we dealing with, Adam? This is..." she waved her hand at the scenario around her, "unreal."

"It's as real as it gets," said Black brusquely. "You can stay, or you can come with me now, and see this to its end. But I'm leaving in two seconds. And to answer your question – we're dealing with killers. Killers who have a real taste for it. This is the world you're in, Rachel."

"Let's finish it." She stared up at him suddenly, her eyes wide with fear. "If we can."

"Believe me." He held her stare, his voice low, firm. "We will fucking finish this."

They left the basement, and the house, glad to be gone. Rachel drove.

"Take it easy," said Black. "Sedate. Let's not arouse suspicion."

"Where are we going?"

"Anywhere. We need to find a quiet place. I have a phone call to make."

She drove in silence. She was perhaps in a mild state of shock, thought Black. He had seen death, in all its many shapes and guises, over many years. Even he was rattled.

They drove for several miles. It was approaching midnight. They were on a quiet country road. No street lamps. The darkness was complete, save details springing up from the glare of the headlights.

"There." Black pointed to a narrow side road. "Up there, and pull over."

She pulled onto a grass verge.

"The number on the girl's chest – you think it was a telephone number?"

"There's only one way to find out," Black said. "May I?"

She handed him her mobile phone.

Black took a deep breath, opened the keypad, his thumb tapping numbers engraved on a dead girl's skin. He put it on loudspeaker.

The mobile on the other end rang once, twice, three times. Someone picked up. No sound, except heavy, rasping breathing.

Then a voice. Loud, harsh, metallic. Blood-curdling. Disguised through a modulator.

"Adam Black."

"Yes."

"I got your attention."

"You don't have to murder people to get that. You have my undivided attention, at all times. Who was the girl?"

"You'll need to ask Chief Constable Divers for that information. The situation's delicate. For him."

"And the Prime Minister's daughter?"

"She's for later. You've been a busy boy, Adam Black."

"I like to keep myself occupied. Though not as busy as you. We should meet up. Where are you now?"

"Divers is the person you need to talk to. He has some explaining to do. And an apology to give."

"To me or to you?"

"To both."

"Where is Divers?"

"I'm going to text you a postcode. It's his secret little place. The Chief Constable's bad at keeping his secrets. And he has lots. He's heading there now. You can go and meet him. He'll be overjoyed at seeing you. A reunion."

"Maybe I don't like being told what to do. Let's you and I meet. Divers can keep for another day."

The voice became strident. "You go to Divers now! You're in no position to argue. This isn't a debate. I'll kill the girl, and then it falls on you."

Black remained silent.

"Good boy. You run to Divers, like a fucking bitch dog. I'm playing you Black, and you know it. Played you from the beginning. You'll dance to my tune. Wherever, whenever. If you don't like it, then I'll peel the girl's face off, and feed it to her. She won't look nice and pretty then, and Mummy will be so displeased!"

Still, Black said nothing.

"Better run, little rabbit," continued the voice. "Tick-tock."

Black spoke. "I might. I might not. You do what you have to do to the girl. She's not my problem. But now I'm yours. I will not stop. And I'll hunt you down. If it takes the rest of my life. You will never know when, or where. Because I'm your worst fucking nightmare. I can become invisible. Off radar. We'll dance all right, you sick fuck. But to my tune. And when the tune ends, I break your fucking neck."

Black hung up. He sat back, released a long breath.

Rachel looked at him, ashen-faced. "What have you done?"

"Nothing. Whoever that was, knows I have no choice. They want me to go to Divers, so there must be a reason. So I'll dance to their tune. For now."

"You went to Divers' house because you thought he might be involved. Care to share? The information could save my life."

"But it might sign your death warrant too. I'll tell you when it's safe. Killing for these people isn't enough. They want their victims to suffer. The less you know the better."

She looked away; her shoulders trembled. She was crying. Black waited.

"That young woman," she whispered. "I've never seen anything like that before. I'm finding this difficult, Adam."

He touched her face, gently. He had kept a lid on his emotions for a long time. Since the murder of his wife and child four years earlier. Locked in, and bound tight. The type of work he was asked to do, and which he craved, got people killed. It was a brutal industry. Already, too many innocents were dead. Also, in Black's line of work, trust led to death.

"You've seen too much already," he said. "You should leave. I can drop you off anywhere you want."

She turned to look at him. "I think you're forgetting something," she said, and through her tears, he glimpsed a ghost of a smile.

"Which is?"

"This is my car."

"I don't really want to get the bus."

"Which means we're in this together."

The mobile buzzed into life. As promised, a text message. A postcode. Then – *love you, Adam.* Then five smiley faces.

Black nodded. "The dance begins."

97

By the time Shaw and Chiltern arrived at the Chief Constable's house, teamed up with eight uniformed police, Black and Rachel Hempworth were ten miles away, heading north.

They confronted the same grisly scene. Forensics were immediately called, and more police were commandeered. A murder in the Chief Constable's basement. A woman no older than nineteen. Tortured, disembowelled. Sensational. On a breathtaking scale.

They searched the house, the grounds. Temporary floodlights were rigged, and suddenly the gardens were bright with light. Dogs were brought. Police combed the extensive gardens, the street outside, the woods beyond, neighbours' gardens. Difficult, in the darkness of late evening. But this was the Chief Constable's house, and the Chief Constable was missing.

Chiltern and Shaw sat in her Ford Mondeo, parked on the driveway with a group of other vehicles, watching people filter in and out. An ambulance had arrived, lights pulsing.

Paramedics disappeared inside. A little later, they re-emerged into the chill air, carrying a stretcher, and on it, a body bag.

"What was she doing here?" asked Chiltern, a rhetorical question, as he watched them transfer her body carefully into the back of the ambulance. It was too late for miracles. The girl was dead. Most of her blood had been used to paint the Chief's walls.

"Ask Divers," replied Shaw, her voice a monotone. "You saw his fucking basement. Not exactly used in the traditional sense. I didn't see many cardboard boxes full of family albums."

"Black's name," said Chiltern. "Written in blood. If he had anything to do with this, then he left a hell of a calling card."

"Kill someone, then write your name a hundred times beside the victim. Somebody hates Black enough to do this. The Chief Constable? Someone's been gunning for Black from the beginning. Ernest Stanford? Why haven't we found him. Why do people keep fucking disappearing!"

Chiltern could offer no sensible response.

"Black confessed to those murders," he muttered. "He still has to be our number one."

"The facts point in that direction. What if.... What if they were all involved? There was a fallout. Squabbling psychopaths. They have the Prime Minister's daughter imprisoned. Maybe taken by sheer fluke. They panic. Argue. Blame. Incriminate. Fuck each other up."

Chiltern ran his hands through his hair. "Christ. The Chief?" It made sense. "And the girl in the basement?"

Shaw took a deep breath. "God knows. Another victim? Doesn't fit the picture."

"Is there a picture?"

Shaw gave a sardonic smile. "Blurred. Incomprehensible. Abstract."

"Meaningless, you mean."

"That's kind of dead accurate."

"What about the numbers?"

They had studied the body, slumped forward, suspended by iron chains. Photographs were taken. Wearing forensic gloves, and with great care, DI Shaw had tilted her head back. The number 8 was carved into her forehead. Other numbers on her chest. Three in all. There may have been more. Someone had made an effort to obliterate them. Pieces of flesh had been scooped out. Possibly by the tip of a knife.

"My guess," said Shaw, "is that something was carved into her skin. An address or phone number maybe. And then it was removed. In a hurry. Gouged out."

"Why?"

Shaw shrugged. "Who knows. Perhaps the whole point of that young girl's death was to convey a message." She turned to look at Chiltern face on. In the glare of the floodlights and the lights from within the house, her face was gaunt, haggard. Her eyes were sunk deep above sharp cheekbones.

"Maybe the message was delivered. And once delivered, the sick fucker came back."

"Came back?"

She gave a brittle laugh. "Like the delete button. To erase. Only this guy didn't press a button. He used a knife."

"Could be," said Chiltern, blowing air through his lips. "I don't get any of this."

"Well get this," she snapped. "We now have the biggest manhunt in Scottish history. We need three men. The Chief Constable, Ernest Stanford. And the most dangerous man we may ever encounter."

Chiltern finished the sentence for her. "Adam Black."

98

Divers got to his lodge in record time. He'd tried to keep his speed down, but fight or flight instinct kicked in, and without realising it, his foot had been hard on the gas pedal for most of the way.

He parked in a tree-lined driveway next to the building, invisible from the road which hugged one side of the loch. The place looked empty. Unoccupied, closed up. He peered through the window of his car. Nothing seemed untoward. He kept his headlights on, to provide some illumination. It looked innocent enough. The heavy wooden storm doors were undisturbed. The rest of the house was a blot of shadow, nestled amongst other shadows. It was 1.30am. The night was still and silent.

He killed the engine, the lights extinguishing automatically. He waited, straining to hear the slightest sound. Nothing. He reached over to the glove compartment, and retrieved a large key. He got out, nerves tingling. He made his way to the main doors, used the key, opened up. The key for the interior door was a normal Yale which he kept on his key ring. There was no alarm to switch off. Here, such a thing was not required. He switched the hall light on. Everything seemed normal. It looked like it always did. It smelled like it always did. He reached to the side, to an antique umbrella stand, and pulled out a heavy club-handled walking stick. He padded through the hall, to the living room, switching lights on, then off. He went from room to room, upstairs to the bedrooms, floor creaking with his weight, knuckles clenched white around one end of the stick. The house was empty.

He got back to his living room. A large window with wide patio doors overlooked a wooden decking set on short columns, and beyond was Loch Laggan. It was too dark to see anything. It was like looking at a canvas of black paint. Even the stars were blanked, covered in cloud. He drew the curtains shut, switched off the main light, switched on a table lamp, poured himself a tall glass of neat whisky from a cocktail cabinet designed in the shape of a globe of the world, gulped half of it down, and placed the glass beside the lamp. He so needed that.

Still grasping the walking stick, he went to a mahogany cupboard on a wall, which he opened. In it was an array of shotguns, resting horizontally on brass mountings. He pulled the top one out. A pump action Winchester. Twelve gauge. Double-barrelled. At close range, powerful enough to punch a hole clean through a man's chest. He opened a drawer underneath and took out a box of ammunition. He fed the rounds in, one by one.

He returned to the side table, and the whisky. He topped the glass up, then sat on an armchair by the window. He rested the Winchester on his lap, and let the booze sink in.

He didn't know what his next move was. He needed time. But time was a luxury he didn't have. He had a strong feeling his fellow police officers were already at the scene, picking over what was left of the dead girl, drawing conclusions. He allowed himself a cold smile. The irony was, this time he was innocent. But it wouldn't look like that. Then questions. A million questions. Divers felt the rising panic bubble up from his stomach, filling his lungs. He took another deep slug.

Number 8. All because of number 8.

For a brief second, he thought of adjusting his body position, and resting the barrel of the gun under his chin. Then a twitch of his index finger. The metal projectile would blow off the top half of his head. So easy. Just a second, and it was over.

He swallowed. He tasted the whisky in his mouth. Images reared up in his mind. Blood and guts. Young women, pale and lifeless. He took a long stuttering breath. If he died, he would not be missed. He couldn't do it. To take his own life would require a bravery he did not believe he possessed. He would have to resort to what he was good at – lying, conniving, manipulating. He was an expert in crawling out of bad situations, and wasn't ashamed to admit it.

He took another drink. Time was not on his side. Blame it on someone else. Blame it on Adam Black. Crucify the bastard.

Tick-tock.

99

"Don't you sleep?" asked Rachel. Black had wanted to drive immediately to the location given. On the satnav, it was north, somewhere in between Spean Bridge and Kingussie. A distance of about a hundred and thirty miles. The Scottish Highlands.

"I don't seem to get the chance," said Black.

"I understand that. Busy day at the office. Riot in the prison, trip to hospital, escape from armed guards and a hundred cops, encountering a murdered woman in a torture chamber, chatting to a psychopath. Now on his way to only God knows what. Presumably a normal day in the life of Adam Black."

He gave a wintry grin. "Quieter than normal. I should think about a hobby. Liven it up a little."

"God, I would love to interview you. I could write a column every week on your exploits, and a year later, people would still want to read more. Maybe I could write a book."

"We'd split the royalties, of course."

"I could call it *The Adam Black Enigma*."

"An enigma? There's nothing mysterious about me, I promise."

"You are the most mysterious man I've ever met."

"You ought to get out more."

They were on the A82, ten miles from the village of Tarbet, the great darkness of Loch Lomond on their right shoulder. At this time, the road was dead.

"Do you miss them?" she asked suddenly.

Black sighed. She wondered if she'd pushed it too far.

"You've been doing your homework," he said, without any resentment. Resignation, rather.

She gave a short, humourless laugh. "A by-product of being a journalist. What do you expect?"

"I think about them every day," he said at length. For the first time since they'd met, he sounded weary. "One minute, I was waving them off. By the end of the day, they were both dead. My wife and daughter. Gone, before I had a chance to say goodbye."

"They were murdered," said Rachel.

"Shot. By an assassin. Paid for by a Glasgow criminal. And it was all my fault."

Rachel was skirting on thin ice but she had to keep going. She couldn't help herself, her voice tentative. "Why do you say that?" She wasn't sure he would respond. But he did.

"Because I killed his son. I crossed people who shouldn't have been crossed. And my family paid with their lives. So I guess if you're going to shout at anyone, you shout at me."

She didn't reply immediately, concentrating on the landscape ahead of her, a wall of darkness, lit briefly by the glare of her headlights.

"What happened to those men?" she asked, her voice small, tight. She really wasn't sure she wanted to hear the answer. Yet deep down, she did.

Black spoke, his voice faraway, as if reliving those moments long ago. "I killed the Glasgow gangster. I took my revenge on him. I killed him on the shores of Loch Morlich. I saw to it that he died a painful death." He looked side-long at her. She could feel his stare. "Does that worry you?"

"I don't know," was all she could think of saying. "And the other one? The assassin?"

"I got to him eventually. I found him in France. He knew I was following him, and tried to flee. I stabbed him through the heart in a back alley in Paris, and left him in the gutter to rot."

She concentrated on the road ahead, eyes fixed in front of her.

"I'm a bad man, Rachel. This is who you're helping. I'm no different from the men who destroyed my family."

She didn't reply immediately, as she composed her response. Then she spoke. "You're wrong. There's a difference."

"Which is?"

"You kill the right people."

He gave a soft chuckle. "Not from their perspective."

"They don't count," she said.

"They might disagree."

A silence followed. Outside, shadows and darkness slipped by. It was too dark for landmarks or scenery. She glanced at the satnav. Sixty miles to their destination. She let time drift. Eventually she spoke. "I don't think you're a bad man, Adam. I don't know what to think. I don't even know what I'm doing here."

"You're getting a great story," he said wryly. "Tell me about you, Rachel. You're a journalist. Which newspaper?

"The *Evening Standard*. Chief crime reporter."

"Chief?"

"That's a title I bestowed upon myself. Self-aggrandisement. The real chief is a man called Billy Cosgrove, who keeps me on because I think he still believes in lost causes."

"Are you a lost cause?"

"I'm a perfect example. I was married for six years. It ended badly. I'm still seeping through the wreckage. But then I saw that young woman in Divers' basement. What she must have gone through. Suddenly my problems seem miniscule."

"Nothing's miniscule, if it's in your mind, and it stays there fixed like a lead anchor. The trick is to let it go. When you've learned how to do that, let me know. We all have our demons."

"Do you have demons, Adam?"

She was met by silence. She looked round. Black's head was pressed against the passenger window, his eyes closed. He began to snore, softly.

She allowed herself a small weary smile, and wondered what the night would bring.

100

The Princess Hotel was five-star: sauna, steam room, indoor pool. Heated. Three bars on the ground floor, and a discreet piano bar on the upper level. Ernest Stanford couldn't really have asked for more. He had taken a train back to Edinburgh, after meeting Divers. His mind, however, was not on the luxury offered. He'd taken dinner in the oyster bar, but hardly tasted the food. He'd restricted his alcohol over dinner to a single glass of house red. Stanford was used to the high life, as a high-ranking civil servant from the inner echelons of Whitehall, at the expense of the tax payer and as such, he abused it to the max. And why not, he thought. He worked like a fucking dog.

But tonight – this night – was different. His mind was on other matters. One matter, in fact. The Prime Minister's daughter was missing, which was the justification for staying in Edinburgh, to liaise, analyse, report. But the abduction was not what he was thinking about.

He sat by a real fire, set under a copper flue in the centre of the piano bar. In one corner, a young man played soft melodies on a baby grand. The place was decked out in varnished wood, giving it an intimate feel. People sat on couches and deep seats, reading, conversing in low tones, or simply sipping their drinks, exactly as Stanford was doing. But he took no cognisance of his surroundings. A woman, maybe forty-five, was sitting solitary. She watched him from the corner of her eye. She was attractive, elegant. Stanford smiled at her, an automatic response. She smiled back. He was on auto-pilot. There would be no fucking tonight.

He had a glass of whisky in his hand, which he sipped. He had a flight to catch the following day. He wanted a clear head. The text message had awoken old memories. Some bad, some good. Summer days, running in the sun, through fields, woods, playing hide and seek, stupid games under a blue Scottish sky. Winter brought different memories. Shivering in a cold house; the freezing sea; dark bleak nights. Sometimes going to bed hungry. Poverty.

Memories of his mother, struggling day in, day out. Memories of his brother. Much younger. Small, quiet. A wisp of blond hair, pale oval face. Remote. Distant. Like the island they inhabited.

There was no real relationship between the two. A twelve-year gap. They grew up, but not together. When Stanford left all those years ago, he didn't look back. Any feelings he had for his family vanished. It was like a tap being turned off. One minute they were there, next, they were gone. His visits had grown less frequent. He hadn't seen his mother for over five years. And on that occasion, his mother barely spoke, wrapped in her own bleak thoughts.

But his brother. He hadn't seen him in maybe fifteen years. Maybe more. Hadn't really given him any thought until this night. He didn't know where he was, what he was doing. Neither had reached out.

Like a tap being turned off. His brother had disappeared from his life, and Stanford really couldn't give a damn.

101

They arrived. Their destination reached. It was 2.22am. Black had woken from his brief slumber.

Rachel parked by the side of the road, on a grassy embankment. Outside was gloom and shadows.

"There," said Black, pointing. About twenty yards further up the road, illuminated by the car headlights, was the entrance to a narrow driveway. Easily missed in the dark.

"Kill the lights."

Suddenly, the dark was total, enveloping them.

"What now?" asked Rachel.

He turned to her, her face a ghostly pale shadow.

"I really don't have a clue," he said. "Dance to the tune, I suppose."

"Which means?"

"I pay the Chief Constable a visit. I suspect I'm not the first person on his guest list. You want to stay here? I have no idea how this will pan out. But it might not end well."

"Let's find out," she said.

They got out of the car. To Black, a stillness had settled in the air, the trees, the waters of the adjacent loch. As if the world were holding its breath, just for this moment. He was bone weary. Rachel's sarcasm earlier had a ring of truth. It had been one fucking hell of a day. And it wasn't over.

Adrenalin kicked in. He made his way to the driveway, senses sharpened to a heightened competence. He had the Glock in his hand, a considerable measure of comfort. He had no idea what to expect.

They reached the entrance of the driveway, marked by two broad stone pillars with swept pier caps, and crept down a slight incline, towards the house, hugging the deep shadow. A Jaguar was parked a dozen yards from the front door. They sidled closer, Black first. The outer doors had been opened. The inner door was frosted glass. Through it, he detected a sliver of light, from somewhere at the back. Someone was in. The Chief Constable? Possibly. They had some catching up to do.

Gently, he turned the handle. The door was unlocked. They went in. Slowly, slowly, they crept along a corridor, towards a room at the end, from which emanated the soft glow of light. Black held the Glock before him, ready. He reached the room. He sensed Rachel's presence close behind him. He wished she'd stayed in the car. He should have insisted. Too late now.

The door was half open. He slipped through. He was in a living room. Despite the fire crackling, the room was chilly. Patio doors were opened to a decking, beyond which was solid darkness. Suddenly Black felt exposed. If someone were outside, then Black was an easy target. He took two strides, to the light from a table lamp, and switched it off. The darkness was complete.

He felt the touch of a hand. Rachel had reached out. He nodded, aware she wouldn't be able to see him. He moved carefully to the open patio doors, towards the cool breeze coming up from the loch, sensitive for the slightest sound, the tremor of movement.

They got out to the decking. Black felt the hammer of his heart. *This is no good.* He had been ordered to come, and the person ordering knew he would, because he had no choice. They were like ducks in a barrel. Easy pickings. Fine, he thought. Bring it on.

"This is no fucking good!" he said aloud.

"Not fucking good at all," echoed a voice. They whirled round. Suddenly they were bathed in light.

Divers stood at the patio doors, his monstrous bulk filling the space, pointing a rifle at them. The merest quiver of his finger, and Black's head would be blown into the loch behind him. He wouldn't be able to pull the Glock up fast enough. If he did, Divers would shoot him dead on, right there and then. And after that, Rachel.

"Of all the people," said Divers. "Adam Black. The villain of the piece. You don't know how good it is to see you, Mr Black."

"Why is that?"

"Because I've been praying for a miracle. And here you fucking are."

102

"Drop the fucking cannon."

Black did as he was told, letting the Glock fall onto the wooden timbers.

"Good boy." Divers gestured with his rifle. "Now both of you inside."

Divers backed away into the room. Rachel followed Black in, back through the patio doors.

"Hands up!"

They raised their hands. They stood, next to each other, in the centre of the living room. For the first time during her mad voyage with Adam Black, Rachel felt scared. She felt, at this precise moment, there was a real chance her life might end. She couldn't keep the tremble from her hands, nor her bottom lip from quivering. She took a deep ragged breath, swallowing down her impulse to sob. As if he sensed her distress, Black took hold of her hand, squeezed it gently.

"Touching." Divers was in one corner, rifle trained on them. From this distance, he could be the worst shot in the world, and he'd still hit something. He swayed slightly. His speech was edged with the faintest slur. "You were the very last person I was expecting to see. Last time we met, you were chained to a hospital bed with a half dozen armed police around you. Are you a fucking magician, Black?"

"You really should keep up, Chief Constable," replied Black, his voice cool, unfazed. Rachel marvelled at his composure. "You should talk to your fellow police officers instead of butchering young girls in your chamber of horrors. I escaped. And I went to your house."

Divers nodded. His jowls quivered. Rachel thought of a slobbery bulldog. He regarded Black with slit eyes. "You saw her."

"I did," said Black.

"*We* did," she heard herself say.

His eyes darted from Black, to her. "You're the journalist. You should have kept your snout out of this one. You start sniffing round a man like Adam Black, you end up dead."

"What's going on, Divers?" asked Black.

Divers, still focused on Black, reached for a whisky glass on a side table next to him, took a swig, replaced the glass. Then he turned his attention to Rachel. "Your boyfriend's a serial killer." Divers then focused back on Black. "Was it you? Did you kill the girl?"

Black said nothing.

"Did he tell you we found some of his trophies in his bedroom?" said Divers. "Fingers of his victims. Kept hidden in a box. Did he tell you that?"

"But not the finger of victim number 8," said Black quietly.

Christ, thought Rachel, *how can he keep such a cool fucking head?*

"No," replied Divers, his voice detached, a monotone, as if he were thinking back, his mind revisiting. "Not number 8."

"What happened, Divers?" Black took a half step forward. Rachel stood, rooted, frozen. Time was caught. She was staring down the barrel of a gun, and in the next second, her life could be finished. Her breath felt locked in her lungs.

Divers licked his lips. "I didn't kill the girl in the basement. I came straight from the hospital, after our little... chat. I had her chained there, all fucking afternoon." His eyes glittered from beneath heavy lids. "She was well paid. She knew what to expect. £3,000 for the day. She was hired out. It's what I like, Black. A bit of pain. A bit of slapping about. Some screaming. The screaming soon turns to moans of fucking pleasure, let me tell you." Divers regarded Rachel. She watched him in horror. With one hand still on the trigger of the rifle, he was using his other hand to rub the front of his trousers.

"Some pain," said Black. "You pay prostitutes for something a little more extreme."

"Pain is good," said Divers. "Pain cuts through all the shit. It breaks them down. And sometimes they need breaking down. Pain lets them know who's boss."

"But you got back, to your basement, and the girl was dead."

"With your fucking name scrawled across the walls!" snarled Divers. "You taunting me, Black? Is that what it was? For leaving you to rot in prison?"

"How could I have anything to do with it," responded Black, his voice calm, logical. "You said it yourself. I was chained to a hospital bed, surrounded by armed police."

"But you escaped! You could have..."

"Think, Divers. It wasn't me. And you know it. Rachel and I went to your house because I had a suspicion. A hunch. We confronted the same scene you did. The girl was dead. Somebody knows, Divers. About number 8. About your secret."

Divers reached down again for the whisky, finished it off, let the glass drop to the floor. "Only one person knows," he muttered. "My ex-wife. And she would never talk."

Again, his eyes seemed to focus inwards, as he gazed into his memories.

Now, thought Rachel. *While he's distracted. Black has the skill. Now, he could maybe wrestle the gun out the man's hand.*

But Black didn't move. And Rachel understood why. He wanted an answer.

"Tell us what your ex-wife knows, Divers. Tell us your secret. You've been living with it for so long. Maybe time to unburden."

Divers took a deep ragged breath. "I went too far, that night. Two years ago. A girl. No older than nineteen. A student at Glasgow University. Making a little extra. On the side. As a hostess. A prostitute. She could earn more in two days than her entire student loan for the year. She told me that. We were in my... play area, in the basement. She was laughing at me. Taunting me. Ridiculing me. The fucking red mist came down. I beat her, harder and harder, until she stopped fucking laughing. I wiped the fucking smile from the tart's face."

My God, she thought. *He's stroking himself.*

"She stopped laughing. But I'd gone too far. The bitch was dead." He glared at Black. "What could I do? I had no choice."

"Tell us what you did," said Black, barely above a whisper.

"Seven young women were already dead. The Red Serpent had been busy. His trademark was distinct." He took another deep breath. His eyes were glistening. Not with the light. With tears.

"I cut her up. The way he did it. Cut out her fucking tongue. Cut her fingers off. Did all the other stuff. Did it like he did it."

"And you carved a mark on her face."

Divers nodded. "The circle."

"And then you dumped her."

"Got rid of the parts, burnt them, buried the bones. Left her body in a factory skip. Another Red Serpent victim."

"And your wife?"

Black had inched further forward. Tears were streaming down Divers cheeks.

"She found me, in the basement with the body. She said she would talk, unless…"

"Unless you divorced and paid her off."

"Fucking bitch. Only she knows. I'll hunt her down and rip her fucking heart out!"

"She has nothing to do with this, Divers. The person who does, knows about what you did, and planted body parts in my flat. The same person who took the PM's daughter. Remember – this whole thing is about rescuing her. Let's not lose focus on this, Divers."

Divers straightened, held the rifle tight. "It has fuck all to do with her. This is about you and me. More specifically, how you're going to help me."

Rachel sensed Black tensing. *Any second now*, she thought.

"This is how it's going to play, Black. You escaped, murdered the girl in the basement, then came here to murder me. Both of you, in it together. You're a madman, Black. A killer on a rampage. So the cops know about my little playthings, my fetish. Big deal. But that doesn't make me a killer, Black. You're the psycho. You're both intruders. I'm perfectly entitled to protect myself. So thank you, Adam Black."

"You've forgotten one thing, Divers."

"What?"

"Somebody out there still knows about you. What you did. Killing us won't erase that fact. You'll be looking over your shoulder the rest of your life. No way you can live like that, Divers. And I know who that person is."

Divers stared at Black. The only sound was his heavy breathing. Black was as still as the frozen air outside. Rachel held her breath.

"Tell me," rasped Divers.

"Put the gun down."

Divers blinked away more tears.

"You really going to kill us, Divers?" Black took another step forward. He pointed at Rachel. "You going to kill her! Is that really your plan?"

"Get... back..." he stammered. But Black was close. He could reach out, touch Divers.

"Do you know what happens to cops in prison?" said Divers suddenly. "I can't go there."

"Give me the gun."

"It's over. It's finished. Goodbye, Black."

He flipped the gun up, placing the barrel in his mouth, and fired. Rachel screamed. The back of his skull burst open, blood and chunks of bone and brain stippling the wallpaper behind him. The massive bulk of Chief Constable Divers collapsed to the floor.

Rachel staggered back. Black stooped, picked up the rifle and tossed it to the other side of the room.

Divers lay, half his head a wet tangle of ruptured flesh. Black stared at him, then turned to Rachel, his face expressionless.

"I didn't see that happening." He gave her a crooked grin. "You saved my life."

B lack covered up Divers' dead body with a blanket from one of the upstairs bedrooms. Blood had saturated the carpet, but there was little Black could do about that, nor the fact that the wall was spattered with remnants of Divers' skull. Black had found winter fleeces in wardrobes. It was below zero outside, but neither Black nor Rachel had any desire to be inside with a corpse. And it was way too late and too remote to leave the house. They put the fleeces on – miles too big for them – and sat on chairs on the decking outside. Also, Black wrapped a travelling rug round Rachel's shoulders. It was 3am. Black had brought the remnants of the whisky bottle outside with him, and they both sat, silent as ghosts, watching the gloom, sipping neat whisky.

Surreal, thought Black. Drinking whisky ten yards from a dead man with a rifle slug in his brain. But it was needed. Rachel was in shock. She'd never witnessed anything like this before. Intense violence, close up. Few had. Shock took many forms. Some reacted in complete silence, unable to articulate. Others sobbed and cried, or prattled incoherently. Or acted irrationally. Black had witnessed its manifestations on many occasions, during conflict, after the rage of battle had dissipated, and a man had time to dwell on the situation.

They sat, unspeaking. The clouds had drifted; slivers of pale moonlight glimmered on the black waters of the loch, reflecting back a rippling silver hue. Far away, came a lonesome call. Maybe a fox, maybe a bird. Black did not know, and he was too tired to care.

Rachel sat, looking out into the darkness, a glass cradled in her hands.

"Are you warm enough?" ventured Black.

"What did you mean?" she replied, her voice soft in the night.

Black frowned, but didn't reply, allowing her time to expand. "You said I had saved your life. What did you mean?"

"If you hadn't been with me," he said gently, "then Divers would have shot me. You made him remember."

"Remember?"

"His humanity."

"There's no humanity in this," she said, her voice leaden. "It's just a trail of death. How do you keep going?"

Black responded with a mirthless laugh. "I ask myself that every day. Death has become... commonplace. I was in the army for over twenty years. In the Special Forces. There, if you let your environment affect you, then it's a spiral downwards. I guess we were trained to bury our emotions, somewhere deep. And once buried, move on, until you've forgotten where they're buried."

"You can only move on for so long. And then you stop. And then it all comes crashing down."

"Maybe. But I'll deal with that when it happens."

"I've seen more this day than I have the whole of my life."

"I know. And it can stop right now. You can end this, anytime you want."

"And you?"

"I have unfinished business. There's a young woman out there who needs me to rescue her. It's as simple as that. I can never give up."

Neither spoke, the sounds of the Scottish wilderness filling the gap.

"What was your hunch?" she asked suddenly. "What made you think Divers was involved."

Black let the whisky sit on his tongue before he answered, the taste filling his mouth.

"Victim number 8 was beaten. Her face was marked. Someone had worked her over pretty good. That was not the Red Serpent's style. He wanted their faces perfect, in the final moments. None of the others had so much as a blemish. I knew Divers liked sexual violence. It was a long shot. It was more luck than detection."

Rachel didn't respond immediately. From somewhere close on the loch, the water splashed gently. "How can you be so matter-of-fact by all this?" she said.

Black had no answer to give.

"My marriage," she continued. "It ended after six years. I discovered the bastard had another family, living in Newcastle. Two kids. He travelled back and forth, splitting his time. I promised I'd never trust anyone again."

Black said nothing.

"But I think I trust you. I've never met anyone quite like you."

"Time for you to go home," he said quietly. "You've been through enough already."

She looked at him, her eyes brimming with tears. "I don't have a home to go to, except an empty flat and an empty life. I don't want to be anywhere else. And when that time comes, when you do eventually stop, and if the world should come crashing down, I want to be there too."

Her mobile phone buzzed. A text message. She fished it from her coat pocket, and handed it to Black.

Black took it, swiped his finger across the glass screen, and tapped the message button.

Did you win?

Black responded. Yes. What now?

Several seconds later, a text came through –

The Last Chapter. It's time, Mr Black. Catch the 5pm ferry.
She's waiting for you.
Tick-tock

He was given a set of letters and numbers.

"What is it?" asked Rachel.

"More instructions," replied Black. "Another postcode."

"What are you going to do?"

He gave her a weary smile.

"The only thing I can. I dance to the tune. I have a feeling."

She raised an eyebrow. "What feeling?"

"We're reaching the end."

104

She may have been incarcerated in her prison for a week, or a year. Elspeth Owen had no idea. Either the single strip light on the ceiling light was on, or it was off. There was no daylight. No stars or moon. She had lost track of everything. She was confused. Sometimes, she thought she was dreaming, when she knew she was awake. Sometimes, her dreams were so vivid, she thought they were real.

The constant fear had abated. Now she felt nothing, hollow. Like her soul had been ripped from her body, and only a void remained. Perhaps it was the drugs – she knew her food and drink were laced with something – but whatever it was, it dulled the senses, and as such, it dulled the dread.

She woke from sleep. The light was on. Her head throbbed. The backs of her eyes ached. As usual, someone had taken care to change her into new clothing. Before, it had been red dresses. Different styles, different material, always expensive. This time it was different. She recognised her new clothing. But it wasn't new at all. Blue faded jeans, scuffed training shoes. Also, a thick blue woolly pullover.

She sat up slowly. She felt woozy. She took a deep breath. She experienced a wave of nausea which she swallowed back.

A sound made her jump. Latches being drawn back. She stared at the door only three paces in front of her. The door opened.

She stood. She was no longer manacled. Before her, in the doorway, was a woman. She was maybe seventy-five, maybe older. Dressed in a black, shapeless fleece, dark trousers, a pair of flat brown walking shoes. Her face was weather-beaten and wrinkled, her grey hair cropped short, in no particular style. Her eyes. Elspeth looked into her eyes. Pale blue, ancient, and tired.

The woman took a step back.

"You go up the stairs, into the hall, out the front door. You head round to the back of the house you'll find the woods. There's a path there. You can see it, if you look hard enough. You follow the path for a mile, and you run, girl, until you come to the village. It's called Craighouse. You get there, and you go to the post office. And if it's closed, you go to the pub. And if it's closed, you beat every door you see, until you get someone. And you call the police."

Elspeth took seconds to digest this information.

"You're free. Go."

Elspeth could barely comprehend what she was hearing, and wondered if this was another dream. Or a trap. "Free?" she croaked.

The old woman suddenly opened her eyes wide. "Run!"

Elspeth staggered to the door. She was looking into a cellar, with dust shrouded wooden crates, a boiler, shelves, ancient cupboards, an old Christmas tree. Clutter. Stairs on the opposite side. She took one step in front of the other. Her head pounded; she felt a drum was banging in her brain. She reached them, climbed the steps, each creaking under her weight, one hand grasping a single bannister. She got to a door at the top. She turned the handle. For a fleeting moment, she thought perhaps it would be locked, that the whole thing was a sick game, that it was part of the torture, and the old woman would turn into a witch and screech her head off with laughter. But the door opened. Just as the woman described, she reached a corridor. At the end, the front door. Unlocked.

Daylight! She half-hobbled, half-ran, emerged into a garden of red chip stones, and patches of weeds, enclosed by a low dry-stone wall, and a little gate. Beyond, a flat stretch of long grass and clumps of gorse, stopping at a cliff's edge. And beyond that, the endless reach of the sea, disappearing into a horizon obscured by rolling clouds.

She stopped, and let the scene immerse her senses. She breathed the sharp salty air, felt the cold breeze on her skin, her hair.

Head round the house. Through the woods.

She did as instructed. There was a narrow walkway of the same red stones round the side. She made her way, one hand on the wall of the house, steadying herself. An area of grass. Woods a little further away. To her left, a single lane road. Her heart leapt. She made her way to the trees. They were thick, set close together. She couldn't see a path. The road was better. She would stop a car. She stumbled along, her senses gradually sharpening, the fresh air clearing the fuzziness.

Two hundred yards. She tripped. The road was pot-holed and cracked. She scrambled to her feet. She made her way forward, stepping carefully.

A vehicle approached. A van.

"Help me!" she cried, raising one desperate arm. "Help me!"

She ran forward, but she was weak, her legs shaky. She sank to her knees, gasping. Suddenly she was exhausted. But she was free. And now she had found help.

"Help me," she croaked. She looked up. The van stopped. Someone got out, to stand before her.

Elspeth smiled. Her chest filled with relief, euphoria.

"I can't believe it's you," she mumbled. "Thank God. Help me. Call the police."

The figure remained motionless, then said, "You've been a naughty girl."

Elspeth frowned, tried to get to her feet, confused. The fear returned. "I... I don't understand."

The figure loomed forward, struck her across the face, knocking her back to the ground.

Her vision blurred.

Then her world turned black.

105

I n Edinburgh, the day started with a sharp chill. Frost lay on the cobbled roads of 'Old Town' like a thin veneer of sugar coating. The place was quiet. It would get busier later in the day, but at this time, most people were in bed. Stanford had slept poorly. His dreams were fragments, broken images. Faces, voices, places. A jumble of memories, keeping him awake, and even in the dull morning light, echoes still lingered in his mind. He hadn't visited his mother for such a long time. Now, suddenly, she needed him.

He gazed out of his hotel window, at the grey-black landscape of tiled roofs and stone buildings, and beyond, looming down, the brooding presence of Edinburgh Castle, all walls and turrets and black shiny cannons. He shivered, and not from the cold. Dread. Something was wrong.

Stanford was fit. He worked at it, every day. He felt lousy, but he had a morning routine, ingrained into a habit. If he were at his London home, he'd go out for an early morning jog. He didn't know the streets of Edinburgh, so opted for the treadmill. Breakfast started at 7am. He got changed, took the elevator to the basement of the hotel, to the indoor pool and gym, and ran

5k in just under twenty-six minutes. He had a swim, then twenty minutes in the sauna. He went back to his room, and got changed and ready for breakfast. It was 7.15.

He ate sparingly. Muesli, juice, some toast and scrambled eggs, hot filter coffee. He went back to his room, answered some emails, reviewed papers. Whitehall was still red hot. The story hadn't lost any of its appeal as the days wore on. The abduction of the PM's daughter was still front-page news. He tried to contact Divers a couple of times, but his mobile was switched off. He phoned Pitt Street Police Station, but no one could help him. Strange, he thought. But he moved on to other things. He bought a variety of newspapers, and read them downstairs in the subtle luxury of the hotel lounge, sipping Darjeeling tea. He took a short walk along Princes Street in the cold, killing time. He bought himself mountain boots, thermal trousers, and a waterproof ski jacket from an outdoor retailer. He got back at 11am, packed, and got a taxi to Glasgow Airport. He checked in, made his way to a coffee shop.

The flight left Glasgow Airport at 2pm. The only option was economy class on an Airbus. Stanford wasn't perturbed. He'd only need to ruck it with the plebs for forty-five minutes. Then he'd get the ferry across to Jura, and then the bus. Maybe slightly longer than forty-five minutes, he thought ruefully, all things considered.

His flight was called. He boarded. The journey was smooth and quick. The plane carried about forty passengers. It was a quarter full.

He landed at Islay Airport, in the centre of the island. He disembarked. It was 3pm, and already the sky was darkening. It was bitter cold. He felt the beginnings of sleety rain. He pulled his hood over his head. The terminal looked more like a squat warehouse, and beside it, the control tower. There was little else. He and his fellow passengers scurried the hundred yards to the terminal, checked in, and Stanford picked up a card for the local taxi company. A sixteen-mile journey to Port Askaig. Thirty minutes, in light traffic. The traffic was always light on Islay.

The drive to the ferry brought back hazy memories to Stanford. Rolling green hills, lush even in the dead of winter, derelict stone crofts, and to the east, the highest peak – Beinn Bheigier. He suddenly remembered he had climbed it once with his father, when he was a young boy. He passed two distilleries, and a village called Ballygrant. Places, features, all conjuring up memories.

He arrived at Port Askaig. It was here he would catch the ferry across a narrow stretch of water, to Feolin, a ten-minute boat ride across choppy waters. He looked across at the island, his birth place. The skies were brooding, the clouds low and heavy. But the three mountains known worldwide as the Paps of Jura were visible. Conical, stark, dominating the landscape. Stanford looked at them, and experienced another rush of childhood memories.

He boarded the ferry, the only passenger on it, reached the port at Feolin. A single-deck bus was waiting. He got in, paid three pounds, and took a window seat. The vehicle rumbled into life, heading off south, skirting the coast round the foot of the island, and then north to Craighouse, the capital. A fifteen-minute journey. The view from the window was of the sea and boggy marsh. Clouds were rolling in. The sleet grew heavier.

One night, thought Stanford. Then he would get the hell out.

The bus arrived at the only stop, in the centre of a village with just under a hundred and twenty inhabitants. A cluster of white stone buildings with high peaked grey slate roofs, huddled about the only hotel. As soon as he stepped out, his body was whipped by a blast of cold wind. He stood, hunched against it, clutching his holdall. It was suddenly dark. Darkness always fell swiftly, he remembered. The place was deserted.

He had a choice. He could walk a single-track road, skirting a long four-mile route around woods, taking him to his mother's house. Or he could cut directly through the woods, cutting the journey to a mile.

He knew where to go. A path veered off from the main road, hugging the rocky shoreline, then meandered up through mossy trees forming a canopy under the winter sky. Stanford, by sheer instinct, picked out the path. Old memories, ingrained in the mind. He trampled under frozen sticks and branches, but he knew the way. The old house was on the other side of the wood, perched on a cliff's edge.

He made his way. The ground was hard underfoot. Easy to twist an ankle. He kept to the path. The going was slow, but his sense of direction was sure. He had walked this way hundreds of times as a boy.

After twenty-five minutes, he saw lights glinting through the tangle of trees and shadow. The house. He headed towards it. The wood stopped, and he reached an acre of grass, on a slight incline. The back garden. The house stood before him. A squat mass of stone, wreathed in the windy darkness. The kitchen light was on, but netted curtains prevented him from seeing inside. He got to the back door. He took a deep breath. His stomach fluttered. He was a seasoned and skilled advisor to the government, had the ear of prime ministers. Yet now, at his mother's back door, he felt nervous. Worse – he felt dread. Inexplicably.

He knocked on the door. He sensed movement inside. He glimpsed a figure behind the kitchen curtains.

He waited. Bolts slid open, top and bottom. A key turned. The door opened.

Stanford stared at the figure in the doorway, slack-jawed. He couldn't comprehend what he was seeing. He found his voice. "What the hell are you doing here?"

"Waiting for you."

A sudden sound, like a cough, a muffled punch. He felt an instant mind-numbing pain in his chest, as if his ribs had been crushed, his lungs squeezed. He looked down. A ragged hole had appeared in his new ski jacket from which blood pulsed and pumped.

His mind seemed to drift – this was his own blood, he realised. Pouring out of him.

He fell back, sinking into oblivion.

106

B lack and Rachel spent the night in the lochside lodge of the late Chief Constable Divers. They left his body where it lay, sprawled on the living-room carpet, his huge bulk hidden under a blanket hastily thrown over.

Rachel had fallen into a deep sleep where she sat on the decking. Another symptom of shock. Black carried her to one of the bedrooms upstairs, lay her on the bed, switched off the light, and left her. He went back down to the living room, poured another whisky, and sat back outside, alone, in the dark.

He had never required much sleep. During patrols, especially deep in Afghanistan, he learned to live on small kips. And when he slept, it wasn't real sleep. One finger on the trigger, or clasped round the hilt of a knife. The subconscious always alert for the slither of movement, the rustle of cloth, the click of a gun.

Black stared into the darkness. The loch was only yards away, a silent shape of oily darkness. He imagined Divers waddling his way down to the lochside with his pals, fishing rod in one hand, a six-pack of beer in the other. Now the guy was dead. Then he imagined Divers torturing women in his basement, and was glad the guy was dead.

Divers was connected, after all. He'd murdered a girl, and disposed of the body in plain sight. Pretty smart, thought Black, using the Red Serpent as his cover.

But somehow, the Red Serpent, or those working with him, had found out. First, they had pinned blame on Black himself, and then sent him to confront Divers. Black considered. They wanted him to meet Divers, because they anticipated a fight. A duel. And Black had won. Now they wanted to kill him. Of that he had no doubt.

They.

Black still believed, as had the Colonel, that there were three. The Red Serpent – Pritchard – was one of a trio. Divers was connected, but only as a peripheral.

He swirled the whisky, sipped it, finished it off.

He'd been given a postcode and a time. He had no choice but to follow the instruction. Elspeth Owen could still be alive. And while that hope remained, he would dance the fucker's tune.

The postcode was a house in the Isle of Jura. They'd checked it on Rachel's mobile. He was told to collect the ferry at 5pm from the mainland to the island of Islay, and then he'd need to take a second ferry from Islay to Jura. He knew little about either island. They were remote, Jura particularly.

A good place for a gunfight, he thought grimly.

He rested the Glock on his lap. If the girl was dead, then those responsible would have to brace themselves for a fury they would not be prepared for. They had introduced him into their world. And one thing Adam Black was good at, was destroying people's worlds.

It was a three-hour drive from Loch Laggan to the port at Kennacraig, where the ferry departed from mainland Scotland to Islay. And then a further two-hour journey across the rough waters known as the Sound of Jura. Rachel woke up at midday, and they left soon after. They had no desire to linger. They stopped at a small café in Bridge of Spean, and bought coffee and bacon rolls. Black was starving. They ate in silence. A television was positioned on a top corner, showing daytime viewing. The volume was muted. Rachel suddenly froze.

"Fucking hell," she whispered.

Black looked round, to the television. A news bulletin. A photograph of a face. His face. And a name under it – Adam Black.

Black finished his coffee. "Fame at last," he said. "Time to go."

They left, Rachel driving.

"You need to get away from me," said Black. "If you can drop me off at the ferry terminal, then that's more than enough. Then you go, and live your life. You can still do that. The longer you remain with me, the more danger you're in. I'm a fugitive. There's going to be a lot of cops out there with itchy trigger fingers. If you stick around, then you'll end up collateral damage."

He turned to look at her. She stared fixedly ahead.

"I'm not asking."

"I can't leave you," she said. "Not now. Not after... everything."

"If you stay with me, then everything becomes nothing. Plus, you can write about it."

"What do you mean?"

"I mean, I might need someone to tell my side of the story. Right now, I have few friends. Those who knew about the plan for me to get into Shotts prison are dying off. The Colonel, Divers. You could help me. But you need to stay alive."

"And so do you," she replied.

"I plan on doing that."

They arrived at Kennacraig at 3.30pm, and parked a short walk from the port building.

"I wonder why you had to get the ferry at this specific time." Rachel was staring out the windscreen at the huddle of white buildings perched only yards from the sea.

"So they can prepare. Set the scene."

"Theatrical."

"You could say."

"And you're happy just to walk into this... trap."

"It's only a trap if the victim is unaware. I have Doctor Glock on my side. He usually cures a bad situation. And I'm not averse to killing bad bastards."

"I will be waiting, Adam Black. You've promised me an interview. I have a good story to write. And the only way it works is if the hero lives to tell it."

Black smiled. "The hero never dies. Don't you watch the movies?"

He got out the car. He had relieved Divers of a woollen mountain hat from a drawer in his bedroom, which Black pulled over his head, covering his ears. Also, the money in Divers wallet. One hundred and fifty pounds. You didn't need money in hell, reckoned Black, and that was where Divers surely was.

Black hunched up against the bitter cold wind from the sea, and made his way to the terminal. He glanced back. Rachel had gone.

For the first time in years, he felt maybe he had something to live for.

~

The ferry left for Islay at 5pm, exactly on time. The last one scheduled to leave. It was a long two hours. Black bought a coffee, and sat at a seat in the passenger lounge by a window, trying to be as unobtrusive as possible. He'd bought a book at a small on-board shop, and assumed the pretence of reading, to avoid eye contact. He was acutely aware he was the most sought-after man in Scotland, if not the United Kingdom. The ferry wasn't busy, but all it would take is one suspicious person, and a phone call.

Time dragged. His nerves tingled. He had no idea what he was walking into. Mayhem, destruction, death. The typical ingredients of the Adam Black experience. The edges of his mouth curled up into a sardonic smile. He wouldn't have it any other way.

He sat, and did nothing. He could hear the drone of a television in another part of the room, and heard his name being mentioned. He glanced around. The people there didn't seem to care, wrapped in their own thoughts, conversing quietly, reading, napping. He gazed at the sea outside, a particularly treacherous strait full of whirlpools and strong, icy currents – the Sound of Jura. He saw nothing, save his own reflection on the glass. It was the heart of winter. Here, with low scudding clouds above, covering the moon and stars, the darkness outside was complete.

The ferry docked at Port Askaig just after 7pm. Black disembarked with the other passengers, keeping his hat pulled tight round his ears. Rain whipped around him, a freezing pelt swept in from the sea. Black waited in a rather austere cafeteria in the terminal building. The restaurant section was closed. He bought a coffee from a machine. The last ferry to Jura was at

8pm. He had no choice but to wait. From where he sat, looking out across the narrow strip of water separating the two islands, Jura was a silhouette, an outline, with some lights denoting the opposite port, and then beyond, a blot of shadow.

He had been texted a postcode. They had logged in the details on Rachel's mobile, and got a satellite image. It was a solitary house just north of Craighouse, on the east coast of the island, set apart from the village by trees, probably a wood, approachable by a single road. Black committed the location to memory.

A figure loomed before him. Black looked up. A man stood at his table. He was holding a plastic coffee cup like the one Black had, staring intently at him. Black tensed. Was this it? Was this the start?

"Disgusting," said the man.

He was about forty, well built, wearing a thick pullover, dark jeans. Sandy-coloured hair, cropped to a half inch. Broad, weathered face. In one hand was the plastic cup, over the other arm was folded a waterproof.

Black put on a smile. "I've tasted worse."

The man returned the smile, showing yellowy white teeth. "The whisky's much better than the coffee. You're not a local."

Black shook his head. Was the small talk a ruse, or was it real? The Glock was in his coat pocket, its bulk providing some reassurance. "I'm not local. Here on business."

The man sat opposite, seemingly uncaring that he had not been invited. He raised his eyebrows. "Business? At this time? On Jura?"

Black had no choice but to engage in conversation. "It is what it is," he replied, keeping his answer as bland as possible.

"I work on Islay," said the man. "I live on Jura. I get the last ferry across, same time every night. Have you visited here before?"

"No," replied Black, tersely.

"There's not much to see."

"I'm not here for the views."

The man regarded Black quizzically. "Haven't I seen you somewhere before?"

It was the moment Black had dreaded. "I don't think we've met."

"But you look familiar."

"I have one of those faces."

"Where have I seen you?" continued the man, to himself.

A buzz sounded, then a robotic voice crackled over an intercom, announcing passengers should board the ferry.

Black stood. "Nice meeting you." He left the building. He glanced behind him. The man was following slowly. He was talking into his mobile phone, staring at Black. He raised his mobile, pointing it in Black's general direction.

Black boarded the ferry, heart thumping.

Time was running out.

Tick-tock.

107

The manpower now available to DI Shaw had escalated since the escape of Adam Black. One hundred and fifty police and civilian staff were manning phones, dealing with Black and Elspeth Owen, occupying two entire floors of HQ. Also, to compound the general hysteria which had invaded the atmosphere, the Chief Constable was missing, and a dead woman had been found in his basement.

The whole thing, when added together, was a shitstorm of confusion, thought Chiltern.

"But Black's the key," Vanessa Shaw had pronounced, as they had made their weary way back to Pitt Street in the early morning following the discovery of the young woman. "We find Black, and we find the answer to this whole fucking mess."

Chiltern was exhausted. He needed to get some shut-eye. As did Shaw. They both agreed to head back to their respective homes, and reconvene the next evening.

They did, the following afternoon. Recent pictures of Adam Black had been issued to all major television channels, the press. A photograph of Black was showing in every home up and down the country, every pub and club, every waiting room in every airport, doctor's surgery, hospital ward.

In every ferry terminal.

Plus, a hotline to phone. But the caveat was clear. Don't approach him. The man was a danger to the public.

A young police officer got the call. He took details, said he'd phone back. It was 7.50pm. He caught Chiltern's attention, waving him over, putting the caller on hold.

"A guy on the phone," said the officer. "Says he was talking to the man on the television. Adam Black. He says he's getting on the same ferry. Swears blind its him. Sounds credible."

"Ferry?" mouthed Chiltern. He took the call. "You say you've seen Adam Black?"

"Seen him, up close to him, spoke to him. I swear it's him. And the story he gave me. Cock and bull about going over on a business trip. No chance. It didn't add up."

"Where is it he's going, exactly?"

"He's taking the ferry to Jura. I am literally twenty yards behind him. It's your man. No doubt."

What the hell was Black doing in Jura? Chiltern was sceptical. For him to deploy officers to such a place was a big gamble. The type of thing to embarrass, and scupper promotion prospects.

"I can send you a photograph," continued the man.

"A photograph?"

"Sure. What's your email? I can send it now."

Chiltern gave it to him. He kept him on the line. A minute later, the email arrived on his laptop. He opened it. "Fucking hell," he muttered.

He took the man's details, his location, thanked him for the information.

"Is there a reward?"

Chiltern paused. "There's no reward for this information. But I can give you some advice."

"Yes?"

"Take the next ferry."

Chiltern hung up. He rushed through to the adjacent room, where Shaw was discussing things with other senior officers.

"We've found him!"

He led them back through to the main incident room, and showed them a photograph of a man, walking away from the camera, his head turned back, the profile of a face.

"It's our boy," said Shaw, in a hushed voice. "Careless."

"It was taken at a ferry terminal. The ferry to Jura."

The other officers were silent. They all turned to Detective Inspector Shaw. With the Chief Constable absent, she was in charge.

She nodded slowly, as if debating, then coming to a conclusion.

"If this is correct, and we have to assume it is, then he's trapping himself. He can't get off the island. Not easily. How quickly can we get there?"

Chiltern stammered. "I have no idea. I mean... we would need to drive, and then get a ferry, and then..."

Shaw interrupted him.

"Is there a police presence on Jura?"

"Not on Jura," said someone in the room – a civilian staff member – tapping keyboards on his laptop. "Islay is the closest. Bowmore Police Station. We could contact them now."

"Do it," said Shaw. "We've got the fucker."

"Why the hell would he go to Jura?" said Chiltern.

"Why does a man like Adam Black do anything? He's on the run. He's scared. And he's gone to Jura for a reason."

Chiltern raised his eyebrows, incredulous. "You really believe Adam Black's scared?"

"I don't know anything, except he's the key." She gave him a wild, almost savage look. "He confessed, remember? He's a killer.

356

And right now, he's the closest thing we've got to finding Elspeth Owen. We get him, we get her."

"There's four available men," said the man on the laptop. "They can be at the Islay ferry in twenty minutes."

"Good. Tell them to get there and wait. They don't approach him."

She snapped her head back to Chiltern.

"How long to Jura?"

Chiltern blew out his cheeks, shaking his head.

Shaw answered her own question. "That's what I thought. We take the helicopters."

108

The man did not follow Black on to the ferry. He hung back. Black watched him from a window, as the boat rumbled into life and slowly drew away from port. The man lingered at the side of the boarding ramp. It reinforced his suspicions. The man had alerted the police, and they in turn had alerted him. *Stay away. Adam Black is a dangerous man.*

Black focused on ahead, not what lay behind. He sat on a hard-plastic seat, along with the other passengers. There were only a handful on board. Black felt exposed, vulnerable. Thankfully, there was no television. But everyone possessed a mobile phone. With a tap of a button, his face would flash up. He counted down the seconds, nerves peeled and raw.

The ferry docked on the island of Jura fifteen minutes later. The metal gate rumbled down, resting on the stone ramp with a metallic clang. Only one car drove off. The passengers filtered out. A bus was waiting. People filed on. Black hung back, then got on last. He paid the driver, and sat near the front. The doors closed. The ferry rumbled back across the water. The driver took a call on his mobile. Black couldn't make out the conversation, but detected his voice rising higher in surprise. He switched off the engine. He shouted round to the passengers sitting in the rows of seats behind him.

"Sorry, folks. Slight delay. We need to stay here a short while. Not long."

The announcement was met with low grumblings. Black gritted his teeth. Across the narrow expanse of water, he spied the unmistakable flicker of a blue light. A police car, parked at the Islay Port. Waiting for the ferry to arrive back.

Black got to his feet, and approached the driver's cockpit. He put on an easy, affable smile. "Would you have a number for a taxi?"

The driver looked up at him. "He's not working tonight." He laughed. "He'll be in the pub, no doubt getting smashed. It's about the only pastime in Jura."

"That's inconvenient," replied Black, endeavouring to keep his voice neutral. "Which way to Craighouse?"

The driver laughed again, a wheezy rumble coming deep from his lungs. "You thinking of walking?" He pointed along the only road, running past the terminal. "It's thataway. Eight miles." He glanced at his watch. "Head off now, and you might make closing time." He looked down at Black's shoes. "And you've got your running shoes on."

Black looked over his shoulder at the distant lights, the dark shadow of the ferry slipping across the narrow strip of sea, drawing closer to the opposite side.

"I don't think I'll need my running shoes."

Turning, so his back was to the passengers, he pulled out the pistol tucked in the inside of his jacket.

"This is a Glock 17," he said in a quiet voice. "Semi-automatic. Extremely powerful. I want you to get off the bus, but leave the keys in the ignition. If you don't, then I'll kill you."

The driver stared up at him, wide-eyed. The laughter had vanished. "I don't want any trouble," he whispered.

"Nor do I. So fuck off."

The driver opened the half door between the seat and the aisle, and clambered out, where he scurried away, into the night.

Black turned to the passengers. Three men, three women. They had been chatting. Locals, surmised Black. Probably returning from a shift in Islay. He raised the pistol above his head. "I have a gun. I don't want any trouble, but I need you all off the bus. Now."

They looked at him, uncomprehending. Black knew what they were thinking. *This can't be happening. This isn't real. This type of thing only happens in movies, a million miles from the Isle of Jura.*

One of the men stood. Large, wide-shouldered, square-jawed. The type of man who didn't take shit from anyone.

"You have to be fucking kidding!" he shouted.

Black fired a round into the ceiling. The noise reverberated like cannon fire, puncturing a hole in the metal. "Do I look as if I'm kidding?"

For added effect, he fired at a window. It exploded in a shower of glass, fragments bursting out into the night. Sudden cold air whipped in. "Now fucking move it!" he roared.

Black backed into the driver's area. They filed past him and out the bus, one at a time, not daring to make eye contact, Black training the Glock on them as they slid silently by. Black pressed a button. The doors folded closed. He took up position on the driver's seat, turned the ignition. The engine started into life.

He drove off. He looked at his side mirror, to the small group of forlorn and bewildered passengers. Already, they were on their mobiles, relaying the unbelievable incident they'd witnessed to friends, family, police.

Black didn't have time to dwell on their discomfort. The

police knew he was here. More – many more – would be arriving soon.

Black couldn't allow himself to be captured. Not now.

He needed a distraction.

He needed carnage.

109

There were no lights. The road was winding and narrow. To his right, a rugged coastline, beyond which, the black expanse of the sea. To his left, nothing. A bare landscape of darkness. The going was frustratingly slow. The last time he'd driven a vehicle this size was over ten years earlier, in the army. All the while, the seconds turned to minutes, and every minute which passed brought the reality of capture closer. And if he were caught, then any chance of saving the girl was gone.

If indeed any chance had ever existed.

The rain was heavy, driving in from the sea. The bus rocked in the force of a lashing wind. The windscreen wipers were on full blast, but the view ahead was blurred, the headlights allowing only several yards of vision. Black slowed right down, crawling along at a snail's pace.

Thirty minutes passed – there! Ahead, through the rain and darkness, he glimpsed dots of light. The road dipped. The lights disappeared. The bus climbed up a long incline. The lights reappeared, closer now, maybe a quarter of a mile distant. He saw other lights. High up in the sky. Black recognised them immediately, from his tours in Afghanistan. Helicopter zone lights. Green, yellow, blue, signifying a landing manoeuvre. Two sets. Two helicopters. It made sense. It was the only way to get to Jura quickly. There would be no helipad to land on. Given Adam Black was the most wanted man in Britain, they would land anywhere they could – in a field, in a car park, in the middle of the fucking road. Every few seconds, Black's eyes darted to the rear-view mirrors, expecting flashing blue lights. He reckoned the ferry would have crossed back again, carrying at least one police van in its belly, maybe more.

Cops above, cops behind.

He drew closer to Craighouse. He was on the final stretch, a straight road of three hundred yards before he reached the first street light. He made out buildings, houses, a main road. Perhaps the only road. On his left, coming up, a petrol station. Two pumps illuminated by bright canopy lighting, a small kiosk, which looked closed. The rain suddenly eased a little.

Black pulled the steering wheel sharp left. The bus swerved, tyres skidding on the slick tarmac. He hit the petrol pumps full on, the impact battering them off their concrete mountings, the rear end of the bus tailing round in a quarter circle, smashing into the kiosk, crushing it like paper. He hit the brakes, killed the engine. The bus driver was a smoker, and had left cigarettes and a box of matches on the console. Black grabbed them and jumped out. The petrol station was obliterated. The front and side of the bus were crushed. A strong smell of petrol and diesel filled the air. Fuel gushed onto the forecourt. Black looked up into the night sky. The helicopters were close. He could hear the thump-thump of the rotor blades.

Black backed away from the bus, the flow of fuel pooling out towards him. Hunched against the rain, he struck a match, cupping it in his hands, waiting a second. He stepped back, tossed it. It flared instantly, catching on the gasoline vapour. A rope of fire sprang suddenly into life, spreading under the bus, surging towards the vacant spaces where the pumps stood, and into the tanks underneath. Black sprinted away, towards the village a hundred yards distant. The ensuing explosion almost knocked him off his feet. He glanced back. The bus was turned on its side, ablaze, a pall of heavy black smoke rolling up into the sky. Then, another explosion – the kiosk burst into fragments, wood, metal, glass spewing out through the air.

Already there was commotion. People opening doors, stepping onto the pavement, bewildered.

Black was running on the main road. He passed an elderly couple, squinting in the direction of the flames.

"Bad accident!" shouted Black, passing them. "Call an ambulance!"

He ran on, more people appearing onto the street. He passed terraced houses of white stone on either side. He looked up. One helicopter was honing in on the fire. The other was circling the village, probably searching for a flat landing site.

To his right, a pub, standing a little back from the road, a detached building. The glow of soft lights glimmered through bevelled windows. He entered. Age-blackened beams lined a flat wood ceiling, a real fire flickered in a grey cobbled hearth. Odd chairs around rough-hewn tables. On any other evening, Black might have enjoyed a quiet whisky here. But not tonight.

A bartender dressed in a tartan shirt and grey corduroys looked up as Black entered, eyebrows raised. Strangers were rare here at this time of the year. Other than him, and four other men sitting on high stools at the bar, the place was empty.

"The petrol station's on fire!" shouted Black. "The whole place is up in smoke!"

The men jerked round. "What?"

They clambered off their seats, and bustled past him. The bartender remained where he was, a crooked grin on his face. "I think you're having a laugh, friend."

Black had no time to waste. He pulled out the Glock.

"No laughs here." He fired at a huge mirror above the hearth. The pistol boomed. Fragments of glass showered the room; it fell crashing to the floor.

"Get the hell out of here!"

The bartender stared, slack-jawed. He lurched to the half door of the bar, jostled with the latch, ran out. Black strode to the bar, leapt over it, grabbed a bottle of vodka. He started splashing liquor over the seats, tables, everything he could see. He lit another match, held it to the edge of a hanging drape. It caught instantly, the flames leaping up, spreading to the ceiling. The wood was varnished. The flames spread like an orange wave.

Black ran out into the night. The men who had been sitting there had vanished. No doubt the bartender had warned them – *madman with a gun*. Which was all good.

Already, smoke was creeping out. Flames flickered behind the windows. Suddenly one burst open.

Black looked back down the main street, in the direction he'd come. In the distance, a column of fire and smoke. Another distant explosion. Probably the diesel tank of the bus, reacting at last. Closer, only a short distance away, the helicopter was landing, in the middle of the street. Big enough to carry eight passengers. People had backed away, watching a dreamlike drama unfolding. Doors opened. Armed police emerged.

Hell had come to Jura.

Black ran in the opposite direction. An explosion rattled the pub. Maybe the boiler. Half the roof blew off. Black melted into the shadows of the trees.

He had to be somewhere.

Someone was expecting him.

110

Everyone was jolted by the sudden huge burst of flame. And the sound which accompanied it. Like a bomb had gone off. Not that Chiltern had ever heard such a thing.

"What the fuck was that?" shouted one of the men.

Chiltern watched the flames lick up into the night, the thick plumes of smoke, mesmerised. DI Vanessa Shaw sat next to him, rigid, wide-eyed. With Divers missing, she was in charge. When the positive ID of Black was confirmed, within ten minutes she had requisitioned two Police Scotland helicopters. Chiltern had never been in a helicopter. Now here he was, hovering over a place he'd never been to, witnessing something he'd never seen.

The helicopters were EC145s. Airbuses. The journey from Glasgow had taken thirty-five minutes. To get the armed response unit mobilised took all of a millisecond. Everyone was gunning for Adam Black. It looked like Black was running out of options, Chiltern had assumed. Until he saw the explosion of fire beneath him, and wondered what the hell was going to happen next.

"It's Black," said Shaw in a flat voice. "He's creating a shitstorm. It's what he does." She instructed the pilot to radio the other helicopter to check it out. "We'll land in Craighouse. Park in the fucking street, if you have to."

The pilot nodded. They lowered slowly, Shaw using loudspeakers to warn people back. They piled out. Both she and Chiltern had been issued handguns – Glock 17s, he had learned. His training on weapons was negligible. Yet here he was, rushing out from a helicopter with a semi-automatic pistol.

A crowd of people circled them. Probably the entire population of the island, he suspected.

The ground shook. Another explosion, only yards away. A building was on fire, its roof torn off. People screamed, running in different directions. Bedlam. Panic. He turned to DI Shaw.

"What do we do?"

She gave him a frozen, startled look. She mouthed the words, *I don't fucking know*.

111

Black had an idea of his location, and his destination. He'd studied a satellite map of the area, back at Divers' house, courtesy of Rachel's mobile phone, and the miracle of the internet. There was a wood about a mile long, running from the north of the village, set in a long hollow. He could use the road, but it was much longer. Beyond the wood, a stone's throw from the sea, perched almost on the cliff edge, was the house.

What he was to confront there, he had no idea.

He entered the dark domain of the trees. Behind, not far, the fire had taken hold of the building. Farther away, the petrol station was blazing. The cops were more than a little preoccupied, he thought grimly. The light from the fire was soon lost, consumed by shadows. The screams and shouts died to a leaden silence. The wood was still, save the rustle of leaves at his passing. Easy to get lost. He stopped, the only noise the sound of his own breathing.

Something glimmered ahead. He crouched down, crept towards it, pistol out. A sound drummed in his head – his heartbeat. He reached the broad trunk of a tree. Someone had used red fluorescent paint. It glowed eerily. A single number.

1.

Another faint glow caught his attention, further off, deeper in. Black, nerves stretched, crept towards it.

Same red fluorescent paint, written on the bark of a tree.

2.

Ahead, the next number.

Black was being shown the path.

Carefully, he made his way through the trees. His eyes had adjusted to the darkness. Shadows stretched before him. He lost sense of time. At length, he came to the number he knew would be the last –

10.

Ten victims.

Ten dead women.

The wood had ended. Now, before him, the outline of a house.

Black had arrived.

112

H e was facing a garden, enclosed by a low dry-stone wall. It was sloping, featureless. No flowers grew here. Entry was through a metal gate, and then a path of broken paving, to a door. Black took a deep breath. This was it. Something – instinct, a gut feeling – told him it all ended here. The game was coming to a close. Beyond, he heard the unmistakable sound of waves crashing onto rocks below.

He opened the gate. Its hinges creaked. Black didn't care. Whoever waited inside knew he was coming. Black made his way up the path. There was a light on inside, coming from a ground floor window, hidden by old-fashioned net curtains. Also, a light above the door. A note had been nailed into the wood.

Adam Black
R.I.P.

Black tore it off, scrunched it up, tossed it to the ground. He turned the handle. The door opened. He went in.

He was in a kitchen. White cupboards. Linoleum tiles.

Shelves with pots, crockery, jars, other oddments. A cooker, fridge. A wooden table with two wooden chairs. Clean, simple. In a corner, a single candle was burning on a saucer. One wall was decorated with the same glow paint – an arrow, pointing to an open door, and the words – *keep going, Adam*. Light was coming from deeper within.

Black, his pistol held up to shoulder height, made his slow, careful way into a long hallway. Low ceiling, the walls dotted with pictures. Candles were placed along the floor, on either side. At the end of the hall, a closed door, and written on it a single word – *Enter*.

Black eased his way along, heart pounding. Black was not scared for himself. Fear was something he had mastered. He was, however, fearful of what he might find behind that door.

Black opened it, slowly, slowly.

And found hell.

113

A room with a stone hearth on one wall, a wood fire flickering and crackling beneath. Bare walls, faded carpet, an old chest of drawers, a little side table and on it, a seashell lamp. Candles on the mantlepiece, the floor, everywhere, creating an eerie, quivering glow.

Three chairs, positioned in the centre of the room, in a line, facing Black. The middle one was an armchair. The others on either side were similar to those in the kitchen. Sitting on one was a woman. Maybe eighty, maybe older. Her head lolled back, blank eyes staring at the ceiling, her throat slit. The cut was deep, the throat yawning wide open. The top of her head had been sliced away. She'd been effectively scalped. Her exposed brain glistened in the candlelight.

Sitting on the chair at the other end, was a man, stripped of his clothes. There was a mark in his chest, resembling a bullet entry. His face had been worked on, involving time and effort. His eyes had been plucked out. His nose had been removed; the lower jaw cut away, the skin peeled from the bone, revealing tissue and vein. Long wood nails had been hammered into his knees, his bare feet, his nipples, and into each ear. The pain would have been excruciating, death a welcome friend.

In the centre sat a woman, wearing a white blouse saturated in blood, head slumped forward, blonde hair trailing. Her hands rested on the arms of the chair. At first glance, she could have been sleeping. Black strode forward, lifted her head.

The face he saw was no face at all. The features were disfigured beyond recognition. Skin burnt and scarred; the circle of the serpent cut deep across the forehead.

Black took a step back, exhaled, composing himself.

She groaned.

Elspeth Owen was alive.

114

B lack tucked the Glock in his jacket pocket. Danger was close. Death was a whisper away. He had to get the girl out, and away to safety. He lifted her gently in his arms. She was tall, athletic. She groaned again.

"We're going to get you the hell out of here," he whispered, aware she wouldn't hear him. Maybe more to reassure himself.

He slipped out of the room, into the hall, the girl hanging limp. He would return the way he'd come. Every step created a miniscule creak of the floor, and with every creak, his heart jumped.

Suddenly, a noise – a voice. A woman's voice. Behind the door to his right. From below.

"Help me!"

Black stopped, uncertain. A trick? Perhaps.

Coughing. The voice got louder, finding strength. "Please, someone!"

Black laid the girl on the floor. "I'll be back." He took out the Glock. He opened the door. He met stone stairs, going down, and a trail of candles, one on each side of every step. He crept down, silent as a ghost. The ceiling going down was rough and rounded, as if a giant wormhole had been burrowed into the ground. Thirteen steps. He entered a cellar. Solid stone floor, stone walls. More candles on Gothic-style brackets. There was a solid metal door in the far wall, closed.

In the centre of the room was a chair. Tied tightly to it by rope was someone he recognised instantly, from all the photographs.

Elspeth Owen.

But it couldn't be.

"Please help me!"

Her face was pale, tear-streaked, terrified. But untouched. Black raced to her, tucked the Glock in his jacket pocket, started to untie the rope. A noise. A casual sound, someone clearing their throat.

Black straightened. He turned slowly. He looked at the person standing at the foot of the stairs, pointing a pistol in a two-handed grip directly at his chest – the female he had carried to salvation only seconds ago, her face a ruin of scars and burns.

"Here we are," said Black.

"Here we are," she replied.

"I don't believe we've met," said Black.

"I don't believe we have."

With one hand still holding the pistol, she brought her other hand to her face, peeled the skin off. It was surreal to watch. Like a thin mask of leather, it all came away. Underneath, another face, unblemished, slightly tanned, clear-skinned, shining blue eyes, smiling a radiant smile. She dropped the rag of skin to the ground. She pulled off a blonde wig, revealing short dark hair, and tossed it away.

She placed her hand back on to the pistol, resuming a steady two-handed grip.

"Interesting disguise," said Black. "Novel approach, using a dead man's face. Theatrical."

"Just a little fun upstairs. A distraction, you understand. I had to set a scene dramatic enough for you not to pay too much attention."

"My congratulations. You had me fooled. Aren't you going to introduce yourself? My name is Adam Black."

"I know who you are, Mr Black. I've known about you for a long time."

Black nodded. "I hadn't realised I was so popular. And you are?"

"My name is Katie Sykes. And we brought you here to die."

115

Elspeth Owen gazed up at Katie Sykes with dull, dark-ringed eyes. "I know you," she croaked.

Sykes took a step forward, still training the gun on Black.

"Of course you do," she replied, softly.

"At a party. You were there. In London." Elspeth began to sob. "Why are you doing this?"

Black used the moment to inch closer to Sykes.

"Don't you fucking move!" she roared suddenly.

Black remained still, raising his hands slowly in the air. "Calm it down, Katie. But the lady asked a question."

"Christ, you're a cool customer. Exactly as you'd been described."

Black did not respond. He needed time, a strategy. Right now, the situation appeared bleak. But then, he had faced bleak situations before, and somehow had always won his way through.

Maybe not this time. "Divers is dead," he said suddenly, hoping for a reaction. "The other member of your little trinity. He was the third. Now he's dead. I killed him. Is that what you wanted?"

"Don't be a fool, Black. The man was disgusting. He used us. He took a woman we wanted. We had our focus on her long before he invited her into his chamber of horrors."

"Jesus Christ," muttered Black. Now he knew. "He killed her before you had the chance. You were watching her. That's how you knew it was him. A sheer coincidence."

"And he used us. She was body number 8. But we never touched her. So we made him pay. Compliments of Adam Black. We had a tracker on his car. We sent you after him, to his bolthole in Loch Laggan, in the hope you'd kill him. Thanks for that. But that fat monster was never part of us."

"Us?"

"I'll tell you a story, Black, because you deserve to know. And when I've finished, you'll understand. Understand you were fucked from the very beginning. That you were a puppet, dancing to our tune. And what a fucking tune it was."

Black waited. This woman liked the sound of her own voice. Garrulous. Which is what Black needed. Time.

"We've been killing for many years. It started long ago. We met at Glasgow University. We were students. We were young. The three of us. Oliver Pritchard worked in the library. In the computers. He had access to their records. Where they lived, where they came from, their life. For Oliver Pritchard, it was love. Love for me. And for the glory, of course. But Oliver loved me, beyond anything. He knew I would never love him back, but he didn't care. He completed the finishing touches. Became quite adept at it. We captured them, and had our fun. Then he finished them. But with style. He cut them up, dismembered them, carved his little sign on their poor dead flesh. It was a passion, for him. They were the canvas, he was the artist, creating his masterpiece. He was honoured to be a part of it all. He would languish a thousand years in hell, and never betray me. Us. When he was caught, he was easy. He took it, took everything. He wanted to be the Red Serpent. So we gave him that. We gave him the glory."

"But you didn't," said Black. "Not really. Because you started again. When he was in prison." He gestured to Elspeth. "You resurrected the whole thing. With her."

"Isn't she beautiful? The Prime Minister's child. I met her at a party. She wore a simple red dress. Her hair smelled of peaches. She was to be our last. Our grand finale. But who knows?"

"Why did you kill them?"

"Why? You ask me why? How can I answer that? We met them. They were all beautiful. We took turns, you see?"

"I don't see."

"I suppose it came down to luck. Or bad luck. For them. We offered our bodies, our love. Don't you think my body is beautiful?"

"Undoubtedly. But please continue. I'm all ears."

"Sure you are. Playing for time. I would too, if I were in your position. We met those young girls. Different places. Bars, parties, clubs, anywhere. They were all beautiful. We took turns. When it was mine, then I would ask them the question."

"Question?"

"If they desired me. If they wanted me, as much as I wanted them. If they were willing to be one with me. Complete. Like the serpent, swallowing its tail. Some said yes. Others said no."

"A real lottery," said Black. "And let me guess – those who said no, ended up here, as your guest."

She shrugged. "They deserved their punishment."

"Of course they did."

"Of the two of us," she said with pride, "I was always more successful."

"Except you weren't. Elspeth Owen rejected your advances."

"And so she met the Serpent."

"In the Isle of Jura? You have a peculiar choice of venue."

"Luck, indeed," she said. "We were here, on a holiday, touring round Scotland. We stumbled across this place. The old woman you saw upstairs lived here. I remember it like yesterday. We came out of the wood on a summer's afternoon, expecting a view of the sea from the clifftops. Instead, we saw her sticking a knife through the heart of her son. We saw everything. The colour of his blood is a vivid memory. When she was confronted with that knowledge, and what we could do with it, how it would ruin her and her family, she was putty in our hands. We used her house. Modified it a little. Specifically here, the basement, the room behind you. Where we kept our guests for a while."

"You blackmailed her. Now she's dead."

"Her use had expired."

"And the man without a face?"

"Her other son. You'll remember him. He was one of the few people who knew about your little Shotts prison plan. The late Ernest Stanford. We sent him a text. The fool thought it was his mother." Sykes suddenly assumed a high-pitched whine. *"I need you here, now. I love you."*

"And why would you want to kill him, I wonder?"

"Aren't you pleased? He and Divers conspired to betray you. Leave you in prison. You should thank me. But in the end, he served his purpose. We lured him up here, to be with you, Adam. When the police come – and they most surely will – they'll find you, the fugitive Adam Black. The man with the fingers of dead girls in his flat, the man who confessed. And beside you, dear Ernest. Tortured and killed. An argument, a quarrel. You killed him, and in your confused state, you kill yourself. The trio of murderers dead. Pritchard, Ernest Stanford, and of course, Adam Black. Case closed. The world moves on."

"You're fucking insane!" screamed Elspeth suddenly.

Katie Sykes cocked her head to one side, studying the bound figure. "You really are beautiful," she whispered. "Your death will be something magnificent. I promise you."

"And the Colonel?"

Sykes snapped her attention back to Black. "That had nothing to do with me. In fact, the whole Adam Black scenario was dreamt up by my... partner. The note, the headstone, the evidence planted in your squalid little flat. None of that was my idea. I was merely given instructions, and followed them through. You were to suffer. Like you have never suffered before. The whole world thinks Adam Black's a killer of women. The destroyer of innocence. And you're going to die, now, knowing the world will never know the truth. And the name Adam Black will be seen as a fucking obscenity."

Black met her gaze. All he needed was that split-second of hesitation, a flicker of distraction. Then, perhaps, they had a chance. "You're forgetting one thing."

"Which is?"

"I really am a killer of women."

"Sure you are."

"And that partner of yours knows it," continued Black. "Which is why I'm here. The instructions were simple. I was to come here. I was to kill you. And the girl. £500,000 transferred to my account. Then I disappear. You're the one who's been betrayed."

Sykes' mouth curved into a crooked grin. "You are marvellous, Adam Black. To make up such incredible bullshit." She spread her feet a little further apart, straightened her arms, assuming a firing stance.

"I have a name! Think! You don't believe me, fine. But if you kill me, then you'll never know until there's a bullet in the back of your head. I can give you that name. I wrote it down. It's in my pocket. How could I know this? Let me show you."

She straightened. "You're a fucking liar, Black."

Doubt, sensed Black. *Doubt in her voice. And she hadn't fired.*

"Humour me," she said. "Show me."

Slowly, he put his hand in his trouser pocket. He pulled out the piece of notepaper he had used back in the Colonel's flat, a million years ago. "It has one name on it."

"You are very mysterious, Mr Black. Give it to me."

Black scrunched it up, tossed it on the ground beside her, all the while being watched by Elspeth Owen, her face exhausted, slack. Resigned.

Sykes, with the gun still levelled on Black, bent down, picked it up.

She opened it, glancing at the name written on it, then back to Black.

"This means nothing," she said. "Other than you and that dead Colonel are good at fucking guesswork." Black detected a waver in her words. *She wasn't sure.*

He stretched out one hand, showing her his palm. "I have something else."

Sykes took a long breath. "What?"

"A tape recording. Of a conversation. You'll hear for yourself. The plan for me to kill you."

Sykes blinked. "This is fucking bullshit."

"It's on my mobile phone. Listen to it."

Without waiting for her to reply, he lowered his open hand down to his right-hand jacket pocket, the movement in slow motion.

"Easy," said Sykes.

Black nodded. He manoeuvred his hand inside. He felt the solid bulk not of a mobile phone, but a Glock 17.

With the care of a surgeon applying a surgical instrument, Black curled his index finger in the inside of the trigger guard, carefully levered his wrist up, the barrel pointing somewhere in her general direction. Now, it was all down to lady luck.

Sykes was oblivious. "Show me, Black."

"With pleasure."

He fired once, twice, in rapid succession. The first bullet caught her in the groin, the second, her hip. She staggered back, firing wildly, shots puncturing the ceiling, the walls. Black drew his pistol out, crouched on one knee, and in two seconds fired off three more rounds, two in the chest, the third ripping her throat apart.

She fell back, into some cardboard boxes stacked against a wall, upon which several candles had been placed, in little round holders. The boxes crumpled with the impact, the candles scattering. The cardboard caught instantly, flames sprung up, taking hold.

Black took three long steps towards her, and fired another two shots into her head. As he had been trained.

When you kill someone, no half measures.

And Black was in no mood for half measures.

116

"Who are you?" asked Elspeth.

"Adam Black, and I'm here to get you out of this shithole."

He untied the rope, and helped her to her feet.

Suddenly, it came out. The weeks of fear, dread, undiluted terror. And now this. Her freedom. She sobbed into his chest, collapsed into him.

"You saved me."

Black held her, smoothed her hair. "We need to go," he whispered.

She put one arm around his shoulders, he put his arm around her waist, and together they made their way out of the cellar, and up the stairs. The dead body of the woman she now knew as Katie Sykes remained, sprawled on the ground, in a bed of flame, her face obliterated, her body drenched in blood. Her captor.

"Is she dead?" she asked, knowing the answer, but asking anyway. Needing this man to reassure her.

"Well and truly. Dead and gone forever."

Elspeth sighed. "Am I dreaming this? Will I wake up and still be down there?"

"No dream."

They emerged into the hall, and out through the kitchen door. They were outside. The rain was falling, and the sea brought a chilly, salty wind. The man called Adam Black put his jacket over her shoulders.

"What now?" She looked up at him. He was tall. Darkly handsome.

He glanced behind him. Already smoke was billowing out through the door, flames yellow and orange, the speed of the fire ferocious, accelerated by a thousand candles.

"They'll see the house burning. Then they will come."

"The police?"

Black nodded. "It's not over yet."

117

Someone pointed.

Chiltern looked up. Flickering beyond the inky black of the wood, the orange tips of flame. Another fire, some way off. Even as Chiltern watched, it rose higher, giving the sky an unearthly orange cast.

The world was burning.

"What's that?" he shouted, to a man in the street – a local, watching the events unfold, his face white with shock. He looked to where Chiltern was pointing.

"It's Wilma Stanford's house," he said.

Chiltern looked about, caught sight of DI Shaw, giving orders, frantically talking in her mobile. Men, women, children, were on the street, dazed. A car close to the pub had caught fire, and had erupted in an explosion of metal and engine parts. More confusion, more panic.

He got her attention, and gestured to the woods.

"Another house is burning."

She nodded grimly. "Black's been busy."

"What do we do?"

"We go and get him, and put an end to this. You come with me. We'll take another two."

Chiltern agreed. He double-checked his gun was still in its holster, knowing it was, but checking anyway.

Black had to die. The man was a mad animal, and as such, required to be shot. Like a dog.

And Chiltern was the man to do it.

118

They waited. The fire crackled and roared behind them.

Black didn't know how the night would finish. Good or bad. At least the girl was safe. Mission accomplished. But the ending still had to play out. And he had to see it to the last act, the final curtain.

If he died, then so be it. It was as simple as that. Death had never really frightened Black. He had seen it in all its forms. Both in the army, and afterwards. His wife and child had been murdered. He had tracked the murderer down and repaid the compliment. But revenge was no cure. And when his family were killed, something had given in his soul. Something had broken. After that, he chose to tread a dark path. A path of self-destruction. He had never been afraid of dying. Now, he craved it.

But perhaps it was changing. Perhaps the soul could be repaired, he thought, as he watched the helicopter approach. A picture of Rachel Hempworth formed in his mind.

Maybe there was salvation.

He watched it, a shadow in the night, then landing lights

flashed as it hovered, then slowly descended, round the other side of the house.

"We should meet them."

Elspeth nodded in agreement, managing a weak smile. "The cavalry," she muttered.

Black chose not to answer.

They made their slow way round, Black still propping her up with one arm. She leant heavily on his shoulder. What she had experienced those last weeks was beyond his conjecture. He prophesised intense convalescing and therapy. Probably years of it. She might never recover.

They reached the other side.

There was a clearing of about a hundred yards between the front garden wall, and the cliff edge. The helicopter found the ground, wobbled, then stabilised. People piled out while the rotors still turned. All armed.

They spread out, and advanced. Black counted four. Four silhouettes in the glow of the firelight. Each carrying firearms.

This time, Black wasn't running anywhere. He put his hands up. "Elspeth Owen is safe and well! She's here!"

"Don't move, Black." A woman's voice.

They had halted at the front boundary of the garden, fifteen yards from where Black was standing.

"Don't shoot. Elspeth Owen is right here. She's safe."

Elspeth raised one weak hand.

"Don't you fucking move!" screamed the woman, pointing a handgun at them.

"Doesn't look like he's armed," said another.

"It's a trick," said the woman. "He's a killer."

"No tricks," said Black. Sensing the way of things, he stepped in front of Elspeth, ready to take a bullet for her.

The four entered through the front gate, then spread out three yards apart, only ten yards from Black.

They stopped as if waiting for the command. Behind them, the whine of the rotor blades slowing. The rain had slackened. The moon and the stars were still blanketed by heavy cloud.

The woman spoke. "My name is Vanessa Shaw. Detective inspector. We've met before. You were on a motorbike at Central Station. Remember? You will co-operate with us, Black. What happened in there?"

"She's dead. I killed her."

"Who?"

"Katie Sykes."

A pause. Then Shaw spoke, her voice husky. "You really are a bastard, Black."

"You've not been the first to say that. But there's a consolation."

"What?"

"I enjoyed it."

Vanessa Shaw lowered her head, as if thinking. The three beside her waited. Seconds passed. In the glare and crackle of the burning flames, under that dark sky, here, on a rainy clifftop, Black felt as if he were dreaming. That he would wake soon, into a brighter world.

It was not to be.

"Do we take him in?" asked one of the men at her side.

She lifted her head. She was crying. But she had made a decision.

"No one takes him in."

She turned, almost casually, raised her handgun, and shot the man to her right, direct in the face. He was dead before he knew it. She spun, shot the other standing to her left once in the chest, then the head. He dropped to the ground. The other, standing transfixed, shocked, took two bullets in the upper chest, bouncing him off his feet.

She whipped her gun back to Black.

Elspeth screamed.

"Shut the fuck up!"

Elspeth's voice rose to a hysterical pitch. "You murdered those men!"

Black took a deep breath. It was all down to those last moments. "Katie Sykes was your lover?"

"And you killed her."

"You should thank me. One dead sick fucker is a blessing in my book."

"The fucking book ends here. At least for you. You shot those three cops. Bad boy. Why did you have to kill Katie?"

"It felt good. Plus, it evens up the score. You killed the Colonel. So, I killed your psychopathic bitch."

"He wanted to meet me for a coffee. He confronted me. He knew I was part of it. On his way back to the police station, I killed him. Hit and run. There was nothing personal with that sad old man."

"It was personal to me," said Black, his voice hard and flat. "We both came to the same conclusion about you, but in different ways. We always thought it was someone in the police, working the Red Serpent case. We just didn't know who. We gave you each codes. You were Blue Number 2. Pritchard was very chatty in prison. He told me about the silver-framed photograph in my office. Only you would know about that, given only you had ever been to my office, when you took my statement. The rapist who fled to Poland. You remember? The Colonel drew the same conclusion, but from a different angle. Care to know how? It might interest you."

"You're going to die, regardless."

"The note you asked Katie to send to the police. From the Red Serpent. My name hidden in the text. First letter, second letter. You were too clever for your own good. The Colonel would never have worked that out. No one would. Except you.

DI Vanessa Shaw. By unlocking your own riddle, you revealed yourself."

"You know nothing, Black!" she snarled. "When I found out that it was you going into Shotts prison, then I took my chance."

Black was genuinely intrigued. He was close now. Close to the truth. "What chance?"

"Revenge."

～

The double impact squeezed the breath from Chiltern's lungs. He'd landed flat on his back, on the hard grass. He couldn't breathe. His chest was caught in a vice. The world spun. He would suffocate, and die. He closed his eyes, and everything turned black.

Light flickered. Orange and red. The fire from the building, raging up into the sky. He cracked open an eyelid. He was alive, but in agony. He felt his chest. The body armour had absorbed one of the bullets. The other had lodged into his shoulder. The pain was mind-numbing. But he was alive. He lifted his head. Three people walked past him, towards the cliff. He focused, willing his vision to clear. Black, the girl. And behind them, Vanessa Shaw, pointing a pistol at their backs. He hoisted himself up on one elbow, gritting his teeth, swallowing back the pain.

Somehow, he dragged himself to his feet, and staggered after them.

119

Black held Elspeth Owen's hand, as they walked towards the cliff edge, squeezed it. She squeezed it back.

Have faith in me, he was trying to convey.

I do.

Vanessa Shaw followed them, pistol in hand. Black, only minutes before, had witnessed her marksmanship. At this range, if Black tried anything, she wouldn't miss.

They passed the helicopter. The pilot, his vision possibly obscured by the fire, was unaware of what had happened. As they passed, Shaw rotated her arm, and shot him three times.

"Keep moving."

They reached the cliff edge. Below, the sea swirled and crashed.

"Turn round."

They both faced her.

"Please don't..." started Elspeth.

"Shut up."

"Revenge?" asked Black, trying to keep his voice neutral, calm.

"It's good that you should know this, before you die," said Shaw. "Do you remember France?"

Black thought back, his gears in his mind whirring. "I remember well."

"Why did you go there?"

"To kill a man."

"Why?"

"He murdered my family."

"And did you kill him?"

"Yes."

"I know you did. You are the death bringer. You brought death into my life."

"And how did I do that?" said Black.

"The man you killed was my father."

Black said nothing.

"On your knees," said Shaw. "You first, Black."

Black turned to Elspeth. Her eyes glistened, tears caught in the distant firelight. "You're not going to die. Not today."

"On your fucking knees, Black!"

Black turned back to Shaw. They stood face to face.

"I'm not afraid to die, you sick fuck. And the last thing I'm going to do is kneel before someone like you."

"Goodbye, Adam Black."

She straightened her arms, preparing for the kill shot.

Black met it with a smile. Behind her, as if from nowhere, loomed his salvation.

Chiltern staggered towards her. She was about to kill Black and Elspeth Owen. Nothing made sense. But Chiltern saw what he saw. And he knew what he had to do.

He approached her. "Drop it, Vanessa!"

She twisted round, surprised, and fired automatically. A stabbing pain in his leg. He crumpled to the ground. He was on his stomach. He craned his neck up, and tried to take aim.

But there was nothing more he could do.

It was up to the man they had all wanted to kill. It was up to Adam Black to save their lives.

∼

Black leapt forward. He had two seconds to capitalise on her distraction. She'd shot the man, and was spinning back. Black didn't have time to get the Glock out of his pocket. He gripped both hands round her wrist, pushed her arm away, and upwards. The pistol fired harmlessly into the air. With her free hand, she clawed his face. Black lurched back, perilously close to the edge. Below, a black mass of rock and spume and freezing sea.

She screamed, and suddenly clasped her arm around his waist. Black was unbalanced. She pushed her weight forward. There was nothing he could do. They fell, both of them, off the clifftop, into the abyss.

The last thing Black remembered was her laughter.

And then nothing.

120

For some reason, Rachel Hempworth never found the strength to write about the man called Adam Black. In that brief period she had known him, her life had changed. She had faced death, unparalleled fear. But she wouldn't have changed one second of it. She'd had the fortune to be in step with a man like no other. A man with qualities few others possessed. Courage. Spirit. Honour. Compassion.

He was, to her, and now to many others, a hero. The old-fashioned type.

But in the end, she thought sadly, he had broken his promise. He had never given her that final interview.

Her heart was torn.

Nor did she write about the serial killers, Katie Sykes, whose charred remains were found in a house in Jura, nor Detective Inspector Vanessa Shaw, whose body was found two days later, washed up on a sandy beach on Islay.

Nor Elspeth Owen, who was reunited with her mother, and who publicly thanked her saviour, the angel who had rescued her.

Adam Black.

Rachel hoped his body would never be found. She hoped he would drift forever, on the seas, under blue skies, under a warm sun. He was at rest, at last. Which perhaps was what he wanted, all along.

She was at her desk. It was a Wednesday afternoon, and it was spring. She had a cup of hot black coffee which she was about to sip, when her desk phone bleeped.

"Yes?"

The voice of the receptionist in the foyer outside responded. "There's a gentleman waiting here."

"Yes?"

"He's asked me to tell you that he's sorry."

"For what?"

Rachel heard the receptionist ask, and a muffled response, too far away to make out.

"For being late for his interview."

THE END

Printed in Great Britain
by Amazon

61071469R00241